"A seductiv[e] ... [frien]dship, the exquisite presence of ... —*Publishers Weekly*

D0380947

"Hoffman h... ...ning the mundane, everyday experiences with a touch of the occult and folklore . . . What lifts this novel into the ranks of the memorable is its evocative, lyrical quality of writing. Hoffman swings from the everyday to the otherworldly with ease and conviction. She lays bare the deepest secret thoughts at one moment, then segues into bits of humor mixed with pathos." —*San Diego Union-Tribune*

"This is a novel you'll remember long after you have finished reading it." —*Asbury Park Press*

"One of those rare books that isn't comparable to other books at all." —*Boston Herald*

"Lyrical and full of magic." —*Des Moines Sunday Register*

"Like Anne Tyler, Hoffman spins a story enchantingly, with the undeniable force and vividness of a dream, and a dream's own logic." —*Ms.*

"A savage yet lovely combination of love and loneliness." —*The Macon Beacon*

"Hoffman is a marvelous writer with a painter's eye who takes the landscape of ordinary people experiencing ordinary emotions and colors them in unexpected ways." —*Washington Post Book World*

"Filled with miragelike desert images, modern-day witchcraft and latter-day folktales, *Fortune's Daughter* is . . . rich in emotional detail, artistically refreshing and spiritually edifying." —*Santa Cruz Sentinel*

(continued on next page)

ANGEL LANDING

"Another unusual, impressive Hoffman novel . . . a deceptively simple, touching romance."

—*Kirkus Reviews*

"A satisfying book, one that is hard to lay aside."

—*Pittsburgh Press*

HERE ON EARTH

"Written with great wisdom and compassion . . . one of the finest fictional explorations of family love, and all those forces that threaten to undermine it, that I've read in many years."

—*Washington Post Book World*

"A sound addition to an impressive body of work."

—*Boston Globe*

"Haunting . . . it will enthrall the reader from beginning to end."

—*Library Journal*

SECOND NATURE

"Magical and daring . . . very possibly her best."

—*New York Times Book Review*

"Suspenseful . . . a dark, romantic meditation on what it means to be human."

—*The New Yorker*

"Hoffman tells a great story. Expect to finish this one in a single, guilty sitting."

—*Mirabella*

"*Second Nature* may be best read at full speed, hurtling down the mountain, as if falling in love."

—*San Francisco Examiner-Chronicle*

TURTLE MOON

"Magnificent." *—New York Times Book Review*

"A spectacular novel."
—Susan Isaacs, Washington Post Book World

"Hard to put down . . . full of characters who take hold of your heart." *—San Francisco Examiner*

"She is a born storyteller . . . and *Turtle Moon* is one of her best."
—Entertainment Weekly

PRACTICAL MAGIC

"A beautiful, moving book about the power of love and the desires of the heart." *—Denver Post*

"Splendid . . . one of her best novels." *—Newsweek*

"Charmingly told, and a good deal of fun."
—New York Times Book Review

"Written with a light hand and perfect rhythm . . . *Practical Magic* has the pace of a fairy tale but the impact of accomplished fiction."
—People

"A sweet, sweet story that, like the best fairy tales, says more than at first it seems to." *—New York Daily News*

"[A] delicious fantasy of witchcraft and love in a world where gardens smell of lemon verbena and happy endings are possible."
—Cosmopolitan

FORTUNE'S DAUGHTER

Alice Hoffman

BERKLEY BOOKS, NEW YORK

THE BERKLEY PUBLISHING GROUP
Published by the Penguin Group
Penguin Group (USA) Inc.
375 Hudson Street, New York, New York 10014, USA
Penguin Group (Canada), 90 Eglinton Avenue East, Suite 700, Toronto, Ontario M4P 2Y3, Canada
(a division of Pearson Penguin Canada Inc.)
Penguin Books Ltd., 80 Strand, London WC2R 0RL, England
Penguin Group Ireland, 25 St. Stephen's Green, Dublin 2, Ireland (a division of Penguin Books Ltd.)
Penguin Group (Australia), 250 Camberwell Road, Camberwell, Victoria 3124, Australia
(a division of Pearson Australia Group Pty. Ltd.)
Penguin Books India Pvt. Ltd., 11 Community Centre, Panchsheel Park, New Delhi—110 017, India
Penguin Group (NZ), 67 Apollo Drive, Rosedale, North Shore 0632, New Zealand
(a division of Pearson New Zealand Ltd.)
Penguin Books (South Africa) (Pty.) Ltd., 24 Sturdee Avenue, Rosebank, Johannesburg 2196,
South Africa

Penguin Books Ltd., Registered Offices: 80 Strand, London WC2R 0RL, England

FORTUNE'S DAUGHTER

PRINTING HISTORY
G. P. Putnam's Sons hardcover edition / April 1985
Berkley trade paperback edition / December 1999

ISBN: 978-0-425-16870-7

PRINTED IN THE UNITED STATES OF AMERICA

20 19 18 17

PLEASE VISIT THE AUTHOR'S WEBSITE AT
www.alicehoffman.com

FORTUNE'S DAUGHTER

PART ONE

$\mathcal{I}$T WAS EARTHQUAKE WEATHER and everyone knew it. As the temperature hovered near one hundred degrees the days melted together until it was no longer possible to tell the difference between a Thursday and a Friday. Coyotes in the canyons panicked; they followed the scent of chlorine into backyards, and some of them drowned in swimming pools edged with blue Italian tiles. In Hollywood the tap water bubbled as it came out of the faucets; ice cubes dissolved in the palm of your hand. It was a time when everything you once suspected might go wrong suddenly did. For miles in every direction people just snapped. Lovers quarreled in bedrooms and parking lots, money was stolen, knives were pulled, friendships that had lasted a lifetime were destroyed with one harsh word. Those few people who were able to sleep were haunted by nightmares; those with insomnia drank cups of coffee and swore they smelled something sweet burning, as if a torch had been put to a grove of lemon trees sometime in the night.

It wasn't uncommon to have hallucinations in weather like this, and Rae Perry, who had never had a vision in her life, began to see things on the empty sidewalk whenever she took the bus home from work: a high-heeled shoe left at a crosswalk, a wild dog on the corner of La Brea, a black garden snake winding its way through traffic. Hollywood Boulevard seemed to move in waves. And at home, the white stucco walls in Rae's apartment shifted as if they were made of sand. It wasn't just the heat that was affecting everyone, it was the strange quality of the air. Every breath you took seemed dangerous, as if it might be your last. Even in the air-conditioned office where she worked for an independent producer named Freddy Contina, Rae found she had to take several deep breaths before typing a letter or answering the phone. Toward the end of the day the light coming in through the windows was a sulky amber color that made you see double. It was the season for headaches, and rashes, and double-crosses, and more and more often Rae Perry put her head down on her desk at work and began to wonder why she had ever left Boston.

But after she'd gotten home, and had sat for half an hour or more in a bathtub of cool water, Rae knew exactly why she had run away two weeks before her eighteenth birthday. As soon as she heard the Oldsmobile pull up, she ran to get dressed and open the front door. Sometimes she swore she was under Jessup's spell. He didn't even have to snap his fingers to get her to jump. All he had to do was look at her. Even in this weather Jessup seemed different from everyone else, as if he were above the heat. He had the kind of blue eyes that were transparent, and so pale that his mother had thought they were bad luck. For several summers she had kept Jessup out of the sun entirely, for fear his eyes would be bleached even lighter. But as soon as you touched Jessup you knew how deceiving his appearance was. He might have looked cool, but his skin radiated heat, and it got so that Rae had begun to wait for him to fall asleep so that she could climb out of bed and sleep alone on the wooden floor.

Since the time they'd run away from Boston, Rae had been afraid that one day Jessup would change his mind and ask her to leave. And the truth was something had been happening to him ever since they came to California. He actually went so far as to get an application to the Business School at U.C.L.A., though he never filled out the forms. He continually grilled Rae about Freddy Contina and even had her steal one of Freddy's résumés—Rae found him studying it one night when he thought she was still in the shower. It was as if the ghost of some ambition had suddenly appeared to Jessup. He had begun to want things, and it just wasn't like him.

In the past, Jessup's main ambition had been to keep moving. In seven years they had lived in five states. As soon as Rae began to feel comfortable somewhere, Jessup started to talk about moving to a place where there were more options. He never mentioned a new job or more money, just these unnamed options—as if the whole world would open to him as soon as they put a few more miles on the Oldsmobile.

Whenever Jessup reached for his stack of road maps, Rae had to remind herself that it wasn't her he was tired of, just the place they were in. This time there had been no maps and no talk of options, and yet Jessup's restlessness was so strong it had begun to affect Rae's dreams. At night she dreamed of earthquakes: glass shattered and spilled over the boulevards, the ground pitched and split open, the sky became a sheet of needles. When she awoke from one of these nightmares, Rae had to hold tight to Jessup or else, she was certain, she'd spin right out of the room.

She had been waiting so long for something to go wrong between them that it took a while before she realized that it already had. Each Sunday they went to the beach at Santa Monica, and as they drove along Sunset Boulevard Jessup's mood always grew worse. By the time they reached Beverly Hills it was impossible to talk to him. The funny thing was, it was Jessup who always insisted they take the same route. He claimed to hate the palm trees and the huge estates, but every Sunday he pointed them out as if seeing them for the first time.

"This is truly disgusting," he would say as they neared the same pink stucco chalet. "Who in their right mind would turn their house into such a fucking eyesore."

"Then when you have a house paint it white," Rae finally told him, and she knew as soon as she opened her mouth that it was the wrong thing to say.

"Do you have something to say about the fact that I don't own my own house?" Jessup said.

Rae looked straight ahead. "No."

"You think I'm a failure or something—is that what you're thinking?"

"Jessup, I didn't say one goddamned thing," Rae told him.

"You said paint it white. I heard you."

"Well, paint it whatever the hell color you want to." Rae was practically in tears. "Do whatever you want."

"I will," Jessup said. "I certainly will."

After that Rae had taken to riding with her head out the window of the car. She told Jessup it was because she loved the scent of jasmine in Beverly Hills, but really it was because Jessup's anger was heating up the car until the plastic upholstery just about burned you alive.

On the last Sunday in August they probably should have known enough to stay home. The temperature had risen above one hundred and there was a trace of sulfur in the air. When they pulled into the parking lot at Santa Monica, the asphalt beneath the tires turned to molasses. Jessup wasn't talking as they walked down to the beach; and when Rae spread out the blanket she wondered if there could possibly be another woman, someone he told all his secrets to, because he certainly wasn't telling Rae a thing. She watched him as she tucked her red hair under a straw hat, then rubbed sunscreen on her arms and legs. The water was so blue that it hurt your eyes, but Jessup stared straight at it. He wore a black T-shirt and jeans, and a pair of boots Rae had bought for him years ago. Everything around them shimmered with heat; every sound echoed. If you closed your eyes you could almost imagine that the cars on Route 1 were only inches away, or that the girls who cried out as they dove into the cold waves were close enough to touch.

Rae was flat on her back and nearly asleep when Jessup finally spoke.

"Guess how many Rolls-Royces I counted?" he said suddenly.

Rae had to crane her neck to look up at him; she kept one hand on her straw hat.

"Go ahead," Jessup urged. "Guess."

Rae shrugged her shoulders. She could barely tell a Ford from a Toyota these days.

"Two?"

"Eighteen," Jessup said triumphantly. "Eighteen fucking Rolls-Royces between Hollywood and Santa Monica."

For some reason that number frightened Rae. In the parking lot, their blue Oldsmobile baked in the sun. In the seven years they'd had the car they hadn't put a scratch on it. In fact, it had been one of the reasons Jessup had wanted to come to California in the first place. A car could last forever in Los Angeles, he had told Rae. No snow, no salt, no rust.

"I don't care about Rolls-Royces," Rae said. "I'd rather have our car any day."

She could see the muscles in Jessup's jaw tighten.

"God, Rae," he said to her. "Sometimes I swear you get stupider all the time."

He left her there on the blanket, just like that. Rae propped herself up on one elbow and watched him walk down to the water. He stood at the shoreline, looking far out into the Pacific, as if he were the only one on the beach able to see the cloudy edge of China. Rae was concentrating so hard, trying to figure out what was wrong, that she forgot to turn onto her stomach so she wouldn't burn. By the time they got home, Rae's fair skin had burned to nearly the same shade of red as her hair, and that night Jessup had the perfect excuse not to come near her.

The following Sunday, Rae didn't dare ask Jessup to go to the beach. The heat was worse than ever, and people with respiratory problems were warned not to go outdoors. Jessup spent most of the day Simonizing the Oldsmobile; he tied a red bandanna over his mouth to filter the air, and took off his T-shirt. At noon, when Rae brought him a beer, Jessup seemed less upset; he stopped working long enough to pull down his bandanna and kiss her. That night Jessup insisted that they go out to dinner at a Mexican restaurant where the air conditioner was turned up so high you could actually feel brave enough to order the extra-hot chili. Rae wore a lavender-colored cotton dress and silver earrings. It seemed more important than ever before that Jessup notice how good she looked, and while he never actually said anything, he did reach across the table to take her hand.

In the dark booth of the restaurant, Rae managed to convince herself that the trouble between them was over. But when they got home, Jessup ignored her. He went into the kitchen, and, without bothering to turn on the light, he sat there and stared out the window. Rae wondered if it was just that Monday was so close. Jessup worked for several studios—he picked people up at the airport, he messengered film, he delivered platters of shrimp cocktail and pastrami up to the executives' offices whenever there was something to celebrate. On his tax returns Jessup listed himself as a driver, but whenever someone asked what he did, Jessup would smile and say, "I'm a slave."

At the beginning of the heat wave, when he'd first started to act so peculiar, Rae had made the mistake of asking Jessup how his day had been.

"How was my day?" Jessup had mimicked in a too sweet voice. "Well, I spent most of my time picking up an order of cocaine that cost more than I've earned in my entire lifetime. That's how my day was. If you want me to continue, I'll be glad to tell you about my week."

She hadn't wanted to know any more. But when they got home from the restaurant no one had to tell her that Jessup was feeling cheated. He sat by the kitchen window and gave the parked Oldsmobile a murderous look. It was then Rae knew he was still thinking about Rolls-Royces, and that thinking about them was just about driving him crazy.

The worst part was that Rae couldn't think of a single thing she could do to make him happy. On Monday morning she got up early, so she could bring him breakfast in bed. The heat was still pushing down as she boiled water for coffee and switched the radio on to a low volume. Listeners were calling in to a talk show that followed the news, each with a way to predict the next quake. As Rae poured water through the coffee filter, she knew she shouldn't be listening to a program about earthquakes—she was so suggestible lately that she could already feel the buildings crumbling around her. But she was hypnotized by the heat, and by the scent of coffee, and as she put some bread in the toaster she continued to listen as a caller insisted that if birds were tracked by radar, entire cities could be saved. It was a well-known fact that birds always left an area long before any catastrophe. Rae found herself drawn to the window; at least there was still a line of blue jays on the telephone wire.

She took out the frying pan and heated some butter, but when she cracked two eggs into the pan she found blood spots in both yolks. Rae panicked and immediately poured the eggs down the drain, then washed out the pan with hot water and soap. But even after she had started over again with two fresh eggs, Rae kept thinking about the spots of blood. She actually had to sit down and drink a glass of ice water and tell herself that anybody could have brought those eggs home from the market—they just happened to have been in the carton she chose.

She watched the clock, afraid to wake Jessup. Although how he could sleep in this heat was beyond her. Other people tossed and turned, but Jessup lay perfectly still beneath a thin cotton quilt. Finally, Rae set out his breakfast on a white tray, then poured two cups of coffee. What was the worst that could happen? Freddy could fire her. Los Angeles could be devastated. Jessup could whisper that he'd found someone new.

"Why is it you people stay in California?" a long-distance caller from Nevada asked on the radio. "Don't you know that birds can't save you? Don't you know that by staying all you're doing is tempting fate?"

Rae climbed back into bed with a cup of coffee in either hand.

"Don't move," she warned Jessup.

Jessup opened one eye and reached for his coffee. Rae put her cup on the night table, then went back into the kitchen. By the time she had returned with the tray, Jessup had finished his coffee and had lit a cigarette. As Jessup tapped ashes into his empty coffee cup, Rae stood by the foot of the bed. There was one thing she knew for sure: Jessup had quit smoking two years ago, when they lived in Texas.

"You don't actually expect me to eat that, do you?" Jessup asked when he saw his breakfast.

"You're smoking a cigarette," Rae said.

"Golly, Rae, that's what I like about you," Jessup drawled. "You're so observant."

There had been a time when Rae had made it her business to find out everything she could about Jessup. Of course, that was when the really important things were whether or not Jessup liked long hair, or if he preferred her to wear blue or green. When Rae was fourteen she taped a photograph of Jessup to her closet door so that she could memorize his face. This was one of the reasons Rae's mother, Carolyn, had decided to move the family out to Newton. It was one thing for Rae to moon over him when she was still in junior high, and quite another to continue this infatuation now that Jessup had graduated, and she was about to go into high school herself. They hadn't even told Rae until a week before the moving van was set to arrive. She locked herself in the bathroom and refused to come out.

"I'm not leaving Jessup," she told her mother through the locked door.

"Oh, yes you are," Carolyn had said. "And years from now you'll thank me."

"Oh, please," Rae said.

"It's not just that I don't like him," Carolyn said. "It's that he's dangerous."

Something in her mother's tone made Rae curious. She turned the lock and opened the door.

"Please believe me," Carolyn said, "because I know about dangerous men."

For Rae that was the limit. Her father was a lawyer who was home so rarely that Rae was actually surprised whenever she ran into him in the kitchen or the living room. Was he her mother's "dangerous man"?

"You can't tell me anything," Rae informed her mother. "You don't even know Jessup."

Once they had moved to Newton, Rae continued to see Jessup even more than before. Her friends found him threatening or mean, and they dropped away from her. It was just the two of them, and even Jessup's mother had to telephone Rae whenever she wanted to locate her son.

Rae had always been sure that if she knew anyone in this world it was Jessup, but now his suddenly starting to smoke again spooked her. Immediately, she had the sense that this was only one of the things he kept hidden from her.

"I'll tell you something else," Jessup said, as he lit another cigarette. "I don't eat breakfast any more—you should know that."

Rae tried to remember—hadn't they had pancakes only a few days ago?

"You have to watch out for things like breakfast when

you get old," Jessup told Rae. "Otherwise you wake up one day and there you are—fat and over the hill."

Jessup still wore the same blue jeans he had worn when he was eighteen years old, but he was turning thirty this year, and the only thing that bothered him more than turning thirty was realizing that he cared about his age.

"I wish you would stop talking about getting old," Rae said. "It's ridiculous."

She was about to go into the kitchen and get Jessup a second cup of coffee, when he reached over and pulled her down on top of him.

"It's just a joke to you," he whispered. "You've got five more years. You've got time. I'm the one who has to hurry."

Jessup kissed her, and Rae wrapped her arms around him. Other women who had kissed only one man in their entire lifetimes might think they were missing something, but Rae certainly wasn't one of them. Instead, she found herself pitying women who had to settle for anything less.

"Wait a minute," Jessup told her.

Jessup walked down the hallway to the kitchen, and when he returned he was carrying a blue-and-white mixing bowl. As soon as Rae saw that the bowl was filled with ice cubes, she sat up in bed. He did have a mean streak sometimes, and the first thing Rae expected was that he'd dump the ice on her as a way of letting her know it was time for her to get up and get dressed for work.

"Oh, no you don't," she told him.

Jessup held the bowl of ice and grinned.

"I mean it," Rae said.

"You don't trust me any more," Jessup said. "And if you don't trust me, I don't see the point in staying together."

Maybe he meant it, maybe he was having doubts—Rae pulled Jessup back down on the bed. She closed her eyes and forgot about the ice. But later, when they were making love and Rae was so hot she couldn't stand it any more, Jessup reached for the mixing bowl. He took an ice cube in each hand and then traced the ice along Rae's skin. Nothing had ever seemed as delicious and cold, and Rae begged him not to stop. But there was something in the way Jessup made love to her that felt desperate; and what made Rae shiver wasn't the ice, it was noticing that, as he held her, he was looking at the front door.

It was nearly ten o'clock by the time Jessup started to get dressed. The phone had rung several times, but they hadn't answered. Jessup didn't talk to Rae. He pulled on jeans, then went to the oak dresser for a clean shirt. Rae sat up and watched him get ready. Jessup never bothered with a comb; instead he stared into the mirror and shook his head until his dark hair fell into place.

"I'm going to have to make up the time I just missed," Jessup told her.

He spoke into the mirror as he put on a white shirt. Rae found herself wishing that he would look over his left shoulder—then their eyes would meet and Jessup might see how much she wanted him to stay home with her. If he agreed, she'd be willing to take the whole day off. But that morning the temperature was already at one hundred and two, and the car exhaust on Sunset Boulevard had begun to form a pavilion of clouds, and Jessup simply didn't have the time to look over his shoulder.

"Don't bother to wait for me," he said.

* * *

Rae didn't know why she always had the feeling she'd been the one to force Jessup into something—he had been the one who kept coming to see her. Even on the coldest New England day, when the sidewalk was a sheet of ice, she'd look out her window and there he'd be, waiting. But then, after Rae had managed to get out of the house, he always seemed annoyed to see her. And so, Rae never really knew what it was that brought Jessup out to Newton so often.

That winter, when Rae was sixteen, was the last time Carolyn tried to separate them by force. When she realized who it was out there on the sidewalk nearly every day, Carolyn Perry called the police. After they'd taken him down to the precinct house, Jessup was threatened with charges that made him laugh out loud: loitering. But from where she stood in the driveway, all Rae could see was Jessup being hustled into the rear seat of a patrol car. She was certain they were driving him straight to the penitentiary. She ran upstairs, locked her door, and tried to slit her wrists with a nail file.

Carolyn, of course, gave up. She stopped questioning her daughter each time she left the house, and now whenever she looked out the living-room window and saw Jessup outside, Carolyn simply drew the curtains. Rae was delighted with her own courage, but when she told Jessup about the nail file, he wasn't impressed.

"You'll never kill yourself that way," he told her.

But the nail file had changed one thing—Rae and Carolyn no longer spoke to each other, they didn't even fight. In the mornings, Rae left for school before her mother came downstairs; at night she sat up in her bedroom on the third floor and waited for Jessup to call. Whatever shred of control Carolyn had had before disappeared. Now Rae did as she pleased, and whenever she wanted money she simply took it. If Carolyn noticed the dollar bills missing from her purse, she never said a word, and the silence between mother and daughter grew deeper and deeper, until finally, even if there had been anything for them to say to each other, it would have been impossible to speak.

Then one day, Rae couldn't find any change in her mother's purse and she decided to look through the bureau drawers in her parents' bedroom. In Carolyn's sweater drawer, between two wool cardigans, Rae discovered a red leather wallet. She knew she had found something important, but she had never expected so much—fifteen hundred-dollar bills, all folded neatly in half.

Without stopping to think, Rae telephoned Jessup and told him she had to see him. That night she ran all the way to the parking lot of the Star Market.

Jessup was crouched by a brick wall; as soon as he saw Rae he jumped to his feet. It had just begun to snow and the parking lot was deserted; it was the kind of night when you didn't go outside, unless your life depended on it.

"My mother has money hidden," Rae told Jessup breathlessly.

"Is that what you got me out here to tell me?" Jessup said. "Look, Rae, everybody's mother has money hidden. My mother has fifty bucks in a plastic bag in the freezer."

"No," Rae said. "I mean a lot of money."

"Oh, yeah?" Jessup said, almost interested.

"Fifteen hundred dollars," Rae whispered.

It was so cold in the parking lot that Rae could feel her toes freezing through her wool socks and her boots. But she didn't dare hurry Jessup; she just watched as he stood there and lit a cigarette and thought about her mother's money.

"I'll tell you what we'll do," Jessup said finally. "We'll keep that money in mind."

Rae didn't know whether to feel disappointed or relieved—she had half expected Jessup to suggest she go right home and steal the money that night. But even if Carolyn's bankroll was safe for now, when Rae walked Jessup down to the bus stop, she knew she had betrayed her mother. She told herself it didn't matter; after all, her mother was her enemy now. And in no time Rae forgot all about the money—although maybe she let herself forget because she knew that Jessup was remembering. And two years later, when Rae was nearly eighteen and they were about to leave Massachusetts together, Jessup reminded her.

"I want you to take that money now," he whispered.

Jessup's arm was around her and they were sitting in the dark, on the bleachers behind the high school. Rae found herself wishing that she had never told him about the money in the first place. But when she suggested they didn't really need it, Jessup took his arm away from her, so quickly you'd think he'd been stung.

"Listen, I've had that money in mind all along," he told her. "If you want us to get a car we need that money." Jessup had been working at gas stations and construction sites ever since he left high school. "How much money do you think I earn?" he asked Rae now. "If you think I earn enough to buy a car, think again. Your mother doesn't need that money, Rae. We do."

Rae swore she would do it. But for days she put it off. If she imagined she was giving her mother some extra time to move the money to a new hiding place, it just didn't work. When Rae finally went to the bureau to check, she discovered that the wallet was in the same exact place, and there was more cash than before, twenty-two hundred dollars. The night before they planned to leave, Rae telephoned Jessup and told him she couldn't do it.

"Oh, great," Jessup said. "Here we go. This is just like when you tried to kill yourself with the nail file. You've got to learn if you're going to do something you've got to do it right. Do you think I want to hitchhike down south with some underage minor whose parents can have me put in jail? Think about it," Jessup told her, "and you'll soon see the attraction of having a car."

Rae admitted that she saw the attraction.

"If we leave Boston together we do it right, or not at all," Jessup said.

Rae could hear him breathing into the receiver. She knew that he had pulled the phone into the hallway so that his mother wouldn't overhear; he was standing there, waiting for her answer—and waiting was definitely something he did not like to do. There was no doubt in Rae's mind that, given one good reason, he would leave her behind.

"It's totally up to you," Jessup told her.

It was her decision, and she chose a night when the sky was so clear that the stars seemed no farther away than the rooftops. As her parents slept, Rae went into their room, carefully opened the dresser drawer, and took out the leather wallet. After that they were able to do it right, just the way Jessup wanted. They bought the Oldsmobile and drove to Maryland, and they never once went back. But even after seven years, whenever Rae couldn't sleep she blamed her mother. On those nights, Rae could open every window in the apartment and still feel haunted by the scent of her mother's Chanel perfume. The odor was everywhere, in the sheets and the curtains, in the dishwater and in every kitchen cabinet. And even though Rae knew it was impossible for Carolyn to have tracked her down after all this time, she found herself searching through the closets and kneeling to peer under the bed—and there were times when she actually believed she might find someone hiding.

The scent of Chanel was particularly strong on that Monday when Rae came in late to work.

"Did you have some woman up here?" she asked Freddy Contina.

"I wish," Freddy said.

Rae turned the air conditioner to fan and opened some windows. It was somehow much worse to smell that phantom perfume during the day; at night there seemed the possibility of an explanation: the woody scent of the bamboo outside the kitchen window, a neighbor's cologne filtering through the walls, the terrible power of nightmares.

"Speaking of someone being up here," Freddy said, "I don't want Jessup in my office while I'm gone."

Freddy acquired films in Europe and redubbed them; he was leaving that day for Germany, and whenever he was away Rae invited Jessup up for lunch. Although the last time, when Freddy was in Italy, Jessup didn't touch his food—he spent the entire hour going through the accounts file, and there wasn't a thing Rae could do to stop him.

"Never bring your personal life into the office," Freddy advised.

"What have you got against Jessup?" Rae asked.

The two men had met only once; Jessup had asked so many questions you'd think he was interviewing Freddy for a job.

"He's the mass-murderer type," Freddy said.

"What's that supposed to mean?" Rae asked, offended.

"Or maybe the lone-assassin type," Freddy reconsidered. "I can just see him up in his room, writing in his diary and polishing his rifle."

The idea of Jessup's keeping a diary made Rae laugh.

"You don't know Jessup," she said.

"That's just it," Freddy said. "I don't want to know him, and I don't want him in my office, Rae."

As soon as the car came for Freddy, Rae telephoned Jessup. She was planning to order up from the deli on the corner and put it on Freddy's account, but Jessup was out on a job and no one seemed to know when he'd be back. Rae could have ordered something for herself, but she felt the urge to escape from the office. She had found a woman's turquoise earring on the couch in Freddy's office, but the scent of Chanel was so unnaturally strong that even if Freddy had spent all night with a woman who had doused herself with perfume the aroma would have been gone by now. And yet there it was, in the filing cabinets and the carpeting, just as if Carolyn was in the office. And so Rae went out, even though the air itself was orange and so thick it seemed as if thousands of butterflies had settled above Hollywood Boulevard.

The minute she left the building, Rae knew she had made a mistake. It was noon, and so hot that the few people there were on the sidewalk seemed stunned. When Rae walked past a jewelry store she found herself staring at a tray of gold chains in the window. In all the years they had been together Jessup had never given her any jewelry, not even a cheap silver chain or a semiprecious stone. All at once, Rae ached for a ruby ring. She nearly walked inside and asked to look at a tray of uncut stones, but suddenly she felt as if she was drowning. On the hot sidewalk, in the middle of a city built out of the desert, she was going under. Maybe it was just that she couldn't get enough air in her lungs, or that the shadows along the boulevard were deep blue. The edges of things had begun to blur, and had she been submerged in ten feet of murky water it wouldn't have been any harder to take another step.

This had happened to Rae once before, when she was seventeen and had come down with pneumonia. Even after she was released from the hospital everything looked funny, as if bleach had been added to the air, and a hazy filter hung between Rae and the rest of the world. Jessup telephoned her every night, but after he'd called, he hadn't had much to say. They stayed on the phone for hours, in silence, as if the only way for them to communicate was by telepathy. But once, Jessup had actually said that he missed her.

"What?" Rae had said, certain that she'd misunderstood.

"Are you trying to embarrass me?" Jessup had said. "I said it once, don't ask me to repeat it."

There was something about her illness that made Rae fear she would never get well. She could only see white things: the sheets on her bed, the cream-colored walls, the ruffled curtains at her window. Everything else was fading; when she squinted, she couldn't make out the titles of the books on the shelf.

"I think I may be dying," Rae told Jessup one night when he called. She could practically hear him smirking. "I mean it," Rae said. "I think I may be going blind."

"I'll tell you what your problem is," Jessup said. "I'm not there, and the only thing worth seeing is me."

A few days later a dozen roses arrived. Carolyn considered throwing them out; even though there was no card, she knew who they were from. But she made the mistake of opening the cardboard box, and once she saw the roses she couldn't bring herself to put them in the trash. Instead, she filled a tall glass vase with water and carried them upstairs. As soon as she saw the expression on Rae's face when those flowers were brought in, Carolyn knew that she had lost her daughter.

All that week Rae watched the roses, and as they turned from scarlet to a deep, mysterious purple, she felt her vision returning. But when she was allowed to go out again, and she shyly thanked Jessup for the flowers, he acted as if he didn't know what she was talking about. By then, the roses had withered and Carolyn had tossed them into the trash, and Rae was left wondering if she had imagined the glass vase on her night table. After all, she had imagined other things when her fever was at its highest: a plane that was circling above the ceiling turned out to be just a buzz in her head; a green lion that sat by her clothes closet was only a sweater that had fallen onto the floor. It was possible that there had never even been flowers in her room, and once she was well again, roses really seemed too trivial a thing for Jessup to send.

Even though she had no fever now, Rae couldn't continue on to Musso Frank's, where she'd planned to put her lunch on Freddy's tab. The sidewalk was like quicksand, the next corner seemed miles away. Rae ducked into the closest doorway, the entrance to a place called The Salad Connection. When she leaned against the plate-glass window she could feel the shudder of an air conditioner's motor; each time a customer walked through the door a rush of cold air escaped, then was swallowed by the heat of the boulevard. Quickly, Rae began to count. She hoped that by the time she reached one hundred, she'd feel strong enough to walk back to the office and lie down in the dark. But she hadn't even gotten to thirty when she noticed a sign offering free psychic readings every Wednesday and Friday. And that was when Rae stopped counting.

Ten years earlier, when Rae and her mother were engaged in the worst of their fighting about Jessup, they had gone to a tearoom near the Copley Plaza Hotel to have their fortunes read. They'd been arguing about the curfew Rae always ignored, when Carolyn had thrown up her hands, turned, and walked into the tearoom. Rae had followed and they waited, side by side and in silence, until the fortune-teller signaled them to a table. The fortune-teller was hidden beneath fringed shawls and thick rouge; she offered them poppyseed cakes and mint tea, then proceeded with a reading that was dead wrong. To Carolyn, who had a real distaste for boats, she promised a sea voyage. For Rae, a miserable student, there was a scholar's future. Rae and her mother had looked at each other across the table; in spite of themselves, they smiled. Clearly, this fortune-teller would tell them whatever she imagined they wanted to hear. Of course Rae asked about Jessup. "What about my boyfriend? Will we stay together?"

"Oh, yes," the fortune-teller had said, and for a moment Rae saw her mother draw back. "Your boyfriend," the fortune-teller had gone on, "is tall and handsome and extremely shy. Polite, wonderful with children, could become a doctor or a lawyer—an all-around darling boy."

That misreading had made Rae and Carolyn so giddy that they'd fallen out the door of the tearoom and into each other's arms. Afterward it was a joke between them: when things seemed dark there was always a place near the Copley Plaza Hotel where it was possible to hear good news for only five dollars.

Good news was exactly what Rae wanted to hear right

now, so she went to The Salad Connection, past a buffet table offering only the coolest food—lettuce leaves, cucumber, slices of avocado. Sitting in a leatherette booth, she ordered lunch and decided to skip dessert—if Jessup was thinking about gaining weight, she might as well think about it too. After she'd finished her salad, the waitress brought an empty cup and a pot of Darjeeling tea. There was a white business card on the edge of the saucer:

LILA GREY
47 Three Sisters Street
Readings and Advice—Limited Private Consultations
25 dollars per hour

Good news, Rae saw, had gotten more expensive.

After scanning the room for the fortune-teller, Rae realized that the psychic was at the next table. She had expected something more than a few silver bangle bracelets and a small silk turban. The psychic appeared to be in her forties, with thick gray hair cut on an angle at her jawline, so that when she leaned over to peer into a teacup no client could see her expression or her eyes. But across the aisle separating them Rae could see the psychic's hands resting on a tabletop, and the long, delicate fingers made Rae uneasy. A woman who picked up a teacup so cautiously might actually be searching for more than good news.

By the time the psychic sat down across from Rae it was nearly one o'clock, and Rae had the sense that if she weren't careful she might just believe anything she was told. Out on

Hollywood Boulevard it was now so hot that the asphalt melted. Whenever people crossed the street their shoes got coated with tar, and the smell of tar made them remember summers in whatever town they grew up in, and they found themselves yearning for lemonade, just as they had on hot days back home when the air hung above them and clouds had the burning, sooty edge of August. Inside the restaurant the air conditioner was turned up higher, and as the psychic raised her arm to pour the tea, Rae felt an odd chill along the backs of her legs.

"You can ask me anything," Lila Grey, the psychic said. "Just don't ask me when the heat wave will break because I don't do weather."

The fortune-teller in Boston certainly hadn't asked them for questions; she had taken one look and had quickly decided what they wanted to hear.

"I'll bet everybody just pours out their whole life story to you," Rae guessed.

"Not really," Lila Grey said.

"I'll bet once they start talking about themselves, they can't stop," Rae insisted.

Lila Grey, who had three more tables to go, a dentist appointment in the late afternoon, and a stop at the market before she went home, was not as careful as she might have been. She might have at least looked at her client, but instead she glanced down at her watch. While she thought about having dinner with her husband that evening, out on the patio where it was cooler, Rae just couldn't seem to stop talking.

"You know, maybe they've got a boyfriend, and they don't know if he's really in love with them . . . "

Lila Grey cut her off. "Is that your question?" she asked.

Rae leaned her head against the booth and considered. "I guess it is," she said finally.

"If you don't drink your tea, we'll never know the answer, will we?" the psychic suggested.

As Rae gulped the lukewarm tea, Lila Grey finally took the time to look at her. The booth suddenly seemed uncomfortable, if only because there was now the odor of some strong perfume that was a little too sweet. When she had drained the cup, Rae offered it to the psychic. Lila Grey knew that something was wrong as soon as she touched the handle. She couldn't even bring herself to lift the cup. Already the tea leaves had begun to settle, and Lila was certain that if she hesitated, even for an instant, she would soon see the outline of the darkest symbol you can find at the bottom of a cup. She pushed the teacup away, then quickly reached for a saucer which she placed over its mouth.

Rae leaned forward. "What is it?" she said.

Lila had always been able to identify the women she had to avoid. The first time the symbol had appeared during a reading she'd taken it as a warning; the second time she'd been tricked by the absence of a wedding band on her client's left hand and by the dim light in her own living room. She shoved the teacup even farther away, and each one of her silver bracelets slipped down to her wrist. The effect was a sound like a wind chime, one you hear from a very great distance when you're in the center of the desert and are out of everything: water and hope and luck.

Rae's throat was dry. "It's something awful, isn't it?" she whispered.

Lila didn't answer. And after all, what was this woman's unhappiness to her; she had seen misery before, and she'd reworked it, turning bad luck into whatever fortune her client wanted to hear. But this was a fortune no one deserved.

Lila knew enough not to look at Rae. She concentrated and closed her eyes. A wall of blue ice sprang up around her, it was hard as diamonds, impossible to penetrate. Lila was still there in the booth at the restaurant, but she was moving farther and farther away from Rae. She had thought she'd lost the ability to escape, but all Lila had to do was imagine that she was a crow. Her wings were so black they looked wet; beneath her the earth was a small blue globe. Her feathers were unfolding, one by one; and the air was as thin and cold and as pure as glass.

"Please, tell me what you see," Rae called to Lila, but her voice was tiny, as if she was standing at the edge of the planet calling up into the limitless sky.

"Even if it's horrible, I don't care. I want to know," Rae called.

Her words were pieces of crystal, and Lila was too far away to be pulled back down. To her, gravity was nothing. She could feel the moonlight on her feathers, that cold, white light. It was so beautiful and lonely; it was impossible to be touched by another soul. And with the compassion of one so very far away, Lila looked back down at Rae; she knew the mercy in not telling more than the smallest shred of truth.

"It's nothing so horrible," Lila Grey said. "It's just that I see you won't be able to sleep tonight."

. . .

That night, Jessup didn't come home. Rae tried to tell herself that the studio had forced him to work overtime, but she knew no one could force Jessup into anything, and they certainly couldn't stop him from making one phone call. If early in the evening Rae suspected Jessup might be cheating on her, by midnight it no longer mattered. She'd forgive anything, as long as he came home.

Turning on the radio just made things worse. People in Hollywood were warned to keep their windows closed at night if they didn't have screens. A band of wild dogs gone crazy with thirst roamed the boulevards; they had begun to push open back doors and circle houses. On Sweetzer Avenue, in a backyard where birds of paradise grew, the dogs had attacked a six-year-old boy in a fight for his wading pool. By the time the police had arrived the boy's neck was broken. They had managed to shoot a collie, and when an autopsy was performed the oddest things were found in its stomach: a silk scarf; small bones, which had not yet been identified; blue water the color of sapphires; three gold rings.

At two in the morning, Rae was certain she heard the dogs outside her window. The trash cans rattled and fell, and something that sounded like claws hit against the cement walkway. Rae double-locked her windows, and she huddled in an armchair where Jessup usually sat to watch her undress for bed. Tonight, Rae didn't take off her clothes, because she could tell already, long before she watched the sky grow light, that the psychic had been right.

At seven the next morning Rae made a pot of coffee, and as she poured herself a cup she noticed that her hand shook. She went back to the armchair and waited, and at seven forty-five she finally got what she was waiting for. The telephone rang, and she picked up the receiver before the first ring was through. But after she answered, Rae found she couldn't speak; staying awake all night had robbed her of her voice.

"Rae, are you there?" she heard Jessup say.

She could tell from the metallic sound of his voice that he was calling from a phone booth. At the very least, he wasn't in another woman's bedroom.

"Are you going to speak to me, or what?" Jessup asked.

"I'll speak to you," Rae agreed, and she was amazed by how calm she sounded.

Whenever he hurt her, Jessup acted like he was the one who'd been wronged.

"I didn't come home last night," Jessup said now. "If you bothered to notice."

"Oh, I noticed, all right," Rae said.

Usually, not pressuring Jessup was the right thing to do—but now it backfired, and by the time Rae's voice traveled to the broiling metal phone booth where Jessup was standing, the cool flatness of her tone infuriated him. He decided it was his right to be cruel.

"I'll give you a hint as to where I am," he said. "I'm in the desert."

She knew he expected her to question him.

"Do you mind telling me in what state?"

"California," Jessup said. "Outside Barstow. You think it's hot where you are."

"Do you mind telling me with who?"

"With who what?" Jessup said. He was enjoying this, she could tell.

"Who are you with?" Rae said.

"Maybe I just wanted to see the desert," Jessup said. "Maybe I wanted to be by myself."

Jessup let her sit there in agony for a moment, and then he told her the truth—he was out with a location company that had needed a driver at the last minute. He actually seemed to think this announcement warranted congratulations.

"That's the reason you didn't come home?" Rae asked.

"Every jerk in the world is making a movie, and I'm driving them around," Jessup said. "Do you think that's fair?"

Rae found herself wondering if it was the coffee that now made her feel so sick.

"Rae?" Jessup said. "Are you still there?"

That was when she knew.

"You're not coming home," Rae said, "are you?"

"The shooting schedule is eight weeks, and I think that's enough time for me to set up my own deal with the producer. I don't see why I couldn't direct."

"Tell me right now, Jessup," Rae said. "Are you coming home or not?"

"Well, sure I am," Jessup said. "Eventually."

The future was so close Rae could feel it; it hung from

the white stucco ceiling, and draped itself across the furniture.

"How can you do this to me?" she asked.

"Wait a minute," Jessup said. "Don't start pulling this guilt shit on me. Maybe I want to be somebody, Rae—this is a chance for me."

"Oh, really?" Rae said. "What about me?"

"What about you?" Jessup said, surprised.

She hung up on him. Even after she turned on the cold water in the shower and stood under the spray, Rae could still hear the crash of the phone receiver hitting against its cradle. She stayed in the shower until she was shivering, but after she turned off the water, she felt too exhausted to move. She sat down in the tub and cried. It wasn't so much that Jessup had left her, it was that after seven years together, Rae felt as if she had never had him in the first place. Outside, the bamboo that grew near the apartment building swayed in the hot wind; when the stalks rubbed together you could swear you heard singing. How could it be that Jessup now seemed like nothing more than a stranger who had telephoned from the desert? Unless he was someone she had dreamed up, and in that case Rae had been sleepwalking for seven years. And she could sit in that empty bathtub from today until tomorrow, and that still didn't change the fact that only the most dangerous of men would go off and leave you in Los Angeles, to wake up alone.

■ ■ ■

Outside the front door of a bungalow on Three Sisters Street was a white arbor where roses bloomed all year long. It certainly wasn't Lila Grey who took care of them; it was all she could do to remember to water the potted geraniums out on the patio. Her husband, Richard, was the one who took care of the yard, and the truth was, he didn't have much luck. The lemon tree out back was crooked, ivy crept into the windows, the hibiscus dropped its salmon-colored flowers on the walkway.

The entire block seemed ill-fated; once it had been an estate belonging to three young women, a gift from one of the early directors to his sisters. But the gift had not been enough for them; they'd withered there, grown old and sick, and finally they'd refused to leave their house. When the block was sold at auction in the thirties, the grounds were so overgrown that bulldozers had been brought in, leveling everything. Bungalows were built, and as the neighborhood slipped—more crime and more roofs that needed patching—the one thing that remained constant was that it was nearly impossible to grow anything on Three Sisters Street.

But Lila's husband was a BMW mechanic, and he insisted that plants had to be simpler than a German-made car. He refused to give up. During the heat wave, when the city allowed hoses to be turned on for only an hour each day, Richard became a maniac for water. He scooped out bathwater and soapy dishwater with a metal pail and rationed a little for each of the trees. He joked that working with plants was a part of his heritage—his father was a Shinnecock Indian who had long ago been a migrant worker, his mother a Russian Jew who could never keep a begonia alive on her window sill. When Richard was nine, his parents bought a gas station on the North Fork of Long Island, and Lila knew that the only things that had ever grown there were wildflowers and weeds.

Sometimes, when Richard was out mowing the grass, Lila could look out the window and actually see the grass turning brown beneath the blades. She had the urge to run outside and beg him to give up: they could brick over the lawn, extend the slate patio, chop down the twisted trees and use them for firewood on rainy winter nights. But Lila forced herself to keep quiet, and when she went outside it was only to take Richard a glass of lemonade. If he wanted to believe he could turn the lawn green and force strawberries to appear on the few spindly plants, who was she to tell him he was wrong? But anyone could see that the only thing that would ever grow in their garden were the huge scarlet roses, and they seemed not to need any care at all, not even water—in the neighborhood it was rumored that the roses had once grown by the Sisters' front door, that they were the last remnants of the hundreds that had once been on the estate.

Lila held with the idea of letting people believe whatever they wanted, no matter how foolish. Her husband believed at least a dozen false things about her, and that was just the way Lila wanted it. Just as Richard imagined himself to be the first man she had ever loved, he believed his wife to be psychic. If he came home early and found Lila giving a private reading in the living room—the lamps turned down, the red silk cloth spread out on the table—he tiptoed down the hallway. Lila didn't see any point in explaining that her readings depended less on the arrangement of a little water and Darjeeling than they did on the dark circles under a client's eyes, or the way some people twisted their wedding bands on their fingers, as though the gold irritated their skin. Those moments when she felt some sort of strange, pure knowledge she credited to intuition, no more and no less than anyone else might have. Privately, she felt her clients' preoccupation with the future was foolish, a sport for schoolgirls and lonely women. But the past, that was another matter. The past could press down on you until every bit of air was forced out of your lungs; if you weren't careful, it could swallow you up entirely, leaving nothing but a few fragile bones, a silver bracelet, ten moon-shaped fingernails.

Lately, Lila couldn't look in a mirror without seeing a young girl whose hair was so thick she had to brush it twice a day with a wire brush made in France. When she stood at the sink washing dishes, she could feel herself falling, pulled backward into a well so deep it might be impossible to ever climb back out once you let go. It was pure luck that Richard had managed to pull her back each time. He'd simply be looking for a magazine or a pair of pliers, he'd decide to have a piece of pie and slam the refrigerator door. That was all it took—his presence would bring Lila back and there she'd be, safe in her own kitchen.

But at night she was too far away for Richard to reach her, and Lila found herself dreaming about the apartment in New York where she'd grown up. It was a place where there were heavy drapes on all the windows, and at night the steam heat made a peculiar crying sound that quickened your heart. Lila was eighteen and still living at home. In the mornings she attended an acting class held in a deserted theater on the Lower East Side, but when her parents had had enough—talk of Broadway and Hollywood until they were dizzy—they insisted she find a job. Lila became a waitress at a restaurant on Third Avenue, and it was there, in the late afternoons, that an old woman named Hannie read fortunes in exchange for fifty cents. The cooks in the kitchen were afraid to tell Hannie to leave—they told each other that she wore long, black dresses to hide the fact that underneath she had chicken's legs. Instead of knees she had knobby yellow flesh, around her ankles there were white feathers. Her eyes, the waitresses all agreed, could put you under a spell and before you knew it you'd be barking like a dog.

Whenever Lila brought over the pots of hot water and raisin buns Hannie ordered, she made certain never to look the old lady in the eye. Lila couldn't help but notice that for every one in the restaurant who feared Hannie, there was a client who thought the world of her. In June so many girls about to become brides wanted to hear their fortunes that a line formed outside the restaurant on Third Avenue. Nearly all of her clients were women, and each had a slightly dazed look on her face as Hannie opened the purple tin in which she carried her tea. There were times when everyone in the restaurant had to work hard to ignore the weeping that came from that rear table, and on days when a bad fortune was read, everyone in the restaurant grew moody, and to cheer themselves the waitresses munched on chocolate bars, and butter crumb cakes, and figs.

ALICE HOFFMAN

Lila found herself drawn to the old fortune-teller. Each time she took a break, she wound up at a table in the rear of the restaurant, and as she drank a Coke with lemon and ice, she listened in to the tea-leaf readings. It was oddly thrilling to face in the other direction and still hear a tale of heartbreak or hope right behind your back. But though she could hear each client's complaints quite clearly, Lila could never make out Hannie's advice. The words were all garbled, too private and low; and Lila found herself moving closer and closer to the fortune-teller's table, until one day Lila realized that it wasn't the wall her elbow was resting on, but Hannie's bony spine. Lila moved away in terror, convinced that before the night was through she'd be howling at the moon. But the old woman smiled at her, then motioned for her to come to her table, and Lila could hardly refuse.

"As long as you're eavesdropping," Hannie said when Lila had sat down across from her, "you might as well sit here and learn something."

From that day on, Lila sat with the old fortune-teller whenever she could, and she no longer had to strain to hear Hannie's advice. Every time a new symbol appeared in a teacup during a reading, Hannie jabbed Lila's arm with her finger. On the back of a menu Hannie listed the most important signs: A flock of birds was always sorrow. The flat line of a horizon meant travel. A four-pointed star was a man who would betray you, and a five-pointed star was a man who was true.

Lila began to practice her new skill on her family and friends. She had a natural talent for guessing what was wrong with someone's life, and in no time she had a following. Some of her mother's friends slipped her a dollar for good luck when she read for them; the other girls who took classes at the theater brought in Thermoses of hot water and tins of loose tea and they offered Lila earrings and hair clips in return for their future. In the restaurant there were some clients who began to prefer Lila's readings to Hannie's, and they sat patiently, ordering cheese danish or mushroom soup, until Lila could take her break. But even after several months, whenever Lila looked into a client's cup she saw only murky tea leaves, never the future. She began to feel that each time she gave a reading she was committing a robbery. No matter how hard she tried, she couldn't see into the future, and when she asked Hannie why this was, the old woman made a sound in the back of her throat that startled Lila, for it sounded exactly like a chicken clucking.

"You could see the future if you wanted to," Hannie said. "You've just decided to ignore it."

Lila had just fallen in love with her acting teacher, and the future was practically all she did think about.

"Answer me one question," Hannie demanded. "Why do you think it is that after all this time you never asked me to do a reading for you?"

"Maybe I don't believe in readings," Lila admitted. "Maybe that's why I never really see anything."

"You think that's the reason?" Hannie said. The old woman's black skirt crackled as she leaned forward and took Lila's hands in her own. That day the luncheon special in the restaurant was pot roast, and the smell of burnt onions was everywhere. It stuck in your throat and brought tears to your eyes. All afternoon, Lila had been wondering if she'd have time to go home after work and wash her hair before she met Stephen. Stephen not only taught acting—he was the second lead in a play off Broadway, and every Thursday night they met in his small dressing room. Lila had already decided to wear a cotton dress with a lace collar, but now, with Hannie holding her hands, Lila wondered if she should wear something warmer. Suddenly she was freezing, and when Hannie closed Lila's fingers, so that each hand made a fist, Lila could feel the chill all the way from her fingertips to her heart.

"Let me give you some good advice," Hannie said. "Be careful—otherwise you may discover that you've lost the one you love best."

But at eighteen the only thing more impossible than being careful is listening to an old woman's advice. "You can see the future," Hannie had insisted. "All you have to do is open your eyes." There was the smell of burnt onions, the rattle of dishes in the kitchen, the rustling of the fortune-teller's black skirts.

And now whenever Lila dreamed, it was of New York. When she woke, she still heard the steam heat, and as she sat in the dark and watched her husband sleep she couldn't help but wonder if perhaps she did have some talent as a fortune-teller after all. There was no doubt in her mind that Rae Perry was the age her own daughter would have been. And she hoped that Hannie had been wrong all those years ago, because if this was what seeing into the future was like, Lila could do very well without that gift.

• • •

Jessup had been gone for a week when Rae began to suspect that even more was wrong than she'd thought. A rush of cool air swept the city, but Rae barely noticed the change in the weather—she still felt burning hot. She drank pitchers of water and took her temperature, convinced that she must have some terrible fever. During the day she couldn't stay awake: she locked the office door and curled up on Freddy's couch. Then at night, she couldn't sleep. She tossed and turned until the sheets were as twisted as snakes. She grew afraid of the dark, afraid of dreams and noises in the night, and clouds that covered the moon. No matter where she turned in her apartment she always found herself staring at the telephone, even though she already knew that Jessup wouldn't be calling her again.

On the day she went to see Lila Grey, Rae started out to go grocery shopping, and had made it as far as the vegetable aisle. But the checkout lines were all too long, and the peaches were bruised, and the milk not yet delivered, and Rae wound up deserting her cart near a display of radishes and scallions. After that it was easy—she didn't even have to think about it. Instead of turning right and walking home, she turned left, and in no time at all she found herself on Three Sisters Street.

Rae knocked on the front door, but as she stood on the

porch the scent of the roses overwhelmed her, and before she knew it she was weak in the knees. By the time Lila opened the door, Rae was doubled over.

"I don't know what happened," Rae said as Lila helped her inside. "I just collapsed."

"And you decided to do it here," Lila said.

Actually, Lila felt panicky, and the only reason she went into the kitchen for some water was to get Rae on her feet and out of the house as quickly as possible. Lila stood at the sink and gulped down a glass of water herself before rinsing out the glass and filling it for Rae. In the living room, Rae took the water greedily, and she didn't notice that Lila was staring at her until she was done.

"I came to have my fortune read," Rae explained.

Lila was wearing blue slacks and a white cotton shirt. Without her turban and her silver bracelets she looked like someone you'd meet on line in the market, and Rae felt somewhat ridiculous asking her to see into the future.

"I work by appointment," Lila said sternly.

She would have said anything then to get rid of Rae.

"It's an emergency," Rae confided. "The man I'm in love with left me."

"If you consider that an emergency, half the women in Hollywood would be here right now."

Rae could feel herself sinking. "You won't believe this," she said. "I think I'm going to faint."

"Oh, no you don't," Lila said. "Not here."

Lila went back to the kitchen for a bottle of vinegar to hold under Rae's nose. When some of Rae's color returned, Lila went to the front door and opened it.

"You're right—I need air," Rae said gratefully. "And maybe some more water."

"Anything else?" Lila snapped, taking the empty glass.

"A cracker?" Rae called after her.

Lila brought out a box of Wheat Thins and a fresh glass of water. She told herself that in less than five minutes Rae would be deposited back on the street.

"This is fabulous," Rae said as she took out a cracker and bit it in half.

"I don't think you understand," Lila said. "I do readings by appointment only. I can't have anyone just walk in off the street."

"Oh," Rae said. She had the other half of her cracker in her mouth, but now she was too self-conscious to chew. The Wheat Thin expanded, swelling her cheek.

If Rae hadn't looked so pathetic, Lila might not have sat down in the rocking chair and reconsidered.

"When did he leave you?" Lila asked.

"A week ago," Rae said. "If I knew he was coming back I wouldn't mind waiting. I really wouldn't."

"Twenty-five dollars," Lila said. "And I don't take personal checks."

Rae reached into her purse and counted out two tens and a five.

"I hope you understand that you may not like what I have to say," Lila warned her.

"I don't care," Rae said. "I'm ready for anything. You can tell me everything you know."

Lila had no intention of doing that. This reading was not for Rae, but for herself. A simple thing like going into the kitchen and filling the teapot was suddenly an act of courage. Lifting the teapot onto the stove's front burner seemed to take forever; time was moving in that odd way it does when you are terrified of what may happen next, and your senses are slow and dull. As the water began to heat up, Lila looked out into the yard. Richard stood on a stepladder and picked lemons off the tree. A neighbor called across the hedge and Lila could hear the two men discuss fertilizer. But after a while Lila could no longer hear their voices; she couldn't hear the thud of lemons as they dropped into a wicker basket. Instead, she heard the flare of Hannie's stiff black skirts as the old woman shrank back and moved against the wall. Lila had brought Stephen to the restaurant just to meet Hannie, but now she could see that she shouldn't have. Hannie looked right through Stephen, even after he had given her his most winning smile, the one that worked on nearly everyone. When he asked the old woman for a reading, she laughed out loud—but it was a hollow sound that echoed in the kitchen and made the cooks put down the knives they were using to cut up potatoes for soup and stare at each other uneasily.

"Lila talks about you all the time," Stephen said to Hannie. "Don't tell me that now you won't tell my fortune."

Hannie hadn't answered. Instead, she gave him one long look, and the heat she threw off nearly burnt a hole right through him.

"I don't need tea leaves to tell you his future," Hannie said to Lila, just as if Stephen weren't there.

Stephen stood up; he went to the counter and didn't look over his shoulder. And there Lila was, in the middle.

Now, Hannie wouldn't look at her either, and when Lila reached for the old woman's hand, Hannie's fingers seemed to retract, and Lila was left holding on to the table. Lila made her decision then and there; she got up and followed Stephen to the counter—although when he put his arm around her, Lila swore he was doing it for spite, more for Hannie's benefit than anything else. Of course, Hannie's rejection only made Stephen even more curious, and from that time on he was after Lila to read his tea leaves. But even then, Lila must have had some hint as to what would happen, because she refused him again and again.

Stephen had grown up in Florida, and when she was with him Lila found herself dreaming about oranges and salt water and endless white beaches where there wasn't a soul. There was nothing she would not do for him, and when Stephen decided that Hannie was a bad influence—a madwoman who could do nothing but harm an impressionable girl—Lila stopped sitting at the old woman's table during her breaks. Soon, Lila stopped telling fortunes; she threw away the tins of tea she kept in her mother's kitchen, she told her aunts and her girlfriends it had just been a game. But as she served customers in the restaurant, she could feel the old woman watching her and she grew clumsy, spilling tumblers of water and bowls of boiling-hot soup. What she missed more than anything were those late hours when business in the restaurant was slow, and she'd sit at Hannie's table, asking for another story about the village where the fortune-teller had grown up—a town nearly cut off from the rest of the world by forests where nothing but pine and wild lavender grew. Now she dreaded that time of the day, and although she tried to stand up to the disappointment on Hannie's face, it grew clear that the only solution to the distance between the two women was more distance. Lila quit her job at the restaurant and took another, at a Chock Full o' Nuts around the corner, where there wasn't the slightest danger that a waitress might talk to a customer.

Lila had to admit there were problems in her love affair: Stephen was married. But people did divorce, and all his marriage meant to Lila was that they couldn't go to his apartment. Instead, they met in a dressing room, or in the borrowed apartment of an actress friend who was often on the road. They stole things when they were in the actress's apartment: tins of sardines, pints of cream, earrings made out of glass. These small thefts bound them together, and when they were in the actress's bed Lila could almost envision their future together. They would sleep late on Sundays once he was free, a kiss would last forever, every cup of tea they drank would be sweetened with two spoons of sugar and utterly free of tea leaves.

But most of the time they were forced to meet in the dressing room, and whenever they were there it didn't seem to matter how hard Lila tried not to look—she always found herself staring at the small photograph of Stephen's wife. Not that he had ever lied to her or led her on. When the run of his play ended, Stephen planned to go to Maine for the summer—his wife's family had a house there. Stephen called it a cottage, but Lila had seen a photograph. It was a huge white house on the edge of a peninsula which jutted into a bay that froze solid from October to May. In her dreams, Lila was haunted by this house; a cold wind moved through the rooms turning every object to ice. Even the arms of the wooden rocking chairs on the porch were coated with frost. That summer house became Lila's enemy, and she knew that it was just a matter of time before it claimed Stephen and Lila would be left with even less than she'd had before.

She did everything she could to prolong the run of his play. She used up her salary buying tickets which she gave away to distant cousins and neighbors. Every night she called the box office, and every night more tickets were available. At last, Stephen told her that the play was about to close. A part of Lila believed that if she just had time enough she could persuade Stephen not to leave her for that house in Maine. But the idea of battling that cold, empty house was simply too much, and her weapons too fragile— nothing more than desire and youth. Since she was about to lose him anyway, she decided she wouldn't ruin their last night together. But of course, it was ruined even before it began: when she got to the dressing room, Stephen had already boiled water for tea and he begged her to tell his fortune. Lila knew enough to be sure that if she refused him this time, they would argue and she would wind up in tears. And then Stephen would softly whisper that he could never stand to see a woman cry, and he would ask her to leave. So she sat across from him at a small wicker table and watched him drink his tea, although just the movement of his hand as he reached for the teacup nearly broke her heart.

"I especially want to know if I'll be famous," Stephen said. "Of course, I wouldn't mind being exceedingly rich."

He had come around so that he stood behind Lila. He put his hands on her shoulders and bent down. As he spoke, Lila could feel his breath on her neck. And she knew, even before she looked, that in the center of the teacup there would be a four-pointed star.

Lila told him exactly what he wanted to hear.

"I can see that you'll have everything you ever wanted," she told him, but then, the moment Stephen looked away, Lila dipped her finger in the teacup and stirred up the leaves. She still did not believe in the symbols Hannie had taught her, but it was so much easier to invent a future when the only distraction was the heat of her lover's breath. The predictions she offered Stephen were each more delightful than the next. His children would swim like fish and recite the alphabet before their second birthdays; his summers on that cold, glassy bay would be endless; and as for fame, his name would be remembered forever and ever.

To tease her, Stephen tossed a dollar down on the table, and then he pulled her down on the couch. But although she embraced him, Lila couldn't look at him. Instead, she stared up at a small window that was screened with heavy black mesh. That night the moon was so huge that it broke through the screen and filled the room with light. As they made love, Lila felt her spirit being pulled out of her. The sheet of moonlight was wrapping itself around her. Her bones were as brittle as ice, and the skin beneath her finger-nails turned a startling blue. The tighter Stephen held her, the more lost Lila was. She was farther and farther away from the earth, up where the air was so thin it was always winter, and breathing alone hurt your lungs and left tears in your eyes.

When Lila reached up her arms it was the moon she reached for. To embrace this lover she had to leave her body behind. She could see herself on the couch with Stephen—her arms and legs covered with a watery film, her mouth wide open. It seemed a pity for Stephen to think she was there with him. Up in the air she was weightless, and her hair turned into feathers that were so black you couldn't see them against the night. That was when the light entered her, and as it did Lila could see the future. It unfolded to her cell by cell, second by second. At first she thought she heard the rapid flapping of a bird struggling for flight, but when Lila listened closely she knew it was the sound of another heart beating.

The very next evening, Lila waited outside the restaurant at closing time. She couldn't bring herself to go in like some customer off the street, and so she decided to follow the old woman home. It was a cool night, and the air was damp. Lila made sure to stay a block behind Hannie; she was frightened of being discovered, then having to beg for a reading on a street corner. They walked for a very long time, Hannie leading the way through a maze of streets, behind Chelsea, near the river. The streets were made of cobblestones—no one had ever bothered to tar them over. There was no traffic here, not even the underground shudder of the subway. No one lived here except for a few old women who carried their belongings in paper bags and pillowcases, and, in the abandoned buildings, feral cats, quick, underfed animals who hunted for pigeons on the fire escapes.

When Lila could no longer tell east from west, Hannie stopped outside the door of an old rowhouse and let herself in. Lila watched as the lights inside were turned on; in the window sat a huge, tawny cat—no relation to the wild cats on the fire escapes—and, Lila was sure of this, there was the impossibly delicious smell of bread baking. As she stood there, Lila imagined what it would be like to follow Hannie inside: the house would be warm and silent, there would be bread and butter and tea. You could sleep here all night and not even hear the wind. And if others missed you, they'd never find you unless you wanted them to. Not in a million years.

Lila began to think of her own mother, and of her own bedroom, where she had slept every night of her life. She could tell Hannie was waiting for her, but she felt a sudden wave of homesickness. She panicked and began to run. It was dark now, the sky purple at the horizon, and Lila thought she heard an anguished echo from the rowhouse, like a bird caught between wires. She was terrified that she was lost, but she never once stopped running. After a while she began to feel the rumble of buses, and she realized that she was looking up, and that the position of the stars had guided her back to Tenth Avenue.

That night, safe in her own bed, Lila couldn't sleep. The next evening she returned to the restaurant, but this time when she followed Hannie the fortune-teller disappeared around a corner after they crossed Tenth Avenue. Nothing seemed familiar to Lila, and she had to struggle so hard to get out of the maze of streets that by the time she stumbled across the avenue, she was in tears. She knew then that in turning away that first time, she had lost her chance. She was certain that Hannie had seen her and that she no longer trusted Lila, she didn't even want Lila to know where she lived. For weeks Lila tried to get up the nerve to go to the restaurant and see Hannie. She was obsessed with having her fortune read; she was desperate to know what her future would bring, and each day she grew more troubled, and ten times as lonely as she had been the day before. At night she dreamed of Stephen, asleep in a hammock on the porch of that house in Maine. She dreamed of birds and gold wedding rings, and she no longer felt safe in her own bedroom. She stopped taking classes at the theater. The new teacher was nothing compared to Stephen, and besides, Lila already knew, she hadn't any real talent after all. In July she went back to the restaurant, and although she didn't actually go inside, she felt a little braver. By the end of the month Lila was ready to face Hannie, to walk past the row of waitresses and the cooks, and ask to have her tea leaves read. Lila never once guessed that Hannie hadn't seen her and purposely avoided her in the alleys and cobblestone streets, just as she never knew that when the old woman squinted as she read tea leaves it wasn't in order to see the future more clearly, but because she was blind in one eye. Every day, when business was slow, Hannie sat at the rear table, waiting for Lila. But by the time Lila had the courage to come back she hadn't menstruated in two months, and she no longer needed to have her fortune told.

As she waited for the water in the teapot to boil, Lila

tried not to think of the old fortune-teller. She watched through the window as her husband climbed down from the stepladder, but all she saw was moonlight, all she heard was the sound of cats' claws on the fire escapes, and the cool, damp air left her shivering.

Outside, Richard turned on the sprinkler. Now that the heat wave had passed, the city had lifted all water restrictions, and in every backyard there was the smell of damp earth. It was a heartbreaking scent, one that left you longing for everything you once had and lost. And although the tea was ready to be served, and Rae was waiting, Lila was really too cold to go back into the living room. Twice Lila had read for pregnant women; both times a small, still child had risen to the surface, before being pulled down into the center of the cup. She had lied, of course, and when she wept her clients had thought it was their good fortune that affected her so. If the symbol appeared a third time, Lila would again fail to mention that the child she saw was not moving, that it did not breathe or open its eyes. Whatever the shape of the tea leaves, Lila would advise Rae of her pregnancy, and tell her nothing more. She would fold her twenty-five-dollar fee into her pocket, and then, after Rae had left, she would stand with her back against the front door and cry. But there was never any hurry when you were about to tell someone that her life would be changed forever, and because the sunlight in the backyard was so warm and bright, Lila slipped out the back door, and she ran across the patio to throw her arms around her husband.

. . .

After the reading, Rae had no one to talk to. Jessup had never believed in friends.

"What's the point?" he had always said. "You get yourself a friend and the first thing they want is to borrow something from you. Next they want to tell you all their troubles. Then look out—because then they're mad that they owe you something, plus you know all their secrets, and they're not so sure they want you knowing so much after all."

What Rae wanted more than anything was a friend, a woman who would tell her that Lila's prediction had been all wrong. But when she really thought about it, she had to admit that there wasn't a friend on earth who could have convinced her that her swollen ankles and the wire stretched tight inside her stomach were anything other than signs of pregnancy. Her period was four weeks late, and she had lost her taste for coffee. What frightened Rae was not being pregnant, but having to tell Jessup about it. Jessup didn't even like to be in the same room with a child. He referred to children as midgets, and he had often suggested that orphans be put out on ice floes and left to drift into the cold, blue sea.

Once before Rae had thought she might have to tell Jessup he would be a father. They were living in a garden apartment in Maryland and it was so hot that September that you never saw any people—everyone stayed where it was air-conditioned. It was their first home and Rae wanted it to be perfect. She taught herself how to cook, which was a real accomplishment considering she had learned nothing from her mother. Any time Carolyn started to cook she began to cry—just cutting up a leek or reaching for a bottle of olive oil was enough to set her off. She would have been astounded to discover that her daughter bought fresh blueberries for jam, grew her own tomatoes for gazpacho, melted bars of imported chocolate for mousse. By the time Jessup got home from work the table was always set and candles had been lit. But before she brought the meal to the table, Rae had to wait for Jessup to get ready. He was working with a construction crew building an addition to the local high school, and he came home caked with red dirt. Every evening, while Jessup soaked in the tub, Rae watched the candles burn down and she worried about the high-school girls Jessup was bound to meet. She was sure that if she ever lost him she would stay locked up in the air-conditioned apartment forever; and she always had the feeling she was losing him, no matter how hard she tried to please him.

One night, as they sat down to scallops and fresh string beans, Jessup picked up his fork and moved and the food around his plate, as if he didn't know what else to do with it. His skin was dark from working outside, and his eyes were bluer than ever.

"Boy," he said as he touched a bean with the prongs of his fork, "you really go for this stuff, don't you, Rae?"

Rae had spent the morning searching for scallops; a raspberry tart was still baking.

"I thought you'd like scallops," Rae said shyly.

"Me?" Jessup said, surprised. "I'd rather have hamburgers."

Jessup ate a scallop, but Rae could tell he was forcing himself. She never used a cookbook again—after all, there was no point in cooking for someone who couldn't tell the difference between a *gâteau au chocolat* and a defrosted Sara Lee cake. But once she had stopped cooking there wasn't much for her to do but watch the clock and wait for Jessup. Each day when he came home after work, Rae was so relieved that she hadn't lost him that she didn't wait for him to take a bath—she pulled him down onto the living-room floor where they made love, and when they were through Rae's skin was streaked with the red dirt Jessup brought home. Afterward Rae stayed in the living room while Jessup went into the bathroom to run the water in the tub. She could never figure out why she felt so lonely, and whenever Jessup called to her, inviting her into the bathtub, Rae closed her eyes and pretended not to hear him. After a while he must have assumed that she liked to be by herself after they made love, because no matter how much he had wanted her, by the time they were through, he just walked away, as if she were a stranger.

It was right about that time that Rae began to think she was pregnant. There were certainly signs: her period was late and she had gained five pounds. But the oddest thing of all was that Rae suddenly had the desire to talk to her mother. One day, while Jessup was at work, Rae called home. When her mother picked up the receiver and said hello, the sound of her voice cut right through Rae, and she had to force herself to speak.

"It's me," Rae said casually. "I'm in a garden apartment in Maryland."

"I love it," Carolyn said. "Your father always insists you're in California. He's convinced that people like Jessup always wind up on the West Coast."

"Mother," Rae said, just as if a year hadn't passed since they'd last argued, "I didn't call you long distance to talk about Jessup."

"I've tried to understand why you'd run away with him, but I can't," Carolyn said.

"Stop trying," Rae said. "You'll never understand me."

"If you would just call your father at the office and tell him you're sorry. Tell him you made a terrible mistake."

"But I didn't!" Rae said.

"You're never planning to come home," Carolyn said suddenly, "are you?"

"I don't know," Rae admitted.

"It's just as well," Carolyn said. "Your father would never allow it—not unless you proved to him that you had changed."

Rae felt herself grow hot. "And you'd just agree with him?" she said.

Carolyn didn't answer.

"Mother!" Rae said. "Would you agree with him?"

"Yes," Carolyn said. "I would."

Rae could hear the Oldsmobile pull up. She dragged the phone over to the window and lifted up one venetian blind. Jessup got out of the car and took off his blue denim jacket.

"I have to go," Rae told her mother.

"I'm in the middle," Carolyn said. "Don't you see?"

Jessup was at the front door; he knocked once, and when Rae didn't answer he fumbled for the key.

"I just called to let you know I was all right," Rae said, but she wasn't—she'd never felt more alone in her life. Any second Jessup would walk through the door—if he discovered that she had called Boston there might be a scene. He might tell her to take the bus back home if she missed the place so much, and now Rae knew that she couldn't—by now they had gotten rid of the furniture in her bedroom, they had probably changed the locks on all the doors.

"Is that the only reason you called?" Carolyn said in a small voice, as though she actually expected Rae to say that she missed her.

"I really have to go," Rae said, and she hung up the phone and ran to get the door just as Jessup was letting himself in.

That night she couldn't sleep. She went into the living room and sat in the dark, the phone balanced on her lap. She dialed the area code for Boston, and then the number for the local weather report. It was much colder in Boston—forty degrees—and by morning a pale frost would appear on the lawns and between cabbage leaves in backyard gardens. On nights when she couldn't sleep, all Rae had to do was ask Jessup to hold her and he would; he might even sit up with her and watch a movie on TV if she asked the right way. But right then, the only person Rae wanted was her mother. If she closed her eyes she could smell Carolyn's perfume, she could feel how cold the windowpanes were in her third-floor bedroom on nights when the moon was full and a web of ice formed on the glass.

Later, when it was nearly dawn, Rae went into the bathroom. When she discovered a line of blood on her thigh, she sat down on the rim of the tub and cried. The sky had turned pearl gray and the crickets were still calling when Rae got into bed beside Jessup. She could tell he was dreaming; he held on to the pillow so tightly that his knuckles were white. As Rae pulled the sheet over them, Jessup woke up.

"I was dreaming," he said.

"I know," Rae told him. "I was watching you."

"It was summer," Jessup said. "There were a million stars in the sky and I was waiting outside your house, but you didn't see me."

Rae put her arms around him. "I saw you," she told him, but Jessup was already back asleep.

After that night, Rae risked the subject of children every now and then, but Jessup's reaction was always the same.

"Take a good look at me," he would tell her. "Do I look like somebody's father?"

Rae had to admit that he didn't. Even when she really tried she couldn't imagine him getting up at two in the morning, or changing a diaper, or shopping for a crib.

"All a baby will do is come between us," Jessup warned her. "Is that what you want? Because if that's what you want let's go into the bedroom right now and make the biggest mistake we ever made."

But this time there was a difference. This time Jessup wasn't around to convince Rae that it was a mistake. Jessup was out in the desert where the moonlight turned nights colder than any winter in Boston. He was turning in his sleep, unaware that Rae had already decided. Whether he liked it or not he was about to become somebody's father.

. . .

Rae took the bus to Barstow on a day when it was impossible to look at the sky and not think of heaven. After a while there was less traffic and the road opened up. Now, each passenger who got on brought some of the desert into the bus, so that a fine cover of sand drifted across the aisles. Even through the dusty windows you could tell how blue the sky was, and all along the roadside there were tuberous wildflowers that were so sweet they attracted bees the size of a man's hand.

At noon the sky turned white with heat, and Rae saw her first real mirage. There was a line of coyotes along a ridgetop, but when she blinked they disappeared. There was nothing in the distance but pink sand and low violet clouds, and of course it wasn't the right time of day for coyotes anyway. They waited for the temperature to fall before they came down from the mountains. Then they walked in single file, circling deserted adobe houses, making a noise in the back of their throats that made you think they were dying of loneliness.

When Rae got off the bus the air was so dry that it stung. She found a phone booth and called every motel listed; the film crew was registered at the Holiday Inn on Route 17, but the desk clerk told her that everyone had gone out on location. Rae took a cab to the Holiday Inn. She'd hoped to get into Jessup's room so she could take a shower and order room service before he got back, but the desk clerk refused to give her the key. After all, what rights did she have—they weren't even married.

By the time she had ordered a grilled cheese sandwich in the coffee shop, Rae was furious. It seemed as if Jessup had purposely not married her just so that one day she'd be kept out of his room at the Holiday Inn. She had wanted to get married all along, but Jessup felt it was a meaningless act. What difference did a piece of paper make—he pointed out his own father, who hadn't bothered with a divorce from Jessup's mother before disappearing, and then clinched his argument by bringing up Rae's parents, whom he called the most miserable couple on earth.

"We'd be different," Rae had promised. Carolyn had been married in a blue suit, as if she had already given up hope. Rae planned to wear a long white dress.

"We already are different," Jessup had said. "We're not married."

After thinking about it, Rae had panicked—if Jessup died she couldn't even legally arrange for his funeral. Dressed in black, she'd have to stand on a runway at Los Angeles Airport and watch as his body was shipped back to his mother in Boston.

"Don't worry about it," Jessup had told her. "If you're really concerned I'll send my mother a postcard and tell her you get to keep the Oldsmobile and my body."

Rae left the coffee shop and went to sit by the pool. Had she been allowed up to his room, she would have shown him. By now she would have ordered baskets of fruit and chilled champagne. Instead, she found some change at the bottom of her purse and got a soda from the vending machine. The heat rose higher and higher and no one dared to venture out of the air-conditioned rooms, but there she was, on a plastic chaise longue beside the pool—all because he had never bothered to marry her. The fact that he was out on location was what really upset her, because there was absolutely nothing worse than taking a long bus trip and having it end with no one there to meet you.

The last time Rae had taken such a trip, she was eight years old. She and Carolyn were going out to a rented summer house in Wellfleet; they had left a few days early so that everything could be in order by the time Rae's father drove down for the weekend. The trip had been a disaster—Carolyn got sick and the bus driver had to pull off onto the shoulder of Route 3. As the other passengers watched, Carolyn stood on the asphalt and tried to breathe.

"It's nothing serious," she told Rae when she returned, but Rae noticed that her mother was gripping the upholstered seat in front of them, and that her fingers were swollen and white.

By the time they got to Wellfleet, Rae felt sick, too. Carolyn had misplaced the key and they had to climb into the house through an unlatched window. Rae stood in the middle of the dark living room as her mother stumbled over to the wall to find the light switch. She could actually feel the goose bumps rise on her arms and legs. Later, Carolyn made up a bed for her with clean sheets, but Rae couldn't sleep. She could hear crickets and the hum that lightning bugs make when they're trapped in the mesh of a screen window. The walls in the house sagged and creaked, and there was an owl's nest in the chimney so that a muffled hooting echoed from inside the bricks. Carolyn couldn't sleep either; she came into Rae's room late at night and sat at the foot of the bed.

"It's not an accident that you have red hair," Carolyn said. She lit a cigarette, and in the dark the smoke spiraled up to the ceiling. "When I was pregnant with you I bought a pair of red high heels made in Italy. Even though I couldn't really wear them because my feet had swollen, sometimes when I was alone I put them on and just wore them around the house. That's the reason you have red hair."

"No it isn't," Rae said.

The hum of the lightning bugs was growing fainter, although Rae could still see patches of light caught in the window.

"I'll bet you anything it's the reason," Carolyn said.

"What if you had worn purple shoes?" Rae challenged.

"You would have had black hair that was so dark it would look nearly purple at night."

"Green?" Rae asked.

"Pale blond hair that turned green every time you swam in a pool with any chlorine in it."

By the time she fell asleep Rae had forgotten about the business on the bus, and the sound of the owls had become as regular as a heartbeat. But that weekend, when Rae's father drove down, Rae could tell that something was wrong between her parents. Usually, they argued—now they just didn't speak. The silence in the house was suffocating, but then, on Sunday, Rae found something on the front porch that made her think August wouldn't be so terrible after all. It was a cardboard shoebox, and inside was a pair of ruby-colored plastic beach shoes. When Rae slipped them on they fit perfectly, as if they'd been made for her.

She meant to go inside and thank her mother for the

gift, but the shoes simply had to be used, so she walked past the salt marsh, down to the beach. Even when she ran into the water she kept her shoes on, and she walked for nearly two miles and didn't come home until dinnertime. Rae went around to the back of the house where she could rinse off her shoes under a metal faucet, but she stopped by a mock orange shrub that was covered with white flowers. Carolyn was out there on the back porch, and she was breathing in that same way she had when she'd asked the bus driver to pull over. Rae's father was standing behind the screen door to the kitchen, looking out.

"If you're so miserable why don't you leave," he told Carolyn.

The sky was as blue as ink, and when Rae licked her lips she could taste salt. There was a slight wind, and Carolyn's skirt rose up, like the tail end of a kite. Right then what Rae wished for more than anything was that her mother would have the courage to take Rae and get back on the bus and leave him.

"But if you stay," Rae's father said through the screen door, "I don't want to hear any more complaints. I'd just as soon not talk at all."

In the shadows by the side of the house, Rae crouched even lower and held her breath. She expected Carolyn to call out her name, and when she did Rae would stand up and her mother would grab her hand; then they'd run past the high white dunes, and keep running until they reached the center of town.

But Carolyn didn't call out her name, she just stood at the porch banister, then she turned and went inside, and the screen door slammed behind her. Even then, Rae could tell when someone had given up, and as she stood out in the yard she felt betrayed. Later, when she went inside, Carolyn was setting the table for dinner as if nothing had happened, and Rae's father was starting a fire in the fireplace to get some of the chill out of the house. As they ate canned soup and tunafish sandwiches, Rae could hear the sand crabs outside, scrambling through the dunes. When a log in the fireplace popped Rae was certain that Carolyn shuddered. That was when Rae decided she would never trust her mother again; she could never love someone so weak, someone who couldn't even tell her husband not to light a fire because on the top of the chimney there was an owl's nest made of sea grass and straw.

All that summer Rae kept to herself, even during the week when her father wasn't there. She hid the red shoes at the back of the closet in her room, and when they left Wellfleet at the end of August, Rae left the red shoes behind, relieved to know that even if they rented the same house again, those shoes would never fit her the following year.

As she waited for Jessup by the pool Rae fell asleep and she dreamed about the house in Wellfleet. In her dream, Carolyn stood out on the back porch. It was late at night and the sky was black. As Rae watched, her mother disappeared, slowly dissolving in the salt air until there was nothing left on the porch but some fine white powder. When Rae woke up it was after five and the lounge chair had left ridges all along the side of her face. There was absolute silence, except for the wind and the sound of metal chimes hung along the outdoor balcony.

Every room on the second floor opened out to a painted blue walkway, and each room had a view of the pool. But when Jessup had gotten back an hour earlier, he hadn't bothered with the view. He had picked up a bottle of tequila after work, and as soon as he got into his room he pulled the drapes closed and ran a bath. When Rae knocked on his door, Jessup was sitting in a tub of cool water, his feet propped up on the far rim. He was drinking tequila out of a Dixie cup, and wondering why lifting a few pieces of sound equipment had left him feeling like an old man. He heard the first knock on the door but decided to ignore it. Tonight he didn't care about extra pay, he wasn't working overtime. He leaned his head against the cool ceramic tiles behind him and listened to the echo of water running through the pipes as someone on the floor above him ran the shower.

The longer she stood out there in the sun, the more Rae felt like crying. She had promised herself she would be calm; she had gone over this a hundred times in her head, and she planned to argue her case reasonably. But she didn't feel reasonable. She was certain that Jessup was in because the desk clerk had assured her he had picked up his key, and Rae wound up pounding on the door. When Jessup finally answered he had a towel wrapped around his waist and he was dripping wet. Rae walked right past him and sat in a tweed armchair. The room was small enough for her to lift her legs and reach the bed; she rested her shoes on the clean bedspread and looked up at him. Jessup had closed the door behind her, and now he was trapped. The only way for him to get anywhere was to jump over Rae's legs. And there was something else in Rae's favor—Jessup wasn't wearing clothes and somehow that made things fairer.

He sat down on the bed and put a hand on Rae's ankle. "Look who's here."

"You bet I'm here," Rae said.

The air conditioner was on, and the sound got between them. It was difficult to hear, and neither of them wanted to shout. In spite of herself, Rae thought he looked better than ever—he certainly wasn't wasting away.

"I wish I could explain some of the things I've done lately," Jessup said. "But all I can say is I'm going through some sort of crisis."

They both laughed at that, and Rae laughed a little too long. Before they knew it, she was crying.

"Come on, Rae," Jessup said. "Please."

"Goddamn you," Rae said.

Jessup shook his head sadly. "I know," he agreed.

Rae took a shower while Jessup got dressed. She rehearsed the right way to tell him she was pregnant, but the thing was she didn't quite believe it herself. She didn't look any different; it could very well be a mistake. When Rae got out of the shower and dressed again there was sand in her clothes and it stuck to her damp skin. She couldn't stop herself from imagining the worst. What if a monster was growing inside of her, something made out of blood and flesh that wasn't quite human. It might be her punishment; it had to happen to somebody—somebody's baby had to be misshapen, somebody had to die in a delivery room and be wrapped up in a stained sheet, somebody's lover had to leave her when he found out she was pregnant.

That night they went out to dinner; they ordered hamburgers and played the jukebox and tried to pretend that nothing was wrong. On the drive back to the Holiday Inn a wind came up suddenly; sand whipped around the Oldsmobile and Jessup had to switch on the windshield wipers in order to see the road. Rae heard the sound of wind chimes each time they passed a house or a trailer, and even though Jessup told her that people in the desert believed the chimes brought good luck, the sound put Rae on edge. The temperature had dropped nearly twenty degrees, but when they reached the motel the wind had begun to die down and Rae saw millions of stars above them. Jessup opened the door to his room, but Rae just leaned over the balcony railing. The night was black and white and so breathtakingly clear that she felt she had never seen the sky before.

Finally, Rae went in. She took off all her clothes and got under the covers. Jessup left a wake-up call for seven, then took off his boots, undressed, and turned out the lights. After he'd gotten into bed he didn't touch her.

"I've been trying to think of ways to explain what went wrong," Jessup said. He reached for his cigarettes in the dark, and when he lit a match Rae blinked in the sudden light.

"It's like I've been dreaming all these years and I suddenly woke up," Jessup said. "And here I am. Almost thirty."

The window in the room was open. It was the time

when coyotes came down from the ridgetops; you could hear them howling as the moon rose higher in the sky. As she lay in bed Rae listened to the wind chimes out on the balcony; cars pulled into the parking lot, they idled, then cut their engines.

"I'm glad you woke up," Rae said bitterly.

"Don't take it personally," Jessup told her. "You know what I mean."

"Well, if you're planning to leave me we may have a problem," Rae said. She could feel Jessup's weight on the mattress; each time he breathed they shifted a little closer together. "The problem is," Rae said, "I'm pregnant."

Jessup reached for a glass ashtray and stubbed his cigarette out. When he put his head back on the pillow, Rae knew it was over.

"Are you saying you think you're pregnant or you know you're pregnant?"

"I know," Rae said.

"There are plenty of times you say you know something, and then I find out you've made a mistake."

"Jessup," Rae said. "I know."

Jessup sat up in bed with his back toward her. In the room next door someone turned on the television and muted voices drifted through the wall.

"Look, I'm sorry," Jessup said finally, "but this is impossible. I'm not ready for this."

Lately, Rae had the sense that everything that was happening to her was really happening to someone else. She pinched her thigh until she could feel the bite of her own fingernails.

"I appreciate the fact that this is a serious situation," Jessup said. "I really do. But what the hell do you expect me to do about it?"

She didn't have an answer.

"I'm not going to be somebody's father."

If he were anyone but Jessup, Rae would have sworn he was about to cry.

"Here I am in the middle of some sort of crisis and you come and tell me you're pregnant."

She knew it for sure now, he was crying. She was glad the lights were out and she didn't have to see it. She wasn't angry with him any more, just tired.

"We don't have to talk about it now," Rae told him. "We'll talk tomorrow." She put her arms around him and pretended not to know he was crying.

"It's not like I don't miss you," Jessup told her. "I don't want to, but there doesn't seem to be anything I can do about it."

She held him until he fell asleep, and then she moved back to her side of the bed. Long after midnight, when she was finally able to sleep, Rae dreamed that she left Jessup in bed and went to the window. She opened it wider and climbed outside. She dropped down two stories, and her feet landed in the sand with a thud. Right away, even though it was dark, she saw the pawprints and she followed the tracks far into the desert. The sand was the color of moonlight and the cactus grew eight feet high. All she had to do was sit down, and the coyote came right over to her, curled up by her feet, and put its head in her lap.

It didn't seem to matter if the coyote was her pet, or if

she'd been captured. When she reached down she could feel its heart beating against its ribs, and she felt elated to be so close to something so wild. She stayed in the desert all night, and by morning she had learned all of the coyote's secrets: she knew which cactus were rich with hidden water, and how to follow a path along sharp, bone-colored rocks. She knew how to stand so still on the top of a high ridge that rabbits ran right past you, and hawks mistook you for stone and tried to light on your shoulders. At last she knew the moment when the night was so pure, you could fight it all you wanted and still—sooner or later—you'd throw back your head and howl.

When she got back to the motel she climbed up the railing, then crouched on the window ledge. Everyone in the Holiday Inn was asleep, covered by white sheets, dreaming of home. There was sand all along the window ledge and it spilled onto the wall-to-wall carpeting. Once Jessup turned in his sleep, and Rae held her breath. But even though he opened his eyes briefly, he didn't see her at the window, and he never heard her climb down onto the carpet, where she slept curled up at the very edge of the room.

When Rae woke up it was dawn, and she knew that she had to get out. She needed fresh air, and breakfast, and a change of clothes. Jessup didn't wake up when she ran the shower; he didn't hear the window close, he didn't hear the door. She would think about losing him later, but this morning all she wanted was to get across the desert before noon. She left the motel room exactly as it had been before she arrived. The air conditioner was still on; the pipes in the walls made a murmuring sound; in the bathroom there were a bottle of tequila, a package of disposable razors, a plastic container of Dixie cups. Only two things were missing when Rae left: the car keys were no longer on top of the night table, and out in the parking lot the space where Jessup had left the Oldsmobile the night before was empty. By the time Jessup woke up the asphalt in the parking lot was already beginning to sizzle. By noon it would reach a hundred and fifteen degrees. But by then Rae was already out on the freeway, and with all the windows in the Oldsmobile rolled down, the only thing she could feel was a perfect arc of wind.

PART TWO

$\mathcal{O}$N THE NIGHT LILA GAVE birth to her daughter she had already walked up two flights of stairs before she realized she couldn't go any farther. She held on to the iron banister and slowly sank to the floor. In the middle of a terribly cold winter, there had been an oddly warm week, with rain instead of snow, and everyone in the city seemed sluggish and out of sorts. Lila's parents had come to agree that their daughter's strange behavior was caused by a combination of the weather and the mysterious pains of being eighteen. Ever since autumn, Lila had refused to wear anything but the same wide, blue dress, which hung from her shoulders like a sack. She refused suppers and lunches, yet she looked heavy and she walked as if off balance. At night, the next-door neighbors could hear her crying, and when she finally slept nothing could wake her, not even a siren right outside the apartment building. No one had dared to ask Lila what was wrong for

fear she might tell them. And so, it had not been very difficult for her to keep her pregnancy a secret. But on that day
in January, when her legs gave out and she sat huddled on
the second-floor landing, Lila knew there was just so much
you could hide.

Lila was expected home for dinner, but she sat in the
stairwell for nearly an hour. Outside the sky filled with huge
white clouds. The weather was changing that night, drop-
ping five degrees an hour, and Lila tried to convince herself
that the sudden shift in the atmosphere was what made her
feel so exhausted and sick. In her calculations she had at
least six more weeks to go. Lila was still stunned by what
had happened to her, and every time the baby moved she
was amazed all over again. On those rare days when she
accepted that she was indeed pregnant, she could never
quite believe she would actually give birth. Perhaps after
nine months of pregnancy the process would reverse itself:
the baby would slowly dissolve, forming, at the very last, a
nearly perfect pearl, which Lila would carry inside her forever. But there on the stairs, Lila knew that something was
happening to her. When she found the strength to stand up
a wave began somewhere near her heart; it traveled downward in a rush, and then, without warning, exploded. Suddenly, Lila's dress was drenched, from the waist to the hem,
and as she climbed up the stairs a trail of warm water was
left behind that would not begin to evaporate until the following day.

Lila managed to get into the apartment unnoticed, then
she undressed and crawled into bed. When her parents real-

ized she was home they came to knock on her door, but by that time Lila's voice was steady enough to call that she was really too tired to join them for dinner. She closed her eyes then, and waited, and she was in her own small bed, in that room where she'd slept every night of her life, when her labor pains began. At first it was nothing more than mild cramps, as if she had pulled the muscles in her back. But the cramps came and went in a regular pattern, and no matter how hard Lila willed the pain to stop it rose upward; it was climbing to the roof. The movement of time changed altogether; it seemed as if only two minutes had passed since Lila had managed to sneak into her room—but it was more than two hours later when the pain began to take on a life of its own. There was a steady rhythm it complied to, and as the pain gained control, Lila panicked. She jumped out of bed, pulled a blanket around her, then ran out of her room and into the hallway. Lila's parents had long finished dinner, but her father was still at the table reading the newspaper, and her mother was returning the dishes to the cabinet in the dining room. When Lila's mother saw her daughter in the hallway with a wool blanket wrapped around her and her dark hair flying wildly, she dropped a large platter which broke into a thousand pieces on the wooden floor.

"Something's wrong," Lila screamed. Her voice did not sound at all like her voice, and though her parents were only a few feet away, Lila was certain that she had to yell to be heard. "I have to go to a hospital," she cried. "Something's happening to me."

Lila's mother ran over and put a hand on her daughter's

forehead to check for fever, but a strong contraction came that made Lila drop down and crouch on the floor. Through the wave of pain, Lila could hear her mother shrieking, and the moment she was able to stand again her mother slapped her face so hard that Lila could feel her neck snap backward. It was then Lila's parents began to argue and accuse each other of stupidity, lunacy, and every other parental crime possible. They nearly forgot that Lila was there in the room with them. At last, her mother and father both agreed that an ambulance's siren was too deep a shame for them to endure, and so Lila's cousin, who was a nurse in the emergency room at Beekman Hospital, would have to be called.

At that point, Lila didn't really care what was decided. It didn't matter that her mother was crying hot tears as she telephoned Lila's cousin, or that her father had already left the apartment, even though he had no place to go—too humiliated to sit in the lobby or ask a neighbor for a glass of water or tea, he went to the stairwell and sat there, and prayed that no one he knew would see him. Lila let them make all the decisions. When they refused to take her to the hospital, she went back to her room and knelt by the side of the bed. After a while, she put her face down on the cold sheet and gripped the mattress with both hands. She felt herself slipping into something dark, and each time a contraction came her waist was ringed with a band of fire. Each time the band grew hotter, until finally it threatened to burn right through her spine. One thing Lila knew: she could not live through this kind of suffering. But even now, she didn't dare scream and bring the neighbors running. She simply begged for someone to help her, and although her mother must have heard her she did nothing more than come into the hallway and quietly close the bedroom door.

The night grew so cold that when it began to rain the drops froze the moment they hit the sidewalk. There were hundreds of accidents: cars and buses skidded on the icy avenues, lights in hotel rooms flickered as generators came to a halt, pipes froze and then burst, and every frail tree in the city was hidden beneath a shower of ice. Up in her room, Lila was surrounded by black fire. She might have slipped into the darkness forever if her cousin Ann hadn't arrived a little after midnight. The bedroom door opened slowly, and the scraping of wood against wood sounded like the flapping of some huge bird's wings. Lila gasped when the sudden light from the hallway filled her room. For one calm moment Lila wondered if she had imagined the pain, and she watched as her cousin took off her gray wool coat and her leather boots. Before the bedroom door was closed Lila had enough time to look out and see her mother peer into the bedroom. At least, Lila thought it was her mother—she wore her mother's clothes, and was her mother's shape and size. But if it really had been her mother, wouldn't she have run into the room and thrown her arms around her daughter and tried to save her? Lila blinked and strained to see, but the figure in the hallway just grew shadowier, and when Lila's cousin walked toward the door she blocked the light, and then there weren't even any shadows. There was nothing at all.

When the door closed the sound echoed. Lila could actually feel the sound somewhere beneath her skin. Immediately the room was airless; the heat in the radiator poured out until it was impossible to breathe. That was when Lila knew she couldn't have this baby.

"I'm sorry," she told her cousin. "They made you come here for nothing. I've changed my mind. I'm not going through with this."

Ann had been a nurse for eleven years—long enough to know she had better not tell Lila that every woman in hard labor had made the exact same pronouncement.

"I can't do this!" Lila screamed.

Every neighbor on the floor above could hear her now for all she cared. Her contractions had been coming two minutes apart for some time, but now something changed. She could no longer tell the difference between one contraction and the next; the pain began to run together in a single line of fire. As each contraction rose to its highest peak, hot liquid poured out between Lila's legs. She couldn't sit, or lie down—she couldn't stand. Ann helped her onto the bed and examined her. By the time she was through, Lila was so wet that the sheets beneath her were soaked.

"Give me something," she begged. "Give me a shot. Put me out. Do anything."

The pain owned her now; it owned the earth and the air and at its center was an inferno. She was in the darkest time before birth, transition, and even though she didn't know its name, Lila knew, all of a sudden, that she could not go back.

There was nothing to go back to, there was only this pain—and it was stronger than she was. It was swallowing her alive.

She wanted Hannie, that was all there was to it. In the past few weeks she had considered going to see her a hundred times, but a hundred times her pride got in the way, and now it was too late. She tried to imagine the stiff black skirts, and the clucking sound Hannie made in the back of her throat, and couldn't. There was nothing but this room, and inside the room there was only pain. And even if Hannie had been right beside her, Lila would still have been alone. That was the unbearable part of this pain—no one could accompany you, no one could share it, and the absolute loneliness of it was nearly enough to drive you mad.

Ann went to the bathroom to dampen some washcloths, and when she came back she found Lila standing by the window, looking out. The sidewalk was three stories down, and from this distance the ice that had formed on the cement seemed as cool and delicious as a deep, blue bay in Maine. Ann ran and turned her away from the window. It did no good to think of an escape, or even to wish for one. This was the center of it, and all you had to do was stand your ground—you could not even think about giving up.

When she saw the damp washcloths, Lila grabbed one out of her cousin's hand and sucked out the water. She was dying of thirst. She would have given anything for a piece of ice, a lemonade, a cool place where she could drift into a deep and dreamless sleep.

"Please," Lila said to her cousin.

"Just remember," Ann said, "I'm not going to leave you. I'm going to stay right here with you till the end."

"You can't leave me!" Lila cried, terrified and misunderstanding.

"I won't," Ann told her. "I'm right here."

Lila threw her arms around Ann's neck. She had never wanted to be closer to anyone. Again and again she whispered "please," but she knew there was no one who could save her. And then something let loose inside Lila, and it was simply beyond her powers to hold it back. She felt a terrible urge to push this thing inside of her out, and when Ann told her she couldn't push yet, she started to cry. Ann showed her how to pant—it was a trick to fool her body into believing it was breathing that she must concentrate on—but even then Lila's tears ran into the back of her throat and nearly made her choke. Nothing was working, she couldn't even pant; she took in more and more air until she started to hyperventilate. Ann began to breathe along with her, and eventually Lila was able to slow her panting to match her cousin's. Lila stared into Ann's eyes and the room fell away from her; the city no longer existed. She fell deeper into those eyes—they were the universe, filled with energy and unbelievable light. Lila heard a voice tell her to get back onto the bed. She didn't feel herself move, and yet there she was, on those damp white sheets with her legs pulled up.

"It's time," Lila heard someone say to her. "Now you can push."

For a moment everything was clear. Lila recognized the ceiling in her bedroom, and the face of her cousin who was a hospital nurse. It seemed that a serious mistake had been made. This could not possibly be happening to her.

It was day now, but the air was so cold that the dawn was blue. Lila sat up in bed; she leaned back against the pillows and pulled her legs up as far as they could go. She pushed for the first time, and when she did she was horrified to hear her own voice. Surely, a sound like that would tear a throat apart. She pushed again, and again, but after more than a hour there was still the same enormous pressure. The only difference was now Lila was so exhausted that she couldn't even scream. All she wanted was for this horrible burning thing inside her to come out. She found herself thinking the same odd phrase over and over. It's only your body, she told herself. It was her flesh that had betrayed her, her blood that was on fire. The solution was simple and took only an instant. As her cousin leaned over her and wiped her face with a washcloth, as dawn reflected through windows all over the city, Lila left her body behind.

Her spirit leapt up into the pure white air. The utter joy of such a leap was almost too much for her. Lila rose upward, guided by a perfect beam of light. Below her, she could see her body propped up on two pillows, she could see that her eyes were closed, and that she held her breath as she pushed down with all the strength she had left. But how could she be concerned with a body that twisted and groaned, something that was so far away? Up here, in this strange new atmosphere, everything was silent. The air was so cold it crystallized, and each time Lila opened her mouth to breathe it quenched her thirst. There was the scent of something much sweeter than roses, and Lila wasn't the least bit surprised to find that her spirit had taken the shape of a bird. What else but a blackbird could swoop so gracefully above a room of pain?

"So now you're free," someone was saying to Lila. "Now you know that absolute freedom of leaving your body behind."

"It was so easy to do," Lila said. "How could anything be this easy?"

Far below her, Lila could hear her cousin ask who on earth she was talking to. But Lila didn't bother to answer. Any moment she might have to return to her body, each second was too precious to waste. The blue dawn was nothing compared to the white light that Lila had discovered. And when the time came for her to return to her body, Lila felt such a terrible sorrow that for an instant she thought she might choose not to return at all. She was floating just above herself, still undecided, when she suddenly found herself moved by the struggle beneath her. Her body's shallow breathing and the beat of her own heart filled Lila with pity; with one tender motion she slipped back inside her own flesh.

This time when she pushed, something hard moved so that it was nearly out. Lila reached her hands between her legs and felt the soft hair on the very top of the baby's head.

"Oh, my God," Lila said.

"The next time you push you may feel as if you'll explode," Ann said. "You may feel like you're burning."

But Lila had already been a spear of flame; she could dance on red coals now and not feel a thing. She bore down harder, and suddenly the baby's head was free. Lila panted again to stop the urge to push while Ann untangled the umbilical cord from around the neck, and then, with the next push, the entire body slipped out in a rush.

Blood poured from Lila, but she felt strangely renewed. She leaned her elbows on the pillows and lifted herself up so that she could watch as Ann cleaned off the baby and wrapped it in a white towel.

"Is it all right?" she whispered.

"It's perfect," Ann told her. "And it's a girl."

Lila's father had come home from a night spent out on the stairway, where it was so cold it could freeze your soul. He and his wife sat on the couch in the living room, rocking back and forth as if in mourning. Behind the closed bedroom door, Ann placed the baby in a dresser drawer on a bed of flannel nightgowns. It wasn't until after she had delivered the placenta that she told Lila that her parents had already had her contact a doctor who arranged private adoptions.

"But I have to have your approval," Ann told Lila.

Lila leaned her head back on the pillows and closed her eyes while Ann lifted her legs and put down a clean sheet.

"You have to tell me," Ann said. "What do you want to do about this child?"

What amazed Lila was how fast it was over, how far outside herself she had gone and how quickly she had returned. Already, the pain she'd felt seemed to belong to someone else. How strange that now she didn't want it to fade—she wanted to grab on to the pain and claim it for her own.

"I'll be honest with you," Ann said. "I don't really see how you can keep this baby. If you do, your parents won't let you stay here. Is it fair to keep her, when you can't even take care of yourself?"

Even though the steam heat in the radiator made a gurgling noise, and buses trapped in the ice strained their engines, Lila swore she could hear her baby breathing as it slept in the dresser drawer. It was at that moment that her heart broke in two: she knew she could not keep this child.

"I want to see her," Lila said.

"Take my advice," Ann told her. "If you plan to give her up, don't see her. Let me just take her away."

"I know what I want," Lila said. "Let me see her."

As soon as her daughter was brought to her and she held her in her arms, Lila knew her cousin was right. But instead of turning her away, Lila held the baby even tighter. Her skin was as soft as apricots, her eyes were the color of an October sky. Lila could have held her forever. She begged for time to stop, for clocks to break, for every star to remain fixed. But none of that happened. Up on the fourth floor the neighbors ran the water in the bathroom, in the hallway outside the apartment there was the scent of coffee.

When Lila gave her daughter up to her cousin's outstretched arms, the room grew darker, as if she had given away a star. The dresser drawer where her baby had slept was still open, and it would be days before Lila would be able to close it again. But now, as her child was taken out into the coldest winter morning ever recorded in the city, wrapped in nothing but a white towel, Lila did manage to get one last look, and for the first time she knew the loss she would feel from that day onward, every morning and every night, for the rest of her life.

■ ■ ■

They sent Lila away because she just gave up. By the end of February her milk had gone dry, and the bloody sheets had been cut into pieces and thrown into the incinerator, but Lila still refused to leave the apartment. She couldn't even sit too close to her open bedroom window, because the breeze from outside stung her lungs. She had grown so used to the still air in the apartment that she had come to dread fresh air and light. You couldn't tell the hour of the day in Lila's bedroom when the curtains were drawn. It no longer mattered if it was day or night. If anyone had asked what future she saw for herself at the bottom of her own teacup she would have said endless days without purpose or plans. But then, on a day when the sky was as gray as cement, Lila found herself alone in the apartment. She went into the bathroom and closed the door behind her. And when she opened the medicine cabinet above the sink, it seemed as if she'd had a plan and a purpose all along.

As she slit her wrists with her father's razor she felt nothing at all. Although when she imagined them finding the body she had to smile: her mother could scrub the floor for weeks with every cleanser on the market, and the blood would still never come off the black-and-white ceramic tiles. But Lila didn't cut deep enough, and before she could correct her mistake, she fainted and hit her head on the tub. When her mother came home from the market where she'd bought codfish and potatoes and lettuce, Lila was still alive. Most of the blood had spilled neatly into the sink. But although the bathroom floor wasn't ruined, when the ambulance drivers carried Lila out a trail of blood stained the oak floor in the hallway, and it never washed out.

Two weeks later, when Lila's wrists were still bandaged in white gauze, they sent her out to East China on the Long Island Rail Road. As Lila handed the conductor her ticket a bit of gauze peeked out from the wristband of her glove, and all the way out to East China she kept her hands clasped together in her lap. Her destination was the home of her great-aunt, Belle, a woman in her seventies who was so hard of hearing she was never quite sure if Lila's mother had whispered baby or lazy when she called to ask for a room for her daughter. Certainly, Belle never asked what the problem had been, she just sent a taxi to meet Lila at the small wooden railroad station, and her only demand was that her great-niece never use salt when it was her turn to cook dinner.

All through March, Lila tried to feel something. But everything around her seemed bloodless and cold: the bare maple trees, the sound of bats up on the roof in the middle of the night, the empty two-lane road called the East China Highway that ran right by the house and seemed to go nowhere at all. In her cold bedroom in the attic Lila could sleep, but she had no dreams. Each night before she went to bed Lila went to the window and longed for the deep oblivion of the sky. She had no energy, nothing left to give. Just speaking a few words to her aunt was an enormous effort—afterward, Lila always had to go back to her room where she slept on the old rope bed, covered by a quilt Belle had sewn when she was not much older than Lila.

There was only one thing that attracted Lila, and that was death. The one time she agreed to do readings for her aunt's old friends—having foolishly admitted that she used to tell fortunes—she saw nothing but symbols of death in their cups: hearts that refused to beat, black dogs, poisoned apples and pears. And although she continued to think about Hannie, she never once missed Stephen, the lover she'd thought she couldn't live without. Stephen was a ghost; compared to death he was nothing, and it was death who called to Lila now. He was there with her every night when Lila ran her fingertips over the knives as she stored them in the silverware drawer; when she washed the dishes he was by her side, telling her that under just the right amount of pressure the glass she held could shatter into shards that would cut right through her skin. What was wonderful about these dark whispers was that they left very little room for Lila to think about her child. But at night, when the wind rose off the Long Island Sound to sweep through the potato fields and rattle down the chimneys, the cold air sounded like a baby's wailing. And even when Lila put a pillow over her head and covered her ears with her hands, she could still hear the baby crying, and it cried from midnight till dawn.

Lila became convinced that she wouldn't last through the winter. She lost twenty pounds and her dark hair fell out in clumps—she found it all over her pillow in the mornings, as if a molting bird had visited her in the night. And then quite suddenly, without any warning, it was spring. The ice disappeared, the earth was left steaming, and all over East China the air was silvery, like steam from a kettle. Puddles formed on either side of the East China Highway, and in them were small dark fish and green turtles. Laundry was hung outside on thick rope lines, and as soon as the snow melted there were white flowers and wild strawberries in every backyard.

No matter how hard Lila tried to resist she was drawn outside her room. Even when she closed her window, she could smell lilacs from the tree out in the yard that had not yet bloomed. There was the scent of seaweed in the air, and a feeling of longing in everyone, even in Lila. Early in April, more than a month after her milk had dried up, Lila awoke one morning to find that her breasts had been leaking all night—her nightgown and bedclothes were drenched, and they smelled so sweet that bees came in through the window and followed Lila all through the house until she took a broom and chased them out the front door.

Hannie had once told Lila that a long time ago, in the village where she had grown up, a separate cottage had been built for women who had lost their children at birth. Every morning people brought presents to leave outside the mother's door: bunches of lavender, sunflowers, caged birds, hot black bread. For six nights the mother who had lost her child was not allowed to go any farther than the front door where the collection of gifts had been piled. No one was allowed to see her weeping; anyone who heard her cries in the middle of the night was to light a candle and then think of other things. On the seventh day everyone went out to collect wood, and a fire was lit outside the cottage. As the flames moved closer and closer to the rickety front steps no one could interfere, no one was allowed to run to the pond for a bucket of water. In moments the flames circled the cottage; nesting birds flew away, dragon-flies who lived in the eaves darted into the sky. And then came the hardest part—waiting until the flames leapt up to the roof.

The woman inside always ran out to join the others, although sometimes it was not until the very last minute, just before the cottage collapsed into a heap of flaming twigs. It was in this way that the mother discovered that she still had the will to live, even now, and she was usually the first one to help when the cottage was rebuilt.

Lila could not stand for April to affect her this way. Every day she felt more alive, but if anything this made her more bitter about her own ability to survive. There was nothing that did not remind her of her daughter: the new bark on the lilac tree outside her window was the exact same color as her daughter's newborn slate-gray eyes. The moss that grew near the back steps was as soft as her daughter's hair. It did no good to stay inside because there the lace doilies on the easy chair felt like baby blankets and the small silver teaspoons were exactly the right size for a child to hold as she ate cereal and pears. And so, one day in the middle of April, Lila left her aunt's house for the first time since she'd arrived at the railroad station in February. Each time Lila took a long walk she felt more hopeless: for no reason at all she was terribly alive. In town people smiled at her, as if she was some young girl with her whole future ahead of her. And so, Lila made certain to walk away from town, out by the potato fields where there were nothing but sea gulls, who were so brave they actually swooped down to take bread right out of her hands. And if it was early enough, the time of day when fog rose along the white line in the center of the highway, there were sometimes small deer who stood perfectly still for a moment, before turning to run back into the woods.

What Lila hoped to find, as she walked along the East China Highway, was a reason to go on living. She had turned nineteen only a few weeks earlier, and she'd been surprised to realize that she was still so young. The days were long now; sunlight lasted past suppertime. At night there were falling stars, and even when armfuls of lilacs were cut from the trees more and more blossoms appeared.

Lila was faced with her past each time she chose a long-sleeved blouse from her closet to hide the scars on her wrists. But spring distracted her, she began to feel that her scars were not enough, and so each day she devised a new way to remind herself of her suffering. When she sewed she made certain to jab her fingers with the needle, when she cooked she picked up pots by their handles without bothering to use a potholder. All that remained pleasurable in her life were the long walks she took, until she realized that she could ruin these, too. The very next time Lila left the house she slipped her shoes off and left them underneath the porch of her aunt's house. She would have to walk far, but by late afternoon the tar on the road would be hot enough, and Lila knew that her feet would burn.

She had walked more than eight miles, and was halfway between East China and Riverhead, when Lila stopped at a gas station. She had come so far on the burning tar that there were blisters on the soles of her feet. She bent down and dusted off some of the pebbles and dirt, and when she looked up she saw Richard sitting in the shade outside the office of the gas station. He was twenty-one, and even from fifteen yards away, Lila could tell how handsome he was. She lowered her eyes immediately, angry at herself for imagining she had the right to look at a man.

"The best thing for hot feet is to pour cold water on them right away," Richard called to her.

"I don't happen to have any water with me at the moment," Lila called back. Even though she wasn't looking at him, Lila felt herself grow embarrassed.

When Richard stood up, the metal chair he had been sitting on creaked, and Lila felt herself shudder, as if she'd been touched. Richard walked over, and as he passed the gas pumps he picked up a pail. He handed the pail to Lila, then stood there and watched as she emptied it onto her feet. The water was so clear and so cold that it made her gasp.

"Is something funny?" Lila said, annoyed when she looked up and saw that Richard was smiling.

Richard backed away from her, stung by her tone. He was more than six feet tall, but he was terribly shy. And right now he was also confused—he didn't know what on earth had made him call out to Lila, it just seemed like something he had to do.

"Nothing's funny," he said. "It's just that you're so beautiful I can't stop looking at you."

Lila turned and she ran all the way home. She ran so fast that by the time she reached her aunt's house her feet were bleeding. That night she locked herself in her room, and she swore that she would never again walk west on the East China Highway. But as she sat in her dark bedroom, the constellations in the sky were so bright they burned through the cotton curtains, and Lila knew that if she saw Richard even one more time, she'd be in danger. If she wasn't careful she might just fall in love with him, and that was one thing Lila did not intend to do.

At first, when she heard her aunt's friends talk about Richard's family, Lila assumed it was no one she knew. These friends were old Russian women who had come to East China by accident. All of them had immigrated long ago with hopes of being in Manhattan, but all had in common a cousin who helped pay their fare, and then insisted they come to live in East China. This cousin had raved about the soil that was so rich potatoes seemed to grow overnight, and it was he who first brought a band of migrant workers to the area. Even though their cousin had been dead for nearly thirty years, all of the relatives he had helped to bring over were still in East China. Every one had planned to move into the city after his death, but Manhattan had faded until it was nothing more than a dream; it was less than a hundred miles to the Midtown Tunnel, but it might as well have been on the other side of a black forest guarded by wolves.

Of course there was one woman, the daughter of a distant cousin, who had managed to leave East China, although she hadn't gone any farther than the outskirts of town. Twenty-five years earlier Helen had married a migrant worker, a Shinnecock Indian whom the Russian women referred to as the Red Man. The Red Man had taken Helen to a small unheated farmhouse where the pines were so tall and their shadows so dark that not even potatoes could grow. When Helen came to town to do her grocery shopping everyone said hello, but nobody really talked to her, and there wasn't a soul in East China who didn't know that Helen's mother had died of shame.

In the winter, when the ice was treacherous, many of the old women didn't venture out of their houses. When April came and the old friends were reunited, gossip flowed. On a particularly clear night, when Lila's feet were still bloody and blistered, four of Belle's distant cousins came to visit, and the conversation turned to the Red Man and his wife. It was a well-known fact that Helen had been cursed with a curious inability to have children, except for one, the son. Everyone wanted to know what had happened to the son during the winter—for years the old ladies had been waiting for him to be shipped off to the penitentiary, and none of them would have been surprised if he had murdered both his parents with a shotgun and then disappeared into Connecticut or New Jersey. However, there was not much news, even after the winter: Helen's son was still working at the gas station his father, the Red Man, had somehow managed to buy. And later in the evening, one of the old Russian women admitted that after an ice storm in January, when she was stranded and out of groceries, Helen's son had come to fix the engine of her Ford, which wouldn't turn over. After having a cup of tea laced with whiskey, she shocked them all by adding that he really was quite handsome.

Lila served the tea that night, but when her aunt's friends asked her to read their tea leaves, she excused herself—she said she had a headache and couldn't possibly see into the future that night. But really, Lila was simply too excited to sit still in a room full of old women. She was nineteen years old, and in spite of everything, very much alive. That night, Lila slept better than she had in months. For the first time since the birth of her child she dreamed. In her dream she found that lilacs were growing in the middle of winter, their blue petals pushing through a slick cover of ice. In the morning, when she woke up, Lila got dressed while it was still dark. She went downstairs quietly, even though her great-aunt wouldn't have heard if she had slammed the doors. Before she left, she stood out on the front porch for a moment, not yet ready to leave her sorrow behind. In the middle of nowhere, between East China and Riverhead, there was a man who might be able to make her forget. Suddenly there seemed to be a reason for everything, and although Lila started off walking slowly, she wound up running down the two-lane road which for the very first time seemed like a highway that led you somewhere you might want to go.

• • •

They were married on the edge of East China, in the parlor of Richard's parents' house. It was July and orange lilies were blooming everywhere, even beneath the huge pine trees where the shadows were deep green. Richard's mother, Helen, cried from the beginning of the ceremony to the very end. The only guest was a high-school friend of Richard's, a boy named Buddy who was so nervous about his duties as best man that he nearly fainted during the justice of the peace's speech about fidelity.

After the ceremony Helen took Lila aside in the kitchen and she held her hand. "I hope you understand that no one in town will ever speak to you again," she told her new daughter-in-law.

In fact, Lila's own great-aunt had asked her to leave the house as soon as she was told about the marriage, and Lila had spent the last week and a half at a motel in Riverhead. But after losing both her child and her parents the disapproval of neighbors was meaningless.

"Richard's the only person I need," Lila told her mother-in-law as she reached up into a cabinet for some plates. There was a luncheon following the ceremony, but with the exception of the still shaky Buddy, there were no guests.

"Just wait," Helen said ominously. She took a tub of potato salad from the refrigerator, then sat down at the kitchen table, as if the weight of the potato salad was too much for her. "You'll be the object of every conversation in town. They'll find out every piece of gossip about you and spread it all over the Island."

The screen door was open and they could hear the sound of bees. Lila stood still and held the china plates to her chest. She had not stopped to think about her past resurfacing out here in East China; she had not even thought how she would explain the scars on her wrists when she undressed in front of Richard that night.

"Don't get me wrong—I'm not complaining," Helen said. "But my life hasn't been easy. What saves me is I'm in love with my husband. But sometimes," she admitted, "I'd like to hear another person's voice."

Lila was no longer listening to her mother-in-law. She was sure that if Richard ever found out about her past he would leave her, and she vowed then and there never to let him know about her baby. She came to him without a past, as if she herself had been born on the day she first saw him.

Richard's father, the Red Man who was gossiped about in so many living rooms and parlors, came into the kitchen for champagne and glasses. He was the same height as his son, although Richard was convinced that his father was several inches taller. No one in town cared, but his name was Jason Grey, and when he saw how sad his wife and new daughter-in-law looked he popped the champagne cork right there in the kitchen and the sudden noise and gush of dry champagne made both women gasp and then laugh out loud.

That night Lila and Richard moved in to the bedroom on the second floor. Jason Grey had put up new wallpaper, and Richard had refinished the pine bed. But even after the lights were turned out, Lila refused to get undressed. It was impossible to see any stars through the pine boughs outside the bedroom window, but somehow the moonlight managed to get through. The room was so well lit Lila was certain that the moment she took off her clothes, Richard would be blinded by the scars on her wrists.

As Lila stood by the window, Richard sat down at the foot of the bed and took off his boots. He was so much in love that he was actually afraid to blink, even once, as if Lila might just disappear. Lila's back was turned to him, and in the moonlight Richard could see that her posture was as straight as wire. All of a sudden she seemed shy, and because she was, after all, a new bride who had just moved into her in-laws' house and because she had promised herself to a man who was really still a stranger, Richard felt his heart go out to her. In that moment he fell even more deeply in love.

"I'll tell you what," he said softly. "Since we're married and we've got the rest of our lives together, we don't have to make love yet if you don't want to."

Lila wanted to more than anything. She knew that she was about to cry, and she couldn't imagine an explanation that would satisfy her new husband once he saw that she had tried to take her own life. Because she did not know what else to do, Lila quickly unbuttoned her white dress, let it slip to the floor, then stepped out of it. She held up her hands, wrists together like a hostage. She had not yet unpacked her suitcase, and if Richard insisted she tell him about her past, she had decided she would have to leave him.

When Richard came over to her and held her, Lila closed her eyes and arched her neck, as if getting ready for some great pain.

"I can't believe how beautiful you are," Richard said.

Lila opened her eyes and backed away. Just then she wondered if she hadn't married a fool.

"You're not looking at me," Lila said sharply.

Richard bent down and kissed her. "Oh, yes I am," he said.

Lila pushed him away and she raised her hands until her wrists were directly in front of his eyes. The jagged lines along her wrists grew whiter and whiter; no one in his right mind could ignore them.

"Look at me," Lila urged her husband.

Richard had spent his whole life in the odd circumstance of being both well loved and lonely. His parents were so much in love that no matter how deeply they cared for him, Richard was somehow excluded. He didn't care if he was considered an outcast in East China, all he needed was one person, someone of his own. Now that he had found Lila, he didn't intend to lose her, even if the scars that she now showed him meant he had gotten a little more than he'd bargained for. Richard Grey wasn't a fool, and he certainly knew something about death. When he was ten he accidentally saw a man kill himself. It was out in the woods behind the deserted army barracks used as a camp for migrant workers. Richard had been born in the barracks, and even after his parents had bought the gas station and moved into the house they still lived in, Richard felt drawn to the migrant camp, if only because there seemed to be more deer there than anywhere else in East China.

He was in the woods, late in October, sitting motionless so that he would not frighten off any deer, when he saw a migrant worker walk into a clearing in the woods with a shotgun in his hands. Richard assumed that this man was an out-of-season hunter searching for deer. But then, quite suddenly, the migrant turned the gun on himself and fired.

Even after he had run for miles, Richard could still hear

the shot. And when he had to go to the district attorney's office to testify to what he had seen, Richard humiliated himself by crying in public when he was questioned. Afterward he couldn't seem to make himself go into the woods; he stood at the edge of the backyard where the lawn disappeared into brambles and pines, unable to take another step.

And then one day Jason Grey came out to the yard.

"Let's go for a walk," he said to Richard. He pushed some brambles aside, stepped into the woods, and signaled to his son.

Richard swallowed hard, but he followed. It was darker in the woods than he'd remembered, and each time a branch broke under his father's boots, Richard shuddered. It didn't take long for him to realize that his father was leading him right back to the exact spot where the migrant worker had shot off his head.

"Come on," Jason Grey said when he noticed that his son had stopped walking. "What's keeping you?"

In the shadows of the pine trees, his father suddenly seemed like a stranger. "You can't make me go there," Richard said.

Jason walked back to him. He reached into his jacket pocket and took out a cigarette. "I guess you're wondering what made him do it," he said.

"I don't care," Richard said.

Jason Grey inhaled on his cigarette and then coughed, and his cough made Richard ache with the sudden knowledge that one day his father would be old and sick.

"If we wanted to," Jason Grey said, "we could find out

everything about that man who shot himself. We could find out how much money he owed, and if his wife had left him for somebody else. But we'd never really know what went on in his mind. It's not our right to know what goes on in another man's mind. But whatever it was, we know one thing for sure—he just couldn't fight it any more. And that's his right, too." Jason finished his cigarette and motioned to his son. "Come on," he said.

Together they walked the rest of the way to the clearing. The few leaves left on the trees had turned yellow, and when the sunlight filtered through them the air seemed to shine. Richard felt the urge to grab his father's hand; instead he stood in the clearing and watched the yellow light.

"People have private places in their minds," Jason Grey said. "That doesn't mean they're crazy. It doesn't even mean they're cowards if they run from something awful."

They could hear leaves falling. Jason Grey stared straight ahead, but he reached down and took his son's hand.

"You just remember there's a big difference between not being able to fight it anymore and feeling like you're all alone sometimes," he said.

"Even when you're married?" Richard had asked, surprised that his father knew so much about being alone.

Jason Grey couldn't stop himself from smiling. "Especially then," he had said.

On his wedding night, Richard knew exactly what his father had been talking about. There was a private place in

Lila's mind that was somehow the same as that migrant worker with the shotgun. But if anything, this made Lila seem more precious. When Richard touched the white scars on Lila's wrist he was dazzled by hope—it was as if Lila had died and come back to him, and he held her tight for a moment, before he stepped away.

"I am looking at you," Richard said. "And all I see is my wife."

The rest of that summer seemed to last forever; the air smelled like strawberries and the sunlight was unusually thick. Helen was delighted to have another woman in the house, and she taught Lila all her secret recipes, for cabbage soup and jam cake and sweet potato pie. Just before supper Lila always went outside to wait on the lawn for Richard and Jason Grey to come home from work. At that time of day the sky was deep blue, and under that sky Lila felt brand new. For a brief time she was a woman without a history—even her dreams were filled with ordinary things, fireflies and pearl-edged clouds, and teapots made out of copper. She didn't question her good luck—she didn't dare to. All she knew was that someone had fallen in love with her, and, amazingly enough, that was all she needed.

But when autumn came, something changed. At night, after they had made love and Richard had fallen asleep, Lila found herself shivering with fear. She was certain that she would lose Richard: one day when she went out to wait for him Jason Grey's Chrysler would pull up in the driveway and only her father-in-law would get out. She began to dream about her past; her womb tightened as it had for days after her baby had been born, and the contractions kept her up all night and made her afraid to sleep in the same bed as her husband.

One night, Richard woke up sometime near dawn to find Lila huddled on the floor. He started to get out of bed, but Lila held up her hand, warning him to stop.

"Don't come near me," she said, and the coldness of her own voice filled her with grief.

"Come back to bed," Richard said quietly.

"If you really knew me you would never love me," Lila told him.

"If you're referring to the fact that you once tried suicide, I know that and I don't care," Richard said.

Lila threw back her head and laughed, and the sound went right through Richard.

"Come back to bed," he urged.

"You really think you know me," Lila said contemptuously.

Richard could tell that after only a few months of marriage Lila was drifting away from him, and for the first time he raised his voice to her.

"Then go ahead and tell me the reason why you tried to kill yourself. You obviously want to tell me, so you go right ahead. Tell me."

"I don't want to," Lila said in a small voice.

"Then don't," Richard said. "But either do it and get it over with or let it go, because we can't keep on this way, Lila."

Lila got back into bed and put her arms around him.

"I thought when I met you you said you could read the future," Richard said.

"I said tea leaves," Lila whispered. "That's all."

"Well, I can see into the future," Richard told her. "You might as well stop fighting it, because we're going to be together for a very long time."

Lila wished she could believe him, but by the time winter came she was convinced that if they stayed in New York State they had no future at all. Someone in East China might manage to find out the truth about her; someone might tell Richard. She felt as if the past were right on her heels, and it got so bad that whenever she went into town to shop for groceries with her mother-in-law she wondered if perhaps the doctor had arranged for a couple in East China to adopt her baby. It became impossible for her to look at a child of any age; she swore her breasts were filling with milk again—at night they ached so badly that she had to sleep on her back. As her own child's birthday grew near, Lila thought she might be going mad. Every night the sky was orange and black, and the days were as gray as stone. She grew more certain that if she stayed in East China through the winter something terrible would happen. She began to talk about leaving, but Richard imagined that what she wanted was a house of their own. He promised that in less than a year they'd find a house with a view of Long Island Sound and move out. But then one day when it was cold enough to make her shiver and remember the ice storm, Lila walked to the gas station to take Richard and Jason a Thermos of hot coffee and some lunch. There was a car

idling by the gas pumps; in the passenger seat was a little
girl. The girl's mother had gone into the office to ask
Richard for directions and a map, and when she came back
out she found Lila with both her hands on the passenger
window, weeping as she stared inside.

Lila forced herself not to run after the car. It hadn't
mattered that the child wasn't hers, Lila wanted her. She'd
had the terrible urge to get behind the wheel of the car and
kidnap her, and if the child's mother hadn't come out of the
office when she did Lila might have already been driving
west. She would have turned the radio on to a low volume,
and the heat up to high, and the little girl would have been
right beside her, her sleepy breath filling the car with a deli-
ciously sweet odor.

That was when Lila decided that California was the
answer. Once, she had imagined that she and Stephen
would go there together and live high above Hollywood, in
the hills. Now all she wanted was a place to start over, a
place so free of history that the past barely existed. She
started talking about going west that evening at supper, and
once she started talking she couldn't seem to stop, not even
after the others had put down their forks and turned to look
at her.

"Are you and Richard planning to leave New York?"
Helen asked in a frightened voice. For the first time she
began to know the dangers of having a daughter-in-law.

"No," Richard told her, although he realized that something was about to happen. "We're not planning anything,"
he told his mother.

Helen was relieved, but when Richard glanced over at

his father he didn't look quite sure of himself, and Jason Grey could tell that his son wouldn't be in East China much longer.

Every night Lila begged him to leave. She talked about palm trees and pelicans until Richard began to dream about the Pacific Ocean. In his dreams the ocean was amazingly green, like a thin piece of jade held up to the sun, and blue-eyed pelicans dove into the waves. One night when the snow was falling and Lila was turned away from him, Richard sat up in bed.

"All right," he told his wife. "We'll go to California."

Lila kissed him until his cheeks and his eyelids were wet.

"But you're the one who has to tell my mother," Richard said.

Lila backed away. "You're her son," she said. "You tell her."

"You're the one who wants to leave. You tell her."

Richard put his arms around Lila and pulled her close.

"You don't understand," he told her. "I'm her only child and as far as she's concerned she'll be losing me forever."

Richard felt his wife move away from him, even though she was still in his arms.

"I understand perfectly," Lila said coolly. "And if you're too afraid to tell her, I will."

But that night Helen was already being told. Jason Grey turned to her in their bed and asked, "How would you like for it to be just you and me again?"

"You and me?" Helen said, confused. Then she realized what Jason meant. "Oh," she said, and she started to cry.

"All you had to do was say no," Jason teased her.

"What makes you so sure they're leaving?" Helen asked.

"I'm sure," Jason said. "They just don't know how to tell us."

"Well, if that's what they've decided," Helen said, still crying, "I can think of a lot worse things than being left here with you."

Helen might be losing her son, but she didn't intend to make it easy for Lila to take him away. First of all, she was sweet as pie—every time Lila began to talk about California Helen offered her a wool sweater that just didn't suit her anymore, or a new recipe, or a piece of china, until—piece by piece—Lila had an entire service for eight stored in a cardboard box in the attic. Every day Lila swore she would tell her mother-in-law about their plans, and every day she put it off. Richard unpacked their suitcases, convinced that Lila's obsession with California had been nothing more than a reaction to a particularly cold winter. But when Lila stopped talking about leaving it wasn't because she wanted it any less.

One day in January, Lila went up to the bedroom and didn't come down. She stayed in bed for three days and nights, and every time she breathed she felt a terrible pain in her abdomen. She refused to speak to Richard, and she would not see a doctor. Richard couldn't bring himself to go to work and he wasn't allowed in his own room. He sat for hours at the kitchen table, unable to eat, not understanding why he felt as though he had lost his wife.

On the fourth day Helen spent the morning crying,

then she went upstairs. She walked into Lila's room without bothering to knock and sat at the foot of the bed.

"You don't have to tell me what's wrong," Helen said. "Just tell me—is leaving New York the only thing that will cure you?"

Lila hadn't talked for such a long time that when she spoke her voice was thick.

"It's the only thing," she told her mother-in-law. "If I stay here I'll die."

Helen took the suitcases out of the closet and packed Lila's and Richard's clothes. She telephoned Jason at the gas station and asked him to bring home the station wagon he'd been working on to replace their old Chrysler. Then Helen went downstairs to the kitchen and closed the door behind her. While Jason Grey and Richard packed up the station wagon and helped Lila down to the car, Helen baked a honey cake. She used almonds, and sweet brown pears, and when it was done she carefully placed it in a tin that she carried out to the car. She handed the cake to Lila through the window of the station wagon, and she kissed Richard twice before she let him go. Lila held the cake tin on her lap, as if its heat could make her well. When they had been on the Long Island Expressway for over an hour, she suddenly begged Richard to drive into Manhattan.

"I understand," Richard had said. "You want to see your parents before we go."

But that hadn't been it at all. It seemed so simple now— Lila would run into the apartment and shake her mother by her shoulders until she divulged the name and address of whoever had stolen Lila's daughter. Then all Lila had to do was go back out to Richard and tell him that her mother had insisted they take a little cousin with them to raise as their own. Once they reached the house where her daughter was being held, Lila would slip through the front door, wrap the child in a warm blanket, then run as fast as she could. All the way to California she would hold her daughter on her lap—she wouldn't let go of her, not until the western sky opened up in front of them as they sped past black hills and corrals full of half-wild horses.

When they got to the apartment building, Richard couldn't find a parking space, so he circled the block. Lila got out of the car, but once she was standing on the sidewalk her sense of expectation disappeared. She went inside the building and climbed the three flights of stairs, but when she reached the apartment and knocked on the door there was no answer. She knocked again and again, but each time she did she felt more defeated—in the cold hallway her plans to kidnap her daughter seemed ludicrous, and in the end, when she walked downstairs and back out on to the street, she was relieved that no one had been home.

She could see the station wagon half a block away, stuck in traffic. It was then that she happened to turn back to take one last look at the apartment building, and when she looked upward she saw the curtains moving in the window of the parlor. Up on the third floor, hidden behind lace curtains, Lila's mother gazed downward. As soon as she realized Lila saw her, she dropped the curtains and moved away. But even then Lila could see her mother's shadow, a line of black pressed against the white curtains.

When the station wagon pulled up to the curb, Lila got in, leaned her head against the seat, and wept.

"They may not be the best in the world, but they're still your parents," Richard said. "It's not easy to leave people behind."

Lila reached down and lifted up the hem of her dress to wipe her eyes.

"Are you sure you want to do this?" Richard asked. "We don't have to go to California—we can still turn back."

Without bothering to look, Lila knew that her mother was still watching her. She moved over so that Richard could put his arm around her, then she closed her eyes as they drove toward the Lincoln Tunnel, and in no time at all they had left New York behind them for good.

• • •

At first it seemed as if it was only a matter of time. But a year passed, then two, then three, and Lila still hadn't gotten pregnant. She bathed in tubs filled with warm water and vitamin E, she forced herself to eat calf's liver twice a week, she gave up caffeine and chocolate and spices. Every morning, before she got out of bed, she took her temperature, and she kept a chart of her ovulation taped to the back of her closet door. But in her heart, Lila knew that she'd never be given another chance; each time Richard talked about the child they would someday have Lila grew more desperate, and by the time she turned thirty she had given up hope.

The nights they made love, Lila could never sleep. She

waited until Richard's breathing grew deep, and then she carefully got out of bed. On these nights she went out to the garden, and she sat in a black wrought-iron chair beneath the lemon tree. She never bothered with slippers, even though the patio was cold and snails moved across the slate, leaving slick trails behind. There had been something wrong with the garden from the start; the neighbors had warned them that everything you wanted to grow simply wouldn't, but renegade plants would reappear each time you pulled them out by the roots. At the rear of the yard, along a low wooden fence, the previous owner had foolishly planted a passion flower vine that was now so tangled it had begun to strangle itself with its own flowers. At the time of night when Lila went to sit in the yard it was almost possible to hear the vine growing, wrapping itself tighter around the fence.

In the mornings Lila climbed back into bed, and Richard never seemed to notice that she'd been gone all night. He still talked about the son they would have someday, the daughter who would look just like Lila, but each year he sounded a little less convinced. When they had been married for fifteen years, Richard said, "Let's say we can never have any children. Is that the worst that can happen to us?"

She told him it wasn't, but secretly Lila believed that it was. Childless women began to disgust her—she could sense their brittle presence in the supermarket and the bakery, she could look right through them and see white dust and bones. The worst times were when Richard's parents came out to visit. The older they got, the more they wanted grandchildren, but even they knew enough to stop asking when. The year Lila turned thirty-nine was the first time Helen Grey visited without advising them that the guest room would make a perfect nursery. But every now and then during that visit, Lila would look up and find her mother-in-law watching her, as if she were the only person who really knew just how badly Lila had cheated her son.

That was when Lila began to do readings again. It wasn't for the money—Richard had bought his own shop—it was because of the comfort she found in reaching into someone else's sorrow. She began carefully, starting with her neighbors, who were shocked by her sudden interest in them. In time, Lila's clients swore by her. Her advice was noncommittal but sound, and Lila actually found she was pleased when her clients grew to depend on her, waiting to make travel plans or give a husband an ultimatum until Lila could read their tea leaves. It was one of her regular customers, Mrs. Graham from around the corner, who brought her niece to Lila's one afternoon. The red tablecloth was set out and the water boiled by the time the two women arrived. Lila read for Mrs. Graham first—the question of whether or not to put her ailing dog to sleep was evaded until next time—and then for the niece. The niece had come from a bad marriage in Chicago, and she was already reconsidering the separation from her husband.

"What I want to know is will he walk all over me if I go back?" she asked Lila. "I give in to him a lot, and that's my problem. If he tells me he's spent his paycheck I say, Why that's all right—but inside I'd like to kill him."

Lila nodded and poured the water over the tea leaves;

she could tell that the niece was going back to her husband to give him another chance. She watched the leaves float to the surface without much interest, but when the niece had finished her tea Lila took one look inside the cup and immediately began to cry. Lila's clients sat on the edge of their seats, and they both let out a whoop when Lila informed the niece that she was pregnant.

"Wait till I tell my husband," the niece said. "He is going to flip out when I tell him."

After they left, Lila went into the bathroom and ran the cold water, and from then on she refused to open the door if Mrs. Graham came for a reading. All the rest of that month, Lila felt shaky, and each time she closed her eyes she saw the small motionless child in the center of the cup. It was not as if she had not seen death during readings before, but this was different, this was enough to break your heart. She grew careful; if a client even mentioned that she was considering pregnancy, Lila never read for her again. But she was tricked the following year by a high-school student who had accompanied her mother to a reading. Lila had carelessly poured a cup of tea for the girl so that she'd be occupied during her mother's reading. It wasn't until the reading was over, and Lila reached for the girl's cup to carry it into the kitchen, that she saw the symbol again. At first she was paralyzed, but when the mother went out to start her car, Lila found an excuse to pull the girl back into the house. After she'd told the girl she was pregnant, Lila was so upset she was the one who seemed to need comforting.

"I'll be okay," the girl promised Lila. "Really."

"Did you know you were pregnant?" Lila asked her.

"I sort of thought I was," the girl admitted.

Lila simply couldn't bring herself to tell any more of what she'd seen, and she couldn't bear to listen as the girl confided that she planned to enter a special high school program for mothers, not when she was so certain that the child would not live.

That night Lila had a fever of a hundred and three and when she woke up the next morning the bed was soaked with tears. After that she almost gave up the readings altogether, particularly at times when she happened to look in the mirror and saw how much she looked like the old fortune-teller in New York. But she continued to see her clients. She managed to convince herself that it was just a job like any other and that she couldn't possibly know what the future would bring, although now and then she still seemed to know more than she wanted to.

Late one night, in the middle of a warm, dry winter, the telephone suddenly rang. Lila felt certain that something had happened to Helen. She sat up in bed, rigid, while Richard ran to answer it. The air was so warm that the clothes Lila had hung up to dry overnight were no longer even damp, but when Richard came back into the bedroom he found that Lila had wrapped a heavy woolen blanket around her shoulders.

"It's my mother," Richard said. "She's in the hospital."

He sat on the edge of the bed, but when Lila went to sit next to him he didn't seem to notice.

"She's dying," Richard said.

"Oh, no," Lila said, but what she really meant was *Please don't leave me.*

"I have to go tonight," Richard told her. "Otherwise it may be too late for me to see her again."

Lila called the airline for a reservation; then she took out the suitcase and packed a week's worth of Richard's clothes.

They were standing by the front door, waiting for the taxi, when Lila thought she heard the sound of bees.

"Come with me," Richard said to her.

But for Lila New York had dissolved; it wasn't even on the map any more.

"It's better if you go alone," Lila told Richard. "You're her only son. You're the one she wants to see."

"I'm going to give my father hell," Richard said. "He should have told me before."

"Don't do that," Lila said. "You know your father."

That was when Richard started to cry.

"Oh, don't," Lila begged him. "What good will it do you?"

"I just don't see how he's going to go on without her," Richard said. "That's the part that really gets me."

When the taxi came, Lila walked Richard out to the porch, but she couldn't watch him drive away. It was the first time since their marriage that they had been apart. But although she dreaded being alone, Lila needed this time by herself: this was the week her period was due, and if she missed it again it would make three times in a row. Every morning Lila checked to see if the sheets were stained. On the fifth day there was one wild moment when she actually thought she might be pregnant, but of course she was not. She sat by the open window, and as night began to fall she grew flushed, and her nerves seemed much too delicate—she could feel them jump beneath her skin.

She should have been relieved; for years she had tried to get pregnant just to please Richard, she had never really wanted any child other than the one she had lost. An early menopause simply saved her from trying to love another child in a way she never could. But now that it was truly over, Lila cared much more than she should have. She went into mourning: when neighbors knocked on the door, she didn't answer, she didn't even bother to get dressed, and when Richard phoned from New York, Lila no longer recognized his voice. Eight days later, when Richard returned, Lila knew that neither of them would ever be the same.

It was early evening when the taxi pulled up. Lila was already in bed asleep when Richard came to lie down next to her. He woke Lila by watching her, and she came to him from a dream where all the furniture in her parents' apartment had been replaced with woven mats, and tea was being served from a silver samovar in the middle of the floor.

"Was she in pain?" Lila asked when she woke.

"She didn't remember me," Richard said.

"Of course she did," Lila told him. "You're her only son."

Richard didn't have the strength to unbutton his shirt—he had been wearing the same clothes for two days.

"The hedges are all overgrown," he said. "I noticed it first thing when I got out of the taxi."

"She knew you," Lila said.

"No," Richard told her. "She knew my father and she called him by name, but she didn't remember me."

"You don't understand," Lila said. "The worst thing in the world for a mother is to leave her child. She couldn't bring herself to remember you, because if she did she'd have to leave you behind."

In the morning, when she woke up, the first thing Lila heard was a jet overhead. But when she listened carefully she could hear the rhythm of an ax. She got out of bed and reached for her robe. In the kitchen, the back door was ajar. A few hours earlier it had begun to rain; puddles had formed, and when Lila walked out to the patio the sudden rush of cold water on her feet left her confused for a moment. In the rear of the yard Richard was cutting down the vines that covered the fence. The ax he used had been stored in the garage for years, but it was still so sharp that in no time a huge pile of vines had collected on the ground. There were white flowers with green centers all over the yard, as if an earthquake had torn them from their vines.

At this time of year in East China, nothing grew. Lilies were deep in the frozen ground, peach trees and azaleas were bare. It had been the dead of winter when Lila and Richard left New York, but the sky had been deep blue. The cake tin Helen had given Lila was red metal, and because the cake inside was still warm, the tin seemed to shine. The one time Lila looked back, Helen was following their car. She went as far as the end of the dirt driveway, where in the spring there would be so much deep mud that Jason would have to shovel for hours before he could move his car. Helen stopped, and she stood there waving. Up on the porch, Jason Grey lit a cigarette, then leaned over the wooden railing. He stayed right where he was as they drove away, watching his wife and waiting for her to come back to him.

Out in the rain, Lila pulled her bathrobe tighter around herself. Somehow, she had become forty-six years old, and she didn't know quite how it had happened. She wondered if there was something about California that made the time move so quickly. Without winter to shock you into another year, entire seasons had dissolved in the sunshine; and no one could manage time in a place where even the roses were so confused that they bloomed year round.

Richard was almost through clearing the fence. He worked harder than ever, as though his life depended on the steady rhythm of the ax. Later, Lila would make him a pot of hot coffee. She'd sit on the rim of the tub while he bathed, just to be near him. But for now, she waited. In their own backyard, as the rain washed all the snails out of their garden, Lila and Richard crossed over an invisible line together. Impossible as it seemed, they had become older than Helen and Jason Grey had been on that day in East China when ice was everywhere and the sky was so cold and so blue.

PART THREE

$\mathcal{I}$N NOVEMBER, WHEN THE moon was clear and white and the acacia trees gave off a bitter scent, Rae began to believe that she had lost the baby. It wasn't just that odd look on the psychic's face as she read Rae's tea leaves, it was that she felt so absolutely well. During the first three months she had been exhausted, and so queasy that she couldn't stand to look at boiled eggs. Now she could stay up past eleven, she could eat hot chili if she wanted to, and she had so much energy that she found herself cleaning out closets on her days off from work. The better she felt, the more she sensed something was wrong, and there was one thing she knew for certain: in all these months she had not once felt the baby move.

She went through lists of birth defects and diseases, but in the end she decided that she herself was at fault. She had taken too many hot showers, eaten too much salt, she'd lifted her arms high above her head so that the umbilical cord had wrapped itself around the baby's neck. In her heart she knew that each time she gained another pound it was only because her body had been cruelly tricked. Her pregnancy was a farce, it would never last full term; eventually someone would cut her open and remove whatever was inside her, and that would be the end of it. She put off going to see an obstetrician, and at work she refused to answer any of Freddy's questions about her health. But Freddy had already guessed, and one day he took her out to lunch at a Chinese restaurant and offered her five hundred dollars.

"You're kidding," Rae said. "You want to give me money?"

"I was thinking of it as a loan," Freddy said. "For one thing, Rae, you need new clothes."

"Are you going to fire me?" Rae said.

She and Jessup had managed to save four thousand dollars—the bankbook was hidden in the silverware drawer, under the forks and spoons—and if she really had been having this baby she could have used the savings to cover the hospital bills if Freddy fired her.

"Of course I'm not going to fire you," Freddy said. "But I'll tell you the truth—I'm real uncomfortable about this whole pregnancy thing."

"So am I," Rae said.

"You know what I'd like to know?" Freddy said. "Where's that assassin now that you need him?"

"I'm not interested in your money," Rae said stiffly.

"Oh, come on," Freddy said. "I'd charge you less interest than a bank would."

Rae couldn't help laughing.

"Seriously," Freddy said. "It's a gift."

Rae knew that Freddy was feeling sorry for her, and somehow that made her feel sorry for herself. She put down her chopsticks and watched him write out the check, unable to stop him, unable to tell him the baby would never be born. If she and Jessup had only left California things might have been different. For a while they had talked about using their savings to go to Alaska. Actually, Jessup had been the one doing the talking.

"This country feels too small for me," he had told Rae one night.

"Oh, really?" Rae was amused by the idea.

"Yes, really," Jessup had insisted. "Everything's been overdone and overused in this country. There are no options any more."

"What about Alaska," Rae had teased. "Is that too small for you, too?"

The moment he looked over at her she thought, Oh, shit—he's serious about this.

"Admit it," Jessup had said. "It's not a bad idea—even if it is yours."

"Not Alaska," Rae told him.

"I'll tell you what," he said. "Let's just consider it— that's all."

They had been in bed, and Rae wrapped her arms around him. "All right," she'd agreed. "But that doesn't mean we'll really do it."

Now she wished they had. If it had been just the two of them somewhere in Alaska, they might still be together. Snow would reach the rooftop of their cabin, and at night the ice outside would turn everything blue—everything, the glaciers and the white wolves and the owls that lived in the eaves. A child born there would be so healthy it would reach out its arms to hold you the moment after its birth.

"I think I have to go home," Rae told Freddy.

She took the rest of the day off, and when she got home she opened all the windows in the apartment. She had suddenly begun to miss Boston, and although she had always hated the winters there, she yearned for a real November, and clear, cold air. Once, on the Tuesday after Thanksgiving vacation, she had been sitting in the kitchen, drinking coffee, when Carolyn came downstairs, wearing her camel's-hair coat and a black wool hat.

"Listen," Carolyn had said to Rae, "don't go to school today."

Rae looked up from her coffee, but her mother didn't explain any further. They still weren't really talking to each other, except for those things that had to be said: Pass the butter, Pass the salt, The telephone's for you. But Rae had a math test that day, and everyone suspected a surprise quiz in French class.

"All right," Rae agreed.

They drove downtown, to the Museum of Fine Arts. In the parking lot Carolyn turned to Rae after she took the key out of the ignition.

"I've been thinking about going back to school," Carolyn said. "Maybe even law school."

Rae had heard this before. "Do it," she advised.

"I don't know if I can," Carolyn said.

"Then why do you always talk about it?" Rae snapped.

"You know what my problem is?" Carolyn said.

It had begun to grow cold in the car; Rae shifted uncomfortably.

"I was always afraid to be alone."

"Oh, yeah?" Rae said without interest.

"Now I see you making the same exact mistake with Jessup as I did with your father," Carolyn said.

"Oh, for God's sake!" Rae said. "Could we just go to the museum?"

She got out of the car and slammed the door behind her, then walked ten paces ahead of Carolyn to the door of the museum. All through the Grecian ruins Rae stayed far enough away from her mother to prevent any conversation between them.

"I'm sorry," Carolyn finally said.

They were walking through a room filled with Japanese kimonos. "I don't mean to insult you," Carolyn said. "It's just that I see you running after Jessup."

"I am not running after him," Rae said.

"Well, going after him, then," Carolyn said. "And once he wrecks your life there'll be nothing I can do about it. I'm warning you—don't come running to me."

A young couple had come into the room, and now walked past them. Rae moved away from her mother. Carolyn followed her daughter to the next glass case of kimonos. The material had been painted by more than two dozen women; willows and water lilies washed over gold- and rose-colored silk.

"The one time I didn't feel alone was when I was pregnant," Carolyn said. "After you were born I couldn't imagine how I had managed to live all those years without you. How did I survive before? Who did I love?"

In the gift shop, before they were about to leave, Carolyn had insisted on buying Rae a gift, a poster of Monet's water lilies, which somehow seemed crude after the delicate kimonos. "Perfect for your room," Carolyn had whispered as they waited for the cashier to wrap the poster in brown paper.

Rae had agreed, she had even politely thanked her mother, but she knew that before long she and Jessup would be leaving, and the Monet poster would hang in her empty bedroom.

When they left the museum it was four, and very nearly dark. Rae carried the rolled-up poster under her arm and kept her hands in her pockets. If she had gone to school that day she would have already been home for a half an hour, waiting for Jessup to appear on the sidewalk.

"I don't know why it is, but November smells like smoke," Carolyn said. "Maybe I'm crazy, but I think it's delicious."

When Rae breathed in she realized that her mother was right, the air was delicious. For some reason Rae had the sudden urge to put her arm through her mother's arm, to feel the weight of the camel's-hair coat that Carolyn stored in a cedar closet every summer. But by then they had reached the car and Carolyn was humming as she reached into her coat pocket for the keys. Rae felt something in her chest, and she forced herself to take several deep breaths. As Carolyn unlocked the car, Rae wondered why it was that she should have to feel sorry for her mother, and why, as she breathed in the smoky blue air, one visit to the Museum of Fine Arts could make her feel so lost.

In Massachusetts, Rae could look out her window and see chestnut trees, white stars, clouds that covered the moon. Here, from her kitchen, she saw only the empty street. But the dogs were out there, she knew it. Ever since the heat wave they had been wandering through the neighborhood, looking for water and bones. And sure enough, when Rae pressed her face up against the glass she saw a large black Labrador in the courtyard; she quickly pulled down the shade. Late that night, at ten minutes after twelve, she telephoned Lila Grey.

"Are you crazy?" Lila said after Richard had handed her the phone. "How dare you call me at this hour. I'll tell you something right now—I don't intend to read for you ever again. Got that?"

Richard sat up in bed, concerned.

"It's nothing," Lila told him. "Go back to sleep."

"This is the thing," Rae said slowly, as though she hadn't heard a word Lila had said to her, "I think there's something wrong with my baby."

Lila leaned up against the headboard; she could feel her mouth grow dry.

"Don't ask me why, because I can't tell you," Rae said. "I just know something's wrong."

"Do you want my advice?" Lila asked. She was shaking,

and she wished Richard would turn on his side and stop watching her. That motionless child in Rae's teacup refused to disappear. "Go see a doctor," she told Rae.

"I can't do that," Rae said quickly.

"Tomorrow, as soon as you get up, call an obstetrician and make an appointment," Lila said.

Rae didn't answer; she lifted the windowshade and watched the black dog stretch out in the courtyard for the night.

"Are you going to listen to me?" Lila said. She could hear the edge of panic in her voice, and she took Richard's hand to reassure him; under the sheets their fingers intertwined.

"Yes," Rae said.

"And I don't want you to call me again," Lila said.

"You hate me," Rae said. "Don't you?"

It was really much too late to be talking to strangers, it was the time of night when mothers went to their children who had nightmares, and they held their sons and daughters close, and stroked their hair until they fell asleep.

"Call a doctor," Lila said gently.

"All right," Rae agreed.

"Good girl," Lila said.

After she'd hung up, Rae couldn't sleep, and in the morning, when she called for an appointment at a clinic nearby, her voice was so hoarse she had to struggle to whisper. They made room on the schedule that afternoon. In the waiting room, Rae tried to imagine that Jessup was beside her, but she knew he would have never come here with her. She considered leaving, but before she could the nurse called her name and took her into a small office for blood tests. Rae didn't panic until she walked into the examining room. The doctor was a woman who seemed much too young—and really, Rae knew, this visit was pointless.

"I don't think this is the best time for me to be examined," Rae said.

"You're right," the doctor said. "The best time would have been two months ago."

Rae took off her clothes, put on a paper smock, and lay down on the examining table. She closed her eyes during the internal, and when she was told that everything looked fine, she was sure this doctor was a fool.

Rae answered all the questions for a medical history, but as she did she could feel herself growing colder. If she really thought about it, it was better this way. She wasn't meant to have a baby alone, it was fate; and if there was a good time to lose a baby it was now, before she began to feel it move inside her, before she started to wait for the rhythm of its turning in its sleep.

"Is something wrong?" the doctor asked her. "You just don't seem interested." She had been going over a food chart and discussing the vitamins she was about to prescribe.

"How long have you been a doctor?" Rae asked.

"Four years—is that long enough for you?"

Rae felt herself grow embarrassed. "Oh, it's enough, all right," she said. "It's just that you missed something. My baby is dead."

"I see," the doctor said. "You're positive?"

Rae was so cold that she was certain her blood had

begun to freeze. When she looked closely at herself she noticed that the skin on her arms and legs was faintly purple.

"Don't you think I know?" Rae said. "Don't you think I can tell?"

"Lie down," the doctor said.

Rae knew now—this was the moment when she would be cut open: the doctor would reach her hands deep inside and lift the baby out, then hide it as she sewed Rae back together.

"You'd better not touch me," Rae said.

She could not believe her voice. Her real voice didn't sound that way. The doctor rolled over a tall, metal machine, and when she moved closer to the examining table, Rae sat up straight.

"Don't come near me," she said.

It was her voice after all. God, she was practically squeaking. It wasn't so much being cut open that terrified her, it was the fact that it was now. Now the operation would begin. Now she would lose her baby.

"I don't know what you think I'm going to do to you," the doctor said. "But all I'm going to do is listen to your baby's heartbeat."

Rae nearly laughed out loud; this was supposed to comfort her? A wild search for a heartbeat that wasn't there.

"Okay?" the doctor said.

Rae looked at her coldly, then shrugged. She lay back down on the table and closed her eyes.

"This amplifies sound," the doctor explained as she rubbed some gel on Rae's abdomen.

With her eyes closed, Rae could feel the ice in the room, and it made her think of the time she and Jessup had taken a bus to Rockport one winter. The harbor had been frozen solid, but as they stood by the docks they could see the tide moving beneath the ice, and when they knelt down and peered beneath the dock they could see that the ice itself was shifting.

"That's the placenta you hear," the doctor said.

"If I lived in this town I'd go crazy," Jessup had said. "Imagine trying to sleep with the sound of the goddamn ocean ringing in your ears."

"I'd love it," Rae had said. It was one of the few times she had disagreed with him. She didn't look over at him, but could tell he was studying her.

"Yeah, well, maybe you get used to it if you hear it every night," he had finally allowed her.

"I think I've found it," the doctor said.

Rae opened her eyes. She leaned up, resting on her elbows.

"I don't hear it," she said.

"Just listen," the doctor told her.

That was when she heard it, and at the moment she heard it she started to cry.

"That's it," the doctor said. "That's your baby."

Rae was hit by something as immediate as lightning, but more piercing, whiter, a thousand times more perfect. The heartbeat seemed to come from a very great distance away. She had to remind herself that it was inside her. If she'd ever said she didn't care about this baby she'd been a liar. When the amplifier was turned off and she could no longer hear it, she sat on the edge of the examining table and wept. Later, she apologized to the doctor and got dressed. She filled out her medical forms and drove back to her apartment, but if anything it was all more of a mystery than it had been before: how anything as fragile as a body might suddenly be so strong it could carry two hearts, and not even feel the weight.

• • •

In less than a month, Rae found that she could come home from work, spend the entire evening in Jessup's easy chair reading Dr. Spock, and actually enjoy it. There was a whole new language to learn: colic and cradle cap and expressed milk. She began to wake every night at three a.m., as though she were in training. She bought milk by the quart and drank herbal tea. When none of her clothes buttoned any more, she decided against a secondhand store. Instead, she took two hundred dollars out of the bank account, went to the maternity department at Bullock's, and then spent more money on clothes in forty-five minutes than she had in the last five years. By the time the saleswoman had handed her two shopping bags, Rae was so out of breath that she had to go out to the parked Oldsmobile and lean her head against the steering wheel. There, in the parking lot, Rae felt something move for the first time. It wasn't at all what she had expected, and she picked her head up from the steering wheel and waited for it to come again. She'd been expecting an actual kick, but what she felt was more like fluttering, as if a pair of wings were deep inside her. When it happened a second time Rae realized that she had been feeling the exact same thing for weeks.

"Oh, Jesus," she said to herself in the Oldsmobile. This was really it: her child was moving.

She decided on natural childbirth and discussed it with her doctor. But when the subject of a labor coach came up, Rae found herself lying—her husband, she said, was currently on the road, selling truck tires. It was a career so unlike the ones Jessup dreamed of that for a moment she almost felt as though she had gotten back at him. She imagined him in a VW van, with a load of oversized tires, and she left him stranded on the interstate in Nebraska with a blowout and no tire small enough to fit his van.

The first person she asked to be her coach was Freddy, and he told her it was out of the question. For days afterward he was afraid to talk to her. Finally, he offered her money to hire a labor coach, and he couldn't understand why she refused him.

"It would be totally different to have you as my coach," Rae told him. "I wouldn't be paying you—you'd be there because you wanted to be."

"Oh, no I wouldn't," Freddy said. "Believe me. I wouldn't want to be there. Rae, I don't even want to hear about somebody's birth. I don't want to see a photograph. Is that the kind of coach you want?"

She nearly asked the woman next door, an actress she sometimes arranged to do her laundry with so they wouldn't both have to sit in the laundromat alone after dark. But when Rae met her out by the mailboxes one evening and mentioned natural childbirth, her neighbor looked stricken. She couldn't even step inside a hospital, she told Rae—if she were ever to have a child, they'd have to knock her out at the door.

And so it wasn't as if Rae wanted to ask Lila Grey—she simply didn't have anyone else.

"It's pathetic, isn't it?" Rae said, after she'd phoned Lila and explained what she wanted. "That I have to ask you."

What was infinitely worse, Lila thought, was to be stupid enough to get trapped on the stairwell, and to have your water break right there, in a place that was so dim it was difficult to find your way on an ordinary day. No one had been there to help her on that stairway—but there were times when Lila liked to think that Hannie grabbed at her own side at the very same moment she did, searching each rib for the pain.

"Don't you have anyone else?" she asked Rae. "A friend?"

"If I did would I be calling you?" Rae said.

"I told you not to call me," Lila said, but she didn't sound convincing, not even to herself. If she had only had the nerve to walk into the restaurant on Third Avenue she might not have been in that awful hot bedroom when her labor began, curled up in a bed that had been too small for her since she was twelve. She could have been safe in Hannie's house, and for days afterward someone would have brought her hot tea and thin slices of toast, and she wouldn't even have had to get out of bed, she could have held her daughter close, and watched as she slept.

"Just think about it," Rae said. "That's all I'm asking."

For two weeks Lila thought of nothing else, but she

didn't return Rae's call. She simply couldn't bring herself to say no, not when she knew what it was like to be alone in a room that was so dark it sucked you into itself and filled your throat with so much darkness that every time you took a breath a dozen black plums pushed down on your tongue. When the door to Lila's room had opened, the light from the hallway had saved her. She could still feel the sensation of the light on her skin as her cousin had walked into the room, she could feel each footstep as her cousin came closer, then mercifully put her arms around Lila and helped her up from the floor.

If that symbol hadn't appeared in Rae's cup, if it hadn't been so clear that her child would be either stillborn or so damaged that a future was impossible, Lila might have agreed to help her. But instead, Lila stopped answering her phone. She told Richard she'd been getting crank calls, and the two of them lay in bed, still as stones, whenever the phone rang late at night, with a ring so piercing it cut right through your dreams. Lila's readings suffered—not just because she missed appointments when she didn't answer the phone, but because she had used up so much energy in not telling Rae the truth that she now couldn't seem to lie to anyone else. She told one bad fortune after another: old clients began to cancel their appointments for weekly readings, new clients at the restaurant fled from their tables in tears and complained to the management. But Lila couldn't seem to stop herself. She told old women to draw up their wills, and young women wept when they heard that the lover who was absent on holidays was not with a sick friend but with a wife. The manager of The Salad Connection gave Lila one more chance, and when there were three more complaints in a single afternoon—a divorce, failure at a job, and possible drug abuse—he fired her.

In a way it was a relief. That very same day Lila took all the tins of loose tea from her cabinets and poured the tea down the drain in the sink. She had Richard call the phone company and change their number; she cut up her white silk turban with a pair of garden shears and threw out the red shawl she always used as a tablecloth during readings. When she decided to go into the auto shop each morning and take over the books, Richard was shocked, but Lila explained that she couldn't stand another moment of listening to someone's troubles; adding up the repair bills for BMWs and Audis was exactly what she needed to clear her head. But in the afternoons, when she was alone in the house, Lila was so uneasy that she couldn't sit still. And when she looked out her window one day and saw Rae sitting in her parked car, Lila's throat went dry, but she wasn't surprised. She had been expecting her to appear for days, and, what was worse, she had wanted her to. Lila put on a sweater and went outside; she got into the passenger seat next to Rae and slammed the door shut.

"I've been trying to get up the nerve to come in and let you have it," Rae said. "You could have at least answered the phone. You could have told me that you didn't want to be my labor coach." She stole a look at Lila. "Unless you haven't decided yet."

"I'm not the right person," Lila said.

"It hardly takes any time," Rae insisted. "There are only

six weeks of Lamaze class, and they don't start until February. You wouldn't even see me again until then."

Lila shook her head. "You need somebody else."

"Don't you understand?" Rae said. "I don't have anyone else."

They both looked out through the front windshield. Rae was close to tears, but Lila was the one who was afraid: if Rae reached out during labor and put her arms around Lila's neck, she might be pulled back into the darkness. Already, she could hear the flapping of huge wings.

"I'll tell you what I think," Lila said evenly. "You may not need me after all. Your boyfriend may come back."

"My boyfriend!" Rae said. "That'll be the day." But she looked over at Lila, interested. "What makes you say that?" she asked.

"I just feel it," Lila said. "He's not gone yet."

Lila found herself agreeing to be Rae's labor coach if Jessup failed to return—that's how sure she was that she wouldn't be needed. But afterward, when Rae had driven away and Lila was walking up the path to her front door, she felt a peculiar kind of regret, almost as if she wanted to witness the birth. She stood on the porch, between the two rose bushes. Even though the front door was open, she stood there a little longer, and she looked down the street. But Rae had pressed down hard on the accelerator—just in case Jessup had already come home—and the Oldsmobile was gone. There was nothing to see on Three Sisters Street except for a line of blue clouds in the western sky, a sure sign that before long the weather would change.

The following week it rained every day, but in spite of the weather the superintendent of Rae's apartment complex strung white Christmas lights in the courtyard. The baby seemed more restless than usual, shifting its weight and throwing Rae off balance, so that she had to grab onto furniture and walls to stop herself from falling. It was the worst time of the year, those weeks between Thanksgiving and Christmas when being alone can send you over the edge. Rae had just about given up hope that Lila's prediction was right—expecting Jessup to come back left her lonelier than ever before. Every morning when she got out of bed Rae switched on the TV, just so she could hear someone's voice. After a while she moved the set into the kitchen and propped it up on the counter so she could watch as she ate dinner. It was some time before Rae realized that this was exactly what her mother used to do, and it drove her wild to think that now that she finally was no longer haunted by the scent of Carolyn's perfume she had to go and take on her habits. Once, she actually added mustard to her egg salad before she remembered it wasn't she who liked egg salad that way, but her mother. Too much time alone was what was making her watch the news while she ate dinner and add mustard to things. When she was with Jessup she used to count the hours till the weekend, now weekends meant nothing to her, and there were times when Freddy had to remind her what day it was.

It was a Friday, and still raining, when Rae ran through the courtyard to get to her apartment before she was soaked. The door was slightly ajar, and she knew right away that Jessup was inside. She could hear the sound of the TV and she smelled fresh coffee. For a moment as she stood in the courtyard it was almost as if everything was the same as it had been before that awful heat wave. But as soon as she went inside and saw Jessup in the kitchen, she knew that it wasn't the same. He didn't even look as if he belonged any more: he seemed too big for the wooden chair he sat in, his boots stuck out from under the far side of the table, his denim jacket was hung over the back of the other chair, dripping water onto the linoleum. The oven was turned on so that his jacket would dry, and Rae felt uncomfortably warm. She stood in the kitchen doorway and stared at him and was surprised to find she had nothing to say.

Jessup cleared his throat. "I made some coffee," he finally said.

Rae looked at the table now and saw that he had set out a ceramic mug for her and filled it with coffee. She could not remember his ever doing that for her before, not in seven years.

"I can't," she said. "I'm staying away from caffeine."

"Oh," Jessup said, as if he suddenly remembered her condition. He looked at her dead center, and Rae immediately pulled his old rain slicker more tightly around herself.

"Why don't you sit down?" Jessup said, as if it was his place to invite her in.

Rae stayed exactly where she was.

"I've got myself a room in a place outside Barstow," Jessup said.

"You don't even have the decency to tell me what you think," Rae said.

"Think about what?" Jessup said uneasily.

"About the way I look," Rae said.

She really had to watch herself; she could hear her voice cracking. She went to the refrigerator and poured herself a glass of milk.

"You look great," Jessup said.

"What a liar," Rae said.

She sat across from him at the table and she knew that he hadn't come back for her.

"After the movie wrapped I figured I had two ways to go," Jessup said. "I could try and get my foot in the door of the movie business, which is a joke because once you're a driver they think you're an imbecile. Or I could get involved in a business proposition with a guy I met in Hesperia."

"What business?" Rae said.

"I got lucky for once," Jessup said. "It's an estate sale. Some old guy died and his family is selling the property cheap. Three thousand dollars up front for me, and three thousand for my buddy."

Rae had never heard him call anyone his buddy. She thought of the four thousand they had saved and her mouth tightened.

"You didn't ask me how I've been feeling," Rae said.

"You didn't give me a chance," Jessup actually had the nerve to say.

Rae picked up the carton of milk and threw it at him. He hadn't expected it so he didn't even try to duck. The carton hit him on the shoulder and milk poured down his shirt.

"Oh, Christ," Jessup said. He jumped up and wiped off

his shirt. "It doesn't take much to get you hysterical these days, does it?"

Rae realized that she was exhausted. She reached for her glass of milk and finished it, wondering if they were having some kind of divorce here.

"There are plenty of things you didn't ask me," Jessup said. "Like what kind of business I'm considering." When Rae didn't ask, he told her anyway—it was forty acres with a trailer and a barn. "You know why the barn's there?" Jessup grinned.

Rae couldn't even begin to guess. "Why?" she asked.

"Because I'm going to be raising horses."

She couldn't help but laugh. When they had first run away together Rae had found a cabin for rent in Maryland, but, when Jessup had come to look at it, all he had to do was hear the squirrels running back and forth inside the attic walls and he'd fled. They had rented the garden apartment in Silver Spring instead.

"Laugh," Jessup said. "But they're not any old horses. They're midget horses," he informed her.

Rae let out a shriek that was so piercing Jessup ran over to her. It took a few seconds before he realized that she was hysterical with laughter. He shook his head and poured himself another cup of coffee and glared at her. He watched her, waiting for her to stop, but every time Rae even thought the words *midget horses* she burst out laughing all over again.

"Go ahead," Jessup told her. "But you'll take me seriously when I'm rich."

Rae wiped the tears from her eyes and instantly felt sober. He actually believed in this.

"I swear to God, Rae," Jessup said, "they're no bigger than Saint Bernards."

He spooned sugar into his coffee.

"I need this ranch," he said.

Now she knew exactly why he'd come back. "Not on your life," Rae said.

"Look, you took the car, now let me have the bank-book."

"I would rather give that bankbook to a total stranger than give it to you," Rae said. "I'd tear it in half first."

"You won't give me an inch," Jessup said.

"I gave you a little more than that," Rae said. "Like, try everything. I was in love with you."

"Was?" Jessup said. He came up behind her and put his arms around her.

"Cut it out," Rae said. "I really mean it."

"I could stay here tonight," Jessup said.

Having his arms around her reminded her that the room was much too hot. She stood up and turned off the oven. "I don't want to pay the gas bills to dry your jacket," she said.

They stood facing each other. It was getting dark, but neither of them went to turn on a light. There was still a puddle of milk on the floor, Jessup hadn't bothered with it when he cleaned off his shirt, and the milk looked blue, as if someone had spilled a bottle of ink. Rae could feel the baby shift, and she put one hand against her ribs.

"I could stay," Jessup said.

Rae shook her head. She couldn't bring herself to look at him until he turned away, then she watched as he rinsed out his coffee cup and put on his denim jacket.

"I guess I'll take the bus back," Jessup said.

"I guess you will," Rae shrugged.

You couldn't see a thing out the kitchen window, but Rae could tell from the sound of the rain—it was bad weather for taking the bus back to Barstow, alone.

"I don't want there to be any bad feelings," Jessup said.

"Why should there be?" Rae said. "Because you care more about some horses than you do about your own child?"

"It's all in my head," Jessup said. "Nothing that's happened lately has anything to do with you."

"Nothing you've ever done has had anything to do with me," Rae said.

"You're wrong about that," Jessup told her, and after he'd left she almost believed him. On some of those days when he stood outside her parents' house, it was so cold even Jessup must have felt it. When she couldn't manage to get out of the house she could see him from her bedroom window, waiting for hours. She couldn't help but think of him there on the bus back to the desert; his legs were so long he'd have to stretch them out in the aisle and he wouldn't get to Barstow until after midnight. In all the years they spent together Rae had believed that if she just kept working at it, she could keep him. But she just didn't want to work that hard any more.

That night she didn't have any trouble sleeping: her bed seemed softer than usual and the rain continued till dawn.

In the morning, Rae cleaned the milk off the floor and washed out the coffeepot. But she didn't open the drawer in the kitchen and reach beneath the silverware until two weeks later. She felt like a total fool to just be discovering that the whole time he'd been sitting there with her he'd already had their bankbook in the pocket of his denim jacket, and that his asking had only been a formality—he'd planned to leave her with nothing at all from the start.

• • •

When Rae didn't call back Lila felt herself grow more and more anxious. She wanted to hear for herself that their bargain was sealed, she wanted to know the exact hour of the day when Jessup had come back. Rae's unborn child had begun to haunt Lila: in the shop she thought about foolish things—baby smocks with pearl buttons, tiny silver spoons, bibs embroidered with lace—and each time she added up the columns of figures in the books she added wrong and charged Richard's customers too little or too much. At night she dreamed of stillborn babies whose fingers and toes were as cold as ice. But what terrified Lila most was that there were actually times when she found herself making a list of names, as if this baby was hers.

If she was wrong—if Rae's boyfriend didn't return— Lila knew that she wouldn't keep her part of the bargain. Every day she waited for the phone call that would release her, but the call never came. Richard could tell how upset she was; he asked so often what was wrong that finally Lila told him. But Richard didn't understand; he thought Lila

would make a wonderful labor coach, he urged her to keep
her promise to Rae. His praise only drove Lila away from
him, and it made her realize that if you haven't told someone the truth for a long enough time, after a while you can't
tell him anything at all and expect him to understand.

So many days went by that Lila began to wonder if perhaps she was free of Rae at last. But then one night, as she
was washing the dishes after supper, Lila closed her eyes for
a moment and saw a tall man sitting in the very last row of a
bus, his head tilted back so he could sleep. It seemed to be
very late at night and the sky above the road was so clear
Lila could see the Milky Way. Lila turned the water off in
the sink and went to sit down. When Richard saw the look
on her face, he dropped the magazine he'd been reading and
sat up straight in his chair. Lila looked up at him; her eyes
were so dark it was impossible to tell their true color.

"I've just seen something," Lila said.

Richard tried to get her to explain, but she wouldn't. He
thought what she had seen was the problem, but that wasn't
it. It was the fact that she had seen anything at all. It was
simply that on this night Lila knew that she could find out
things she didn't want to know. And she could feel it—it
wasn't the future she was seeing, but the past, and she grew
so frightened that she couldn't even go back into the
kitchen alone, she had to ask Richard to walk in there with
her and hold her hand.

They finished the dishes together, but Lila wouldn't
talk to Richard, and later when he said he was going to bed
she didn't seem to hear him. He stood in the doorway, waiting; when he called her name sharply, the way you call to

people you can't seem to waken, Lila told him to go on without her. And as Richard walked down the hallway he had the distinct impression that it was Lila who was walking away from him, even though she was still in the kitchen, staring out into the yard.

When Richard got into bed, Lila could hear the springs creak; the light from the crack under the bedroom door disappeared as he turned off the lamp. Lila called Rae at a little after eleven. Rae had already been asleep for an hour, and her voice was thick, but Lila could tell, right away, that Rae had been sleeping alone. She didn't whisper the way she would have if her boyfriend had been there with her. You could hear the raw sound of betrayal in her tone.

"He came back all right," Rae told Lila. "Only he left that same night, and he took all my money with him."

"How could you let him do that to you?" Lila said.

"I didn't let him!" Rae said. "He just took my bankbook and left."

Lila sat down in a kitchen chair. She intended to tell Rae that she couldn't go through with it—Rae would have to find another labor coach. But out of the blue she started thinking about names again, and the most beautiful of the names—Catherine and Jessica and Claire—made her feel like weeping.

"You think I should go after him and get that money back, don't you?" Rae said.

"I don't know," Lila said. She felt dizzy, she really didn't feel very well at all.

"You know, you're right," Rae said admiringly. "I let

him get away with everything, but I'm not going to do it this time."

After she'd hung up the phone, Lila put some water up to boil. She needed something comforting and plain: a packaged teabag, two spoons of sugar, a chipped blue cup and saucer. As Lila poured the water in, the teabag split apart, and she had to wait for the tea leaves to settle before she could drink. She sipped the tea slowly and listened as the rain began. At first there were only a few hard drops hitting the highest leaves in the lemon tree, and then it came down faster. The weeds on Three Sisters Street had gone wild this winter; each time it rained they crept farther into the vegetable patches, they wound themselves around the chain-link fences and around the lowest telephone wires. Tonight, the birds in the trees shivered, and husbands and wives turned to each other in bed beneath extra blankets and quilts. It was the kind of night when no one should be up past midnight, alone in the kitchen.

Lila had finished only half the cup when she realized that there was something wrong with the tea. It left a strange aftertaste in her mouth; her tongue was coated and numb. When she looked down into the cup, the outline of a child was already forming. Lila ran to the sink and spilled out the tea. She stayed there, leaning against the sink for balance. The rain was coming down harder than ever, but Lila couldn't hear its echo on the roof or in the rain gutters. She suddenly knew exactly what she wanted; she didn't even have to think about it, she felt it the way a mother feels her baby's cries somewhere just beneath her skin. It seemed so simple now, she could hardly believe she had waited this long. She was going back to get her daughter, and before the rain slowed down, before the moon returned to the center of the sky, Lila went into the bedroom, and she quietly dragged her suitcase out of the closet and packed nearly all her clothes.

That night Richard dreamed of his mother. She was in the parlor of the old house in East China, with her hands in front of her face, weeping. Somehow, sparrows had gotten into the house; they flew everywhere and got tangled up in the drapes. There was nothing Helen could do to help them; she could only watch as more and more were caught in the heavy fabric, trapped inside billows of linen. As Richard dreamed, Lila packed her suitcase. Then she left the bedroom and closed the door behind her. She put her suitcase in the front hallway and went to make coffee. At exactly three a.m. the birds outside began to sing, and Lila went to the window. But already she was seeing only the things she imagined her daughter saw: bare white birch trees, a thin layer of ice smoothly covering the cement, the morning star in the east.

She was still thinking about her daughter when Richard woke up in the morning and found she wasn't in bed. He went into the living room. Lila was sitting on the couch; her coat was draped over the rocking chair. Richard sat down next to her, but instead of taking her hand he kept his own hands folded in his lap.

"What's happening to us?" Richard said.

Lila knew she should have told him the day she met him, or the night before they got married. She should have asked him to take a walk with her on the East China Highway or told him in the car on the way to California. There were a half dozen times when she nearly begged him to turn back to New York—every time they saw a little girl, in the back seat of a car, at the counter of Howard Johnson's, on a billboard high above the interstate. On each anniversary, during every full moon she could have told him. But all of those chances slipped away, just as this one was slipping away from them now.

Lila turned to him and rested her head against his shoulder. Richard was wearing a blue bathrobe that Lila had given him for his birthday one year. He began to stroke Lila's hair, and each time he did Lila held him a little tighter. But by the time the blackbirds in the yard had flown to the highest branches of the lemon tree, Lila had missed another chance completely. All the way to the airport, in the back seat of the taxi, she kept one arm on her suitcase and thought about the way he'd asked her, at the very last minute, not to go. He never asked why she was leaving, just asked her not to go. After the taxi dropped her off, Lila stopped thinking about Richard, and, after all, she had to. Once the jet had taken off, it didn't really matter if she missed him or not: in less than six hours she'd be back in New York.

• • •

It took Rae three full days to track him down, and at the end of that time she felt as though she could commit murder. It had been bad from the start—when she drove out to

Barstow there were dead animals all over the road: snapping turtles with their shells cracked open, lost dogs, hawks with wingspans of nearly two feet. Every time she passed something dead on the road, Rae closed her eyes and pressed her foot down harder on the accelerator. Then, when she got into town, she found he wasn't listed in the phone book, and she had to waste forty dollars on two nights at a motel where the lumpy mattress made sleeping impossible.

He didn't have a box at the post office, and there wasn't a car registered in his name at the Department of Motor Vehicles. It was almost as if he had never existed. By the third day Rae had just about given up hope of ever finding him again when she heard a waitress mention his name at Dunkin' Donuts.

"Is that my Jessup you're talking about?" Rae said without thinking.

The waitress turned from her friend and looked Rae up and down; even when she was seated anyone could tell Rae was pregnant.

"I don't know," the waitress said carefully. She was eighteen years old and she had the feeling that she might have gone out with a married man. "It's the Jessup that took me out to dinner last Saturday night."

"How many of them do you think there can be?" Rae said.

"One," the waitress agreed.

It didn't take much to talk the waitress into divulging Jessup's Hesperia address, and once she'd gone that far the waitress went on to give Rae exact directions, writing them down on the back of a paper napkin.

On the drive over the hills Rae saw two coyotes turning over crushed turtles with their paws, inspecting the shells passively. It was night when she finally got to Hesperia, and she had to pull over and switch on the light so that she could study the directions. For a while she thought she was lost, but after another twenty minutes of driving in the dark she knew she had found the right place— she saw a flash of silver. Jessup's trailer. She pulled the Oldsmobile off the road, then cut the lights and headed down the long dirt driveway. It was so quiet that she felt herself straining to hear something. There was an old Ford convertible parked near the trailer, and Rae thought bitterly, Jessup's buddy's car. She parked and turned the key in the ignition, and when her eyes adjusted to the dark she made out Montana license plates on the Ford; she could see a row of shovels and hoes leaning against the trailer, and Jessup's old leather boots, the ones she'd bought him, caked with mud, set out on the porch.

A huge antenna was balanced over the trailer, but the air out here had to be too thin for TV frequencies, and when Rae turned on her radio to find out the time, all she got was static. Whatever time it was, it felt late. The lights in the trailer were out, and anyone could tell that whoever was inside was already asleep. Still, when Rae listened carefully she could hear noises. Beyond a small barn was a corral; Rae leaned toward the windshield and narrowed her eyes to see the horses. Jessup was right, they weren't any bigger than dogs, but somehow that didn't seem funny now. They moved in a group along the wooden fence, restless, raising a thin layer of dust. Rae found herself wondering what would happen if somebody opened the gate for them. Probably they would race toward the hills and you'd be able to hear them for miles as they moved like one dark creature, the sound of their hoofs steady in the night.

After two nights of not sleeping well, she just couldn't face Jessup yet. While she was deciding on the best place to look for a motel for the night she fell asleep behind the wheel, and it was Jessup's partner, Hal, who found her when he went out to feed the horses at five thirty the next morning. He hadn't had his coffee yet, and it was still dark, so he didn't notice the parked Oldsmobile until after he'd dragged the bales of hay out of the barn. The horses were waiting impatiently at the gate; Jessup had shut off the alarm clock and turned over, leaving everything to Hal, just as he did every morning. A stranger's parked car just meant one more thing for Hal to attend to while Jessup slept, but when he walked over and saw it was only a woman asleep, he couldn't wake her. He went to feed the horses, and it was the sound of their running to greet him that woke Rae. She knew right away she shouldn't have slept in the car: her legs were riddled with cramps and her ribs hurt, as if the baby had been pressing against them all night long. When she got out of the car she stamped her feet; it was much colder than she'd expected and she wrapped her arms around herself. She went over to the corral, leaned against it, and watched Hal drag the hay inside. The air smelled like peaches, but it was cold enough to give you goosebumps.

"I'm Rae," she said when Hal faced her, but she could tell from his puzzled look that her name didn't mean anything to him.

Inside the corral, the horses were so excited as they ate hay that their bodies seemed to shake. They were shaggier than most horses, and even when they ate they stayed crowded together, as though they were afraid to be alone. Rae couldn't take her eyes off them; the longer she watched them, the more difficult it was for her to breathe.

"It takes a while to get used to the air out here," Hal said after he'd walked out of the corral and shut the gate behind him.

He took her inside the trailer. The place was a mess—kitchen cabinets left open, clothes tossed all over the floor—and everything was so tiny that Rae felt more uncomfortable than usual about her size. She had to turn sideways to get into the kitchen and sit down. At the rear of the trailer was a set of bunk beds; Rae could tell that the person asleep in the lower bunk was Jessup just by his shape beneath the blankets.

"I can't believe this is what he spent my money on," Rae said.

Hal poured himself a cup of coffee and offered one to Rae, but she refused with a wave of her hand.

"I could kill him," she said.

Hal handed her the sugar bowl. "We're out of milk," he said. "We've got Cremora, but I never use it. It always gives me a terrible headache."

Rae looked at him as if he were the stupidest person on

earth. "I'm upset," she said. "Can't you tell how upset I am? Don't you talk to me about Cremora."

Hal took some orange juice out of the small refrigerator and poured her a glass. He sat down across from her without saying a word and watched her drink.

"We've been together for seven years," Rae said. "That's not even counting high school. I don't suppose he ever mentioned me?"

Hal shook his head. "The longest I ever lived with someone was two years and seven months," he said. "Her name was Karen."

Rae nodded, expecting more, but Hal clammed up.

"I left her," Hal said finally. "I guess I'll always regret it."

Jessup moved in his sleep, and Rae and Hal looked at each other.

"He never gets up on time," Hal said. He took a sip of black coffee. "And of all the things he never told me, he certainly didn't mention a wife who was pregnant."

"We're not married," Rae said. And to herself she thought: This is really it. I really could kill him.

In his sleep, Jessup heard Rae's voice, and he dreamed that he was talking to Rae on the telephone in his mother's apartment in Boston. Whenever he used to talk to her, he'd felt as if there was nothing he could not do. Back then, all they'd needed was enough money for gas. Everything was out in front of them, possibilities were endless. Jessup woke up, but he lay in the lower bunk bed without moving and he counted the weeks until his thirtieth birthday. He had been born in the dead center of March, in one of the worst snow-storms ever to hit Boston. He just couldn't wait to be born, his mother had told him. She could feel his head moving downward as the taxi drove to Brigham and Women's Hospital, and he'd been born in the elevator, between the third and fourth floors.

Rae had admitted to Hal that she was starving, and he'd decided to drive into Barstow and get food. Jessup stayed in bed until he heard the trailer door slam and Hal's car start. Then he got up and pulled on a pair of jeans and a sweater. Rae heard him coming up behind her, but she didn't look at him, not until he navigated around the table and faced her.

"I was just thinking about sending you my new address," Jessup said.

"I'm here for my money," Rae told him. "You couldn't possibly have spent it all on a down payment for this."

"I'm just curious," Jessup said. "How'd you find out where I was?"

"If you really want to know," Rae said, "from a waitress in Barstow."

"Paulette," Jessup said. "Well, I think I ought to tell you that she's nothing to me."

"Look," Rae said, "I don't care what she is. I want my money."

Jessup lit a cigarette and leaned against the refrigerator. "I don't have it, Rae. I used half as a down payment, and the rest went to fix this place up. We're going to build a new corral, and we're buying a pickup truck—we've got expenses."

"Get the money back," Rae said stubbornly.

"Let me just tell you my plan."

"Get it from that waitress," Rae said. "She must save her tips."

"I told you already. She's nothing," Jessup said. He seemed pleased every time Rae mentioned Paulette. "Let me just explain my plan. These horses we've got are the perfect pet for people with money. Compared to one of these horses, a dog is nothing. What I'm saying is you'll have to just wait a while for your money. But I intend to pay you back."

"How could you do this to me?" Rae said. "What did you think I needed money for, a trip to Tahiti? I'm having a baby, Jessup."

"Let me just show you the place," Jessup said.

He got her a heavy sweater and opened the trailer door.

"Come on," he urged. "Just take a look."

They went out to the corral; the horses were now huddled at the far side. When he showed her the barn, Rae put her hand to the small of her back and rubbed the muscles that had been aching all morning. She realized then that the baby was pushing down on her bladder and that she'd never make it back to the trailer. She went out behind the barn, crouched down, and peed, and when she got up she saw Jessup watching her.

"Don't look at me," she said.

"Why not?" Jessup said. "You look really good. I never saw anybody pregnant look so good."

"What's that supposed to mean?" Rae said.

"It's a compliment. But then I always thought you

looked good," Jessup said. "I picked you, didn't I? Didn't I ask you to leave Boston with me?"

Actually, he had, and afterward she'd wondered if she'd imagined it. He was walking her home one night; as usual they had stopped on the corner before Rae's block. That was the night he told her that he planned to leave Boston. He hadn't been looking at her, but as she watched Jessup, Rae felt as though she could see the shell around him crack open, and for a second she could see inside him.

"I mean, it's totally up to you," he had said casually. "I'm used to being alone, but if you want to go I'm not going to stop you."

"Maybe I will leave with you," Rae said, trying to sound just as casual. After that she kept sneaking looks at Jessup, searching for that crack in his shell, and at certain angles she could almost see it. But she never again had the sense that she was looking inside him, and it began to seem ridiculous that she had once imagined she could see past his skin to a thin band of light.

Whatever had happened, she had certainly never felt chosen by Jessup, and now it didn't matter who had done the choosing.

"I'll never forgive you for this," Rae said.

"I guess not," Jessup said.

They were at the corral when Hal drove up with the groceries. They turned to watch him carry the bags into the trailer.

"Don't you care that this is your baby?" Rae asked Jessup once Hal had gone inside.

"What if I did?" Jessup said. "What good would it do

ALICE HOFFMAN

me? Even if I wanted to *be* his father, how could I be? I'd just ruin it—I'd end up disappearing and the guy would hate me in the end, so I might as well get all that over with now." Jessup lit a cigarette. It was windy, so he had to cup the lit match in his hand. "If we had planned it, it might have been different," he said. "I could have gotten some place like this ranch before, and by the time the kid was born I would have been rich."

She knew he wasn't going to give her any of the money back, and somehow Rae didn't even care any more. She gave him back his sweater and walked over to the Oldsmobile. The engine took a while to turn over, and once it did Rae had to pump the gas to keep it going. Through the closed car windows she could still smell the horses. If she hadn't been pregnant she might have actually considered moving here, in spite of the waitress and the fact that he hadn't even asked her to stay. Usually, she didn't take up much space—she could have slept beside him in the bunk bed, her spine against the metal wall. It would have been easy enough to wash all the dirty dishes with boiling-hot water, and the clothes left strewn on the floor would have taken a half hour at most to hang up. At night, the horses would run in circles, and the coyotes would come down from the hills to watch them, a little braver and a little closer to the corral each time. But, of course, she was no longer really alone, and Jessup would never be able to understand her putting somebody before him.

Just as she was about to leave, Jessup walked over and tapped on the window. After Rae rolled it down, he surprised them both by taking her hand. For a moment Rae swore she could see the stream of light just beneath his skin, but she forced herself to look away.

When Rae put the car in gear Jessup let go of her hand. But before she drove back onto the dirt driveway Rae turned to him and smiled.

"You're going to miss me," she said, and she didn't even give him a chance to disagree.

In Barstow, Rae stopped at a diner and got herself a sandwich to go, which she ate as she drove over the mountains. There was a thin cover of snow on the ground, and even though the altitude was higher, it was already easier to breathe. By the time she reached the flatlands it was possible to pick up L.A. radio stations. The air grew warm enough to turn the car heater off. She wasn't thinking about Jessup, she was thinking about those horses, and the more she thought about them the more relieved she was that she didn't have to spend another moment watching them move along the wooden fence. The whole time she had been with Jessup she had been seeing those horses. Even when she wasn't looking she could still see them out of the corner of her eye, like a shadow that kept getting in the way of her line of vision.

She got home in the middle of the afternoon. After she'd parked the Oldsmobile and gotten out she noticed a Volkswagen parked in front of the entrance to the apartment complex. As she walked by she could tell that the man in the driver's seat was watching her, and halfway across the courtyard she knew that he was following her. Rae walked faster and kept her keys between her fingers, sharp edge out. When she heard him clear his throat she started to run.

For the first time in weeks she wished desperately that Jessup were in the apartment and that all she had to do was shout his name and he'd open the front door.

"Are you Rae?" she heard the man behind her call.

She kept running.

"Rae?" he called.

She turned and faced him. He was standing in the middle of the courtyard watching her.

"What if I am?" Rae said. She was less than fifty feet from her own door, and if she ran she could make it there before he had the chance to move.

"I'm Richard Grey," he told her. "Lila's husband."

Now that he was here he felt slightly ridiculous. He'd found her address in Lila's phone book, but it was really none of his business.

Rae looked over her shoulder, at her front door. Being afraid had started her wishing for Jessup, and now she found she couldn't stop. It was almost as if the man she wanted was someone other than the one she had just left in the desert. The Jessup she wanted was waiting for her at home. Together they felt so safe they could keep the door unlocked at all hours of the day and night and not feel as if they were in any danger.

"Is something wrong?" Rae managed to ask.

"Lila's gone," Richard told her.

"What do you mean—gone?" Rae said.

"She went to New York," Richard said. "I knew you were counting on her to be your labor coach, so I thought I'd better tell you. I've been trying you on the phone, but no one's ever home."

"Wait a second," Rae said. "She promised me."

"Well, she's back in New York," Richard said. In the empty courtyard his voice sounded hollow. "That's where we come from," he added, as though it explained something.

Rae felt her face get hot. "You can't depend on anybody," she said.

"So what do you think?" Richard said to her now. "Do you think she's coming back?"

Rae looked at him carefully and realized that he was crying. She looked away, embarrassed, but she couldn't help wondering what it would be like to be loved that much.

"Sure," Rae said. "She'll come back."

She was certain that after she'd left this morning Jessup had gone on with his plans for the day. He wouldn't start to miss her till later, and then he'd borrow Hal's car and drive to Barstow. He'd look up that waitress or somebody new, and the whole time he was missing her, he'd be holding somebody else.

Richard had collected himself, and he was particularly grateful that Rae hadn't looked at him while he'd been crying.

"I guess I'll go home," he said.

"That's a good idea," Rae agreed. "Maybe she'll call you."

They looked at each other then and laughed.

"It's hell waiting for a phone call," Rae said.

"How about a drink?" Richard said suddenly, and then he seemed flustered. "I didn't mean alcohol," he explained. "I was thinking about something cold."

Actually, Rae knew that what he wanted wasn't a drink. It was just some company.

"Sure," she said.

Richard followed her across the courtyard, then waited while she unlocked the door and went to turn on the lights. His pain was so evident that Rae almost forgot her own as she led him into the kitchen and poured them both glasses of cold, blue milk. It made it a little easier to come home when someone was sitting across the table, and because neither of them wanted to leave, they drank two glasses of milk apiece, and after a while Rae had to admit she could use a little company, too.

PART FOUR

*I*T WAS SNOWING WHEN LILA first got to New York, and that made her arrival easier. Everything was white, and when she took the limousine from Kennedy Airport into Manhattan she could have been anywhere: in the middle of a frozen city in Europe, deep in the iciest part of Canada. She was dropped off at the Hilton, and it felt so anonymous there that she stayed. She ordered room service and had her dinner at a table by the window on the twenty-third floor. Below her was a grid of lights. Each time a building dared to seem familiar it was swallowed up by snow; this high up above the city it almost seemed as if Lila was farther away from New York now than she had been for the past twenty-seven years.

At midnight Lila got into bed, but every time she closed her eyes she thought she heard something, and at a little after two she got up and turned off the steam heat. In the morning it was so cold that ice formed inside windowpanes all over the city. Lila ordered breakfast from room service, and then, when the waiter had left her alone and her coffee had been poured, she took out the Manhattan Telephone Directory. Her parents were no longer listed, and when she dialed the old number, which she was surprised to find she still knew by heart, a stranger answered and insisted she'd had the number for more than fifteen years.

She would get the information out of them no matter what. She didn't care how old they'd become: she would shake her mother by her shoulders until her fragile bones snapped, she would stare her father down no matter how sightless his eyes had become. She got dressed and went down to the lobby at a little after ten. Her wool coat was much too thin for a New York winter, and even after she had gotten into a cab she was still freezing. She gave the driver her old address and sat on the edge of the back seat. The city seemed much more complicated, and there was so much more of everything: traffic, and lights, and fear. When they got there Lila made the driver circle the block four times before she admitted that her building was gone. The old brownstones had been knocked down and a new co-op had taken their place, and it was the oddest feeling to be back on her old street without really being there at all. She had the driver circle the block one last time while she tried to decide what to do. She could feel herself begin to panic. All she could think of were the smallest details from her past: the numbers of the buses that used to run crosstown, the varieties of flowers their neighbors used to keep in a window box, how many cracks in the sidewalk had to be stepped over and avoided when she walked from the front stoop to the candy store.

"This is costing you money," the driver reminded her. "Not that I'm complaining."

"The building's gone," Lila said. Her voice sounded higher than it should, as if she were still eighteen and so shy she could barely bring herself to ask customers in the restaurant what they'd like for lunch.

"Yeah, well, that happens," the driver assured her. "How about trying another address?"

They drove to Third Avenue, but when they reached the corner Lila told the driver not to stop. As they passed by the spot where the restaurant used to be, Lila rolled down her window. Hannie always walked west when she left the restaurant in the evenings; if Lila worked late she could sometimes look out and see Hannie looking through the wooden boxes of vegetables in the market down the block, choosing the right head of cabbage or pointing to three perfect apples with a bony finger before she reached for the change purse she kept pinned to the inside pocket of her black skirt.

All the time Lila had been away she had imagined New York to be exactly as she had left it. Pigeons still sat on the ledge outside her bedroom window, her mother made pot roast every Friday night in the cast-iron roasting pan she had inherited from Lila's grandmother. At night the sky was inky, apartments were always overheated and hallways much too cold, and on Third Avenue, at the rear table, you could find out everything you had ever wanted to know for fifty cents. It was almost as if Lila had truly believed that she could be eighteen again, and that one ticket on a jet from Los Angeles to New York could buy back all the things she had lost. There was only one more address that might be worth something—her aunt and uncle's apartment on 86th Street. They were her cousin Ann's parents, and by now they'd be quite elderly. Lila had spent holidays at their apartment. The adults had always sat in the living room, drinking wine and eating small apple cakes. The children had been relegated to the bedroom, where they could make as much noise as they liked.

Ann, older than the rest of the cousins, would lock herself away in the second, smaller bedroom. They could hear her radio through the bedroom wall, always the same thing, Frank Sinatra, and the cousins made fun of her behind her back and called her Frankie's girl. Once, when the cousins were being particularly obnoxious, opening the windows and tossing crumpled newspapers onto anyone who happened to walk by, Lila had gone out into the hallway, pushed open her cousin's bedroom door a bit, and looked in. The radio was on and Ann was lying on her bed, writing in her diary. When she saw Lila at the door she rushed over and slammed it shut, so hard that it made Lila jump. Lila was twelve years old, and because she felt that nobody wanted her, she stayed right there in the hallway. Then and there she decided that she would never come to another family get-together again, and when her parents were ready to go and called out her name, they were surprised to find her waiting by the door, already wearing her coat and her hat.

She had never gone back to that apartment again, although when the driver now pulled up it seemed as if she had been there only days ago. She went in through the first set of doors. It was dark in the foyer, just as it had been the last time she'd been there, when her hair was so long it fell to her waist, even after it had been braided. Her parents had been arguing, so Lila was the one to ring upstairs, and she'd stood on tiptoes to reach the buzzer.

All morning Lila could feel the chances of finding her daughter slip away; and there were times, when the taxi was stalled in traffic, when she could not quite remember why she had come back in the first place. Here in the foyer, the black-and-white tiles echoed when you walked across them. The glass shade that covered the overhead light made things seem fuzzy and shapeless, and Lila had to look twice before she allowed herself to believe that the name Weber—her mother's maiden name—was still on the tenants' directory. She had found someone.

She rang upstairs; there was the sound of static as someone on the sixth floor picked up the intercom.

"Yes?" a woman said.

"It's me," Lila said, right away, as though she'd been expected. "Lila."

There was static over the intercom, and then suddenly, the buzzer rang. Lila grabbed the door open and ran all the way to the elevator. She went down the long hallway on the sixth floor, and then knocked on the door, once. She could feel her heart racing, and when someone came to open the door Lila could feel the click of the lock inside her own body, like a bone breaking.

There was a chain inside the door, and a woman looked out, examining Lila. For a moment Lila recognized her aunt; she was just as she had been when Lila was twelve years old.

"It is you," the woman said.

It was Lila's cousin, not her aunt, and for the first time since she'd come to New York Lila felt that same sense of expectation she had had when she had begged Richard to drive into Manhattan one last time. She could actually feel herself getting closer to the past when she walked into the apartment, and if her teenaged cousin had run past them, to lock herself in her bedroom and listen to records, she wouldn't have been the least bit surprised.

"I guess I must look old to you," Ann said. "You get this way living in Manhattan, but when my parents moved to Florida I couldn't pass up a rent-controlled apartment, so I moved back here."

Lila tried to listen to her cousin, but she couldn't. Again and again she reminded herself that she didn't have to scream—all she had to do was ask; she simply wanted a name or an address. She wanted her daughter.

"I was married and divorced and I took back my own name," Ann was saying. "If I were still living in Connecticut you would have never found me. His last name was Starch, which should have warned me right from the start."

Lila wanted to interrupt, but she couldn't bring herself to speak.

"It's just my mother now," Ann said. "My father died two years ago." She looked at Lila carefully. "Do you want to know about your parents?" she asked.

"No," Lila said.

The force of that word felt like a piece of glass under her tongue, and when Ann asked if she wanted a drink of water or juice, Lila nodded. While Ann was in the kitchen Lila realized that she was sitting where her mother always sat when they came for a visit. On holidays her mother never had more than two glasses of wine, but that small amount did something to her, and on the way home from this apartment she always told Lila family secrets: how her brother had been in love with another woman but had settled for his wife, how her father had been such a big drinker they used to hide the wine in a boot kept in the front closet.

"Are they alive?" Lila asked when Ann came back with tall glasses of orange juice.

Ann shook her head. "I'm sorry," she said.

There was a plate of cookies on the table, and that reminded Lila that her mother had packed her a lunch to take along on the train out to East China. She had been unwrapping the cheese sandwich that her mother had made in those last moments before they took her to Penn Station when the train reached the outskirts of East China. She put her sandwich down and moved closer to the window and saw the spot where the potato fields begin, where the earth is so sandy you can feel it whenever you rub your fingers together, and at night the sand gets in between the sheets on everyone's bed, and each time you kiss someone you can feel sand on the edge of your tongue.

"Cancer," Ann said. "Both of them."

They sat on couches facing each other, a coffee table between them.

"I know why you're here," Ann said. "It was all my fault. When they asked me about adoption I should have kept my mouth shut."

"I want her back," Lila said.

It was such a simple thing to say that it was hard to believe it could hurt so much to say it.

"Sometimes I wish I had taken her for myself," Ann said.

"I've wanted her back from the minute you took her," Lila said.

"I thought about keeping her when I had her with me in the cab," Ann said. "She was wrapped in one towel, and it just seemed so cold that night."

That night when she had walked out to the living room both of Lila's parents had turned away, terrified to look at the baby. Out on the street, she couldn't get a cab, so she kept the baby warm inside her coat and walked to Eighth Avenue. The baby was crying and Ann could feel her shivering. The ice storm had stopped everything: no buses were running and telephone lines were out. Stores that were usually open twenty-four hours a day were shut down behind iron bars, trucks were abandoned on the roads, pigeons froze in midair, and their shattered bodies lined the sidewalks.

Some people who were stranded had managed to get cabs, which were driven by only the bravest drivers. They skidded and careened down the avenues, and each time one passed Ann hailed it, but no one would stop for her. She had called Dr. Marshall from Lila's parents' apartment and arranged to meet him in his office at the hospital as soon as the baby was born. Now, she wasn't sure if he'd still be there or if he'd gone home once the ice storm had begun. But where else was there to go? Although her feet were numb and a coating of ice formed around her ankles, she continued walking downtown. After a while the baby stopped crying, and that was what really scared Ann—as long as it had been making noise she knew it was alive. She shook it, but there was no response, and she could tell it was the silence of someone who has nothing more to lose. She had to get to the hospital immediately, and the next time a taxi passed Ann ran out into the street and stood right in front of it. The taxi skidded to a halt when it couldn't avoid her, and as soon as it had stopped, Ann ran to the passenger door and got inside.

"What do you think you're doing?" the cabbie said. "You can't just jump in front of a cab and get in."

"I have to get to Beekman Hospital," Ann told him.

Now that she was sitting down she could feel that, tucked inside her coat, the baby was still breathing.

In the back seat was a couple who had been stranded uptown; because all the hotels were full, they had offered the cab driver a hundred dollars to take them home to Brooklyn. Ann looked slightly crazy to them—every strand of her hair was covered by ice, and under the yellow light of a street lamp they could see that there was dried blood on her hands.

"Take her wherever she wants to go," they advised the cab driver, and that was when Ann considered not giving the baby up, that was when it just seemed too cold.

Dr. Marshall was asleep on the couch in his office. Ann

woke him, then stood by the desk as he called the couple on Long Island whom he'd promised the baby to earlier that night. She didn't hear a word he said to them; she was listening to the baby's even breathing from deep within her winter coat. Finally, she handed the baby to Dr. Marshall so that he could examine her and put her footprint on a birth certificate made out in the adoptive parents' names. He wanted to take the baby upstairs, but Ann wasn't ready to hand her over. She asked if she could be the one to carry her to the nursery.

That night there were nearly a dozen other newborns in bassinets, and for some reason none of them were crying. A night nurse sat in a rocking chair, but she had fallen asleep, and when Ann placed the baby in an empty bassinet there wasn't a sound in all of the nursery. She walked all the way to the apartment she shared with three other nurses. By now, it was a beautiful night, so clear that you could see Orion just above the roofs of the tallest buildings.

After that night Ann just couldn't bear to see Dr. Marshall any more. When he came into the emergency room the next morning to admit one of his patients who had gone into labor, Ann hid in the toilet until he was gone. Later, she went up to the nursery, but the baby was already gone. Whatever spell there had been the night before had been broken—all the babies were crying in unison, and the attention of five nurses couldn't soothe them. A few weeks later, Ann applied for a job at New York Hospital and moved uptown. There were times when she simply refused to meet old friends downtown. And when she got married and was living in Connecticut, she was grateful that she no longer had to walk past the maternity ward or the nursery and feel she had helped ruin somebody's life each time she heard a baby cry.

"I need to know their name," Lila said evenly.

Ann looked over at her, confused.

Lila's voice rose dangerously. "Tell me the name of the people who took her to Long Island."

"I already told you," Ann said. "I didn't listen when Marshall phoned them. It didn't seem to matter."

"It doesn't matter," Lila said. "Can't you remember?"

"I can't," Ann said. "But I know who could—Dr. Marshall."

They went into the kitchen together, and Lila stood right next to her cousin as she called Beekman Hospital. Marshall hadn't been affiliated with Beekman since his residency, but if they waited the address of his private practice could easily be found. Lila couldn't wait; she went back out to the living room and stood by the window. She was so close that she could hear her daughter breathing, buttoned up inside Ann's winter coat; she could hear the taxi skidding across the avenue as the driver stomped on his brakes. If she had been the one in that taxi she would have never let that driver stop, she would have persuaded him to drive all night, and by the time they reached New Jersey her daughter would have been sleeping and the ice on the highways would have melted and refrozen into daggers, so that anyone who tried to follow them would have gotten no farther than the first dangerous corner.

Ann wrote Dr. Marshall's address and phone number on a yellow slip of paper, and Lila quickly folded it and put it in her coat pocket. When Ann walked her out to the elevator neither woman could look at the other; it was as if what had once happened to them was so private they couldn't allow themselves to acknowledge it. But when the door to the elevator opened, Ann put a hand on Lila's arm to stop her.

"I always wondered if you blamed me," Ann said.

"Of course not," Lila said, and when she kissed her cousin goodbye anyone could tell that the only one she had ever blamed was herself.

It was late afternoon and already dark when Lila walked back to her hotel. But once she got to the Hilton, she didn't stop, she continued walking, west and downtown. Each time she put her hand in her coat pocket to feel the slip of paper there, she felt a jolt; she was on the very edge—if she took one more step forward, she could never go back. Each time she tried to imagine going to see her daughter she couldn't seem to get any farther than the front door. When she reached for the bell she was put off by some terrible heat, and when she finally forced herself to ring the bell it left its burning black imprint on her flesh. She was so terrified of her daughter's reaction that she simply disappeared, and each time her daughter opened the door there was no one on the front porch, just two black feathers and a rush of cold air.

If she backed off now she could take the limousine back to Kennedy and be home tonight. She could watch Richard prune the rose bushes and then lead him into the bedroom and lie down beside him as though she had never been gone. And so each time Lila passed a phone booth and considered stopping to phone Dr. Marshall she kept on walking, and she knew that once she had her daughter's address she would have to go on and that nothing would ever be the same again. She walked until it grew too late to call the doctor's office; the streets became crowded with people on their way home from work, and in apartments above her lights were turned on, and ovens were lit to cook supper.

Tenth Avenue was exactly as she remembered it; when the wind came up across the river on a dark January evening it was still the coldest place in the city. If you stood on the corner facing west you could be sure your eyes would tear as you felt the pull of the river. It was colder by only a degree or two, but it was enough to make you feel it, enough to make you shiver as you waited for the first stars to appear in the sky.

If she could have found her way on the cobblestone streets beyond the avenue, if Hannie were still alive, she would have begged the old fortune-teller for advice. She needed someone to tell her what to do: this way hope, this way despair. She stood on the corner for longer than she should have, and when she finally hailed a cab the palms of her hands had turned blue. That night she was still undecided; she phoned the airlines for times of departures to L.A., she took out the slip of paper with Dr. Marshall's address and looked at it a thousand times. She couldn't eat dinner, and she was afraid to sleep. But when it was very late she had to lie down, just for a moment, and as soon as she closed her eyes she could feel herself begin to drift. When she dreamed, she dreamed of Hannie. They were two crows, high above the earth. Lila tried to hide it, but the scent of fear was all over her, and she was ashamed for Hannie to know what a coward she was. They were flying over a place where there were black hills; below them women prepared for a birth. From the air they could see that white sheets had been raised on poles to form a tent. There were ripples in the sheets, and the women had left footprints in the earth that looked like marks made by crows. There were more than a dozen women below them, and even though they seemed not to hurry, they were a hundred times faster than the crows flying above them.

"I can't do this," Lila called to Hannie, but the air was so thin she couldn't be heard. All anyone could hear was the sound of the wind. In the center of the sky the sun grew hotter and hotter, and the wind began to smell like fire.

When the women reached the tent, each one knelt on the ground. In the air, Lila struggled to keep up with Hannie. When the old woman flew lower Lila followed her, even though the air currents were against her and she could feel tiny bones in her wings breaking.

She thought to herself, It's too late, and she watched as Hannie took to the earth so quickly that her feathers were set on fire by pure speed. The women had begun to sing; the sound was closer all the time, and it went right through Lila. She was falling; it was a drop of twenty stories below her. The tent seemed much more beautiful than clouds, whiter than stars. She just gave in to it then, she let herself fall without a fight, even though the heat was getting stronger all the time. She could actually smell the burning feathers, and then the scent of black earth. Above her the air was cool and blue and so much easier to breathe. But it was such an enormous relief to finally let go that she couldn't stop herself from weeping as she floated into her own shadow and, once and for all, gave up struggling against the delirious pull of gravity.

■ ■ ■

She needed to get in to see Dr. Marshall without his suspecting anything, and because he wasn't taking any new patients, Lila had to lie to his secretary. She insisted that she had been a patient years ago, that she had just moved back to the city and was desperate: she had found a lump in her breast. She had to wait four days until he could fit her in. She should have been nervous, there was enough empty time to imagine the worst: medical files lost in a fire, doors slammed in her face, a squad car called to oust her from the doctor's office. But instead, Lila began to feel calmer, and each day she was more convinced that it was only a matter of hours before she would have her daughter back again.

Each time she closed her eyes Lila could see the blue inlets of Connecticut that her daughter must have seen when they first brought her out to Long Island. At night her daughter heard gulls overhead, and in the summertime mimosas grew outside her bedroom window. At the far end of the hallway, in a room where there was a double bed and heavy pine furniture, the people who claimed to be her parents slept, never guessing that in her small white room Lila's daughter closed the door and dreamed about her real mother.

In the morning, when the smell of bacon filtered

ALICE HOFFMAN

through the house and they called upstairs to her, Lila's daughter was still dreaming: somewhere there was a woman with blue eyes who had to brush her hair a hundred strokes each night, just as she did, so that the knots would untangle. She was always polite to them at breakfast, but they could tell she wasn't really with them. On days when there were snowstorms or when she had the flu, she felt particularly trapped—the couple at the far end of the hallway became, momentarily, her keepers. But all she had to do was look up into a night that was filled with stars and she knew that she was leaving them: in her mind she was already with her true mother.

When they finally sat her down in the living room to tell her that she'd been adopted she nodded and smiled; she didn't want to hurt them by telling them she had always known she wasn't theirs. She just continued to do what she'd done all along: wait for her mother to appear. On the day of her high-school graduation, on her wedding day, on the morning after the birth of her first child, she waited. Soon she had another child, and her son and daughter were so talented they could swim like fish and recite the alphabet backward before their second birthdays, and when you held them their skin gave off the scent of oranges. On dark nights she kept a candle in the front window and she had her husband put a spotlight up over the garage so that the path to their house was well lit. Every year on Mother's Day she sat out on the front porch, even when it was pouring rain, and she waited for her mother until long after dark, still hoping that this might be the day.

When they were reunited Lila would give her daughter

everything she hadn't been able to before. She bought a cashmere sweater at Lord & Taylor, a silk scarf at Bloomingdale's, a pair of small opal earrings at a jewelry shop on Madison Avenue. She kept writing checks and didn't even bother to enter the amounts on the stubs, and at night she sat on the floor in her hotel room and carefully wrapped each gift in imported wrapping paper that was so delicate it shredded if you unfolded it too quickly. Only on the day of her doctor's appointment did she begin to feel a sense of dread. She was in the shower, with the water turned on very hot, when she distinctly heard a train whistle. She held on to the metal railing in the shower stall, but the train was so close that the railing had begun to rattle. It was one of the old trains that the Long Island Rail Road still used on routes that were no longer well traveled. There was a long stretch of frozen tracks, and the snow was so blinding that Lila had to reach for her sunglasses. But once she got to East China, once she was standing in the front yard of her in-laws' house, it was so warm that she didn't even need a sweater. She could see herself right there, under the pine trees, but when she opened her mouth to speak nothing came out but a stone.

Lila turned off the water and got out of the shower as fast as she could. She could still taste the cold weight of that stone in her mouth. She quickly got dressed and went down to get a cab, but when she got into the back seat she found that she'd lost her voice and it was a few moments before she could tell the driver where she wanted to go. In the doctor's office she filled out a medical history with false information, then waited for nearly half an hour. A nurse led her into the consultation office, and that was when Lila realized how unsteady she was.

Dr. Marshall had already begun to read her invented medical history. Lila sat absolutely still in a chair across from him; outside, in an alleyway, the garbage was being collected and metal cans hit hard against the pavement.

"You've found a lump in your breast," the doctor said, concerned.

Lila kept her hands folded in her lap, but she could feel the blood running through them until each finger was amazingly hot.

"No," Lila said. "I haven't."

Dr. Marshall was confused, and he looked back down at her history.

"I'm looking for my daughter," Lila said. "You placed her with a family on Long Island twenty-seven years ago, and I want her back."

"I think you've made a mistake," Dr. Marshall said.

"It was during the ice storm," Lila told him.

The door to the office had been left ajar; now the doctor got up and closed it. Lila sat calmly in the leather chair, but she could feel her heart racing.

"What do you want?" Dr. Marshall asked.

"I told you," Lila said. "Just give me an address."

"You don't understand," the doctor said. "I couldn't even if I wanted to."

"You can," Lila insisted.

He told her that it was too late; her daughter was a grown woman, with parents, a history, a life of her own. But he couldn't talk Lila out of it. Nothing he could say would erase her small bed drenched with milk or the three weeks afterward when she bled every time she walked down the hall to the bathroom, and everything she owned became stained with blood.

"You think I don't have any sympathy for you, but I do," Dr. Marshall said. "If you had come to me the next day, or even the next week, I might have been able to do something."

"I was eighteen years old," Lila said. "I couldn't."

"I don't think you're listening to me," the doctor said.

She tried to explain what the moments just before the birth were like, how it was to touch your belly and know that inside there was a perfect mouth, eyes that already blinked, fingers that opened and closed, searching for something to hold on to. Inside your own body was another, you could feel the pressure of its head until the moment when it was half inside you and half lost to you forever, slipping farther and farther away with every second, with each heartbeat.

"I don't see how I can do what you're asking," Dr. Marshall said.

Lila put one hand on her forehead and rubbed her temples.

"I don't see how you can't," she said.

When the nurse in the reception room buzzed the intercom, Dr. Marshall picked up and told her he wasn't taking calls. Then he turned to Lila.

"I have two daughters myself," he said.

Lila looked at him carefully. He leaned back in his chair and took off his glasses, and Lila saw that something was wrong with one of his eyes—it was milky and unfocused. She forced herself to look away so she wouldn't feel anything for him. Lila could tell, already, that he was about to reveal something, and she also knew that afterward there wouldn't be a day when he wouldn't feel he'd compromised himself.

"I raised those girls and I still have times when I feel like they're total strangers. I'm just warning you—you don't know how disappointed you can be after twenty-seven years."

"You don't know how much you can still regret something after twenty-seven years," Lila said.

"How about a cup of coffee?" Dr. Marshall asked Lila.

Lila shook her head no, but the doctor stood up and took two ceramic mugs from the top of one of the filing cabinets behind his desk.

"I strongly recommend some coffee," he told her.

Lila looked up at him. "All right," she said.

"Their last name was Ross," the doctor said. "Naturally, I'm trusting you not to go through my files while I'm out of the room."

"Naturally," Lila said.

"I don't approve of this," Dr. Marshall said.

"I know," Lila said.

"Cream and sugar all right?" he asked.

"Perfect," Lila told him. "Thank you."

He went to the kitchenette down the hall, giving her ten minutes. When he came back to the office, carrying two mugs of coffee, she was gone. The file drawer on the far left had been opened and Dr. Marshall closed it. Then he drank both cups of coffee, even though he never took cream. He was tired, and his left eye was acting up so that things looked blurry. He had four more patients and a train ride to go before the end of the day, and it was one of those winter afternoons when the day already seems over at four o'clock, and everyone is tired and ready to quit much too early. Still, he wished he could have seen the look on her face when she'd finally gotten what she wanted. He never once guessed that Lila didn't even look at the file after she'd found it. She just took it out of the drawer and slipped it inside her coat. She didn't look at it out on the street, or even in the cab back to the hotel. She waited until she could sit down in the chair by the window. She waited until the sky was dark and the lights below her were turned on. And if the doctor had been able to see the look on her face, he would have been disappointed. Lila's face didn't give anything away. And when she really thought about it, she wasn't the least bit surprised to find that her daughter had been given to a couple in East China, and that she had spent her first day on the same train Lila later took out, in that particularly cold winter when the Sound froze over and you could walk over the waves, all the way to Connecticut.

. . .

Jason Grey picked her up from the train in a Ford station wagon that had no muffler and no shock absorbers. Lila walked right past him and went to stand out on the platform. But as soon as she saw the old Ford she knew it was his, and after she turned back toward the station she realized that an old man was watching her. It had been five years since her in-laws' last visit to California, and in that time Jason's hair had gone completely white. But that wasn't what made him seem so much older—it was that he was no longer as tall. When Lila walked over and hugged him they seemed exactly the same height.

"This is one of the best surprises I could have," Jason Grey told Lila as he lifted her suitcase into the rear of the station wagon.

They drove out to the East China Highway. There was no heater in the car and their breath fogged up the windshield. Somehow, he didn't really seem surprised to see her. He took her out to breakfast and they both ordered coffee and eggs, and as they ate they watched the traffic on the highway.

"If you've left Richard, he must have deserved it," Jason Grey said in an offhand way.

"Maybe I just decided I wanted to see you," Lila said.

Jason laughed and paid their bill; he had seen the way she was staring out at the East China Highway, and he knew he wasn't the one she was there to see.

Outside, the air was so salty and cold that it burned. A new layer of ice had formed on the windshield, and Jason took most of it off with a plastic scraper. They drove out to the house, then went down the rutted driveway and sat there staring at the place. The pine trees were taller than Lila had remembered; beneath them the house was drowning in a pool of black shadows. It was too dark even to see the wooden front door.

Jason got her suitcase out of the back, and Lila followed

him up to the house. The air was even colder underneath the pines, and it smelled sweet. Lila could feel something in her throat, and she forced herself to swallow hard.

"I hope you're not here to feel sorry for me," Jason Grey said. He had pushed open the unlocked front door, but now he kept her standing out on the porch.

"Absolutely not," Lila said.

"Good thing." Jason nodded as he led her inside.

He carried her suitcase up to the second floor and gave her the bedroom that used to be his and Helen's. When Lila's mother-in-law was first sick she couldn't manage the stairs. They had moved into the parlor, and ever since Jason had kept the heat in the rest of the house shut off and he'd remained in the parlor bedroom. Now he got out a portable kerosene heater and started it up so that Lila's room would be warm by the time she went to bed. While he poured in the kerosene Lila went to the window and wiped the fog off the glass. Out in the back the lawn had disappeared and the woods now came right up to the back of the house.

"I started to have my doubts about mowing the lawn," Jason explained when he saw her at the window. "It just seemed silly after a while."

Lila had come here without any real plan. She never imagined she'd waste a whole day with her father-in-law. But now that she was in this house, she felt strangely tired. After they'd gone back downstairs she sat down on the couch next to a hospital cot in the parlor. In no time three hours had gone by.

She knew no one could do it for her. She had to walk out the door, start up the Ford, and drive to the other side of town. She was only five miles from her goal, and she was paralyzed. All the time the day was slipping away from her Lila kept thinking: I can do it anytime. But the horizon grew dark, and the birds mistook the parlor windows for the sky, beating their wings against the glass. Lila began to wonder if she would ever be able to leave this house. When she tried to lift her arms she couldn't move. At dinnertime, Lila managed to follow Jason into the kitchen, but then her knees felt weak and she had to sit down.

"This is my big secret," Jason Grey said. He opened the refrigerator and pulled down the freezer compartment. "I eat frozen dinners."

Lila found that if she really tried she could pretend to speak.

"I won't tell," she said, and she managed to stand up, light the oven with a wooden match, and slide two frozen dinners onto the lowest rack.

They ate in the kitchen with the oven left on to heat the room. Every time she swallowed Lila swore the dinners hadn't defrosted and that she was swallowing pieces of ice. Jason Grey seemed to be having no trouble with his turkey and mashed potatoes, although every once in a while he stopped eating long enough to fiddle with the stove.

"I can't stand to give the oil companies any more money than they already have," he explained. "The oven in here isn't too bad, and I put the woodstove in the parlor three years ago."

Lila really didn't know what was happening to her. She put her fork down and covered her eyes.

"I'll freeze to death before I give the oil companies

another cent," Jason said cheerfully. "I'll bet you think I can't make good coffee," he added. "Well, you're wrong."

He got up to start the coffee, and he let Lila cry.

"Thanks," Lila said when he brought over the coffeepot.

"I don't like to see you upset," Jason said.

"Oh, well," Lila said.

"I mean it," Jason said. "I don't like to see it."

He got some milk and sugar and took down two cups from the top cabinet. "We don't have owls any more around here," he told Lila. "Remember how there used to be owls all over East China—in the trees and everywhere? They just took off, and now the only thing you hear at night is traffic. You never used to hear traffic around here."

They drank coffee and Lila took off her boots and lifted her feet up to warm them by the oven. Sitting here with Jason, she could almost forget why she had come back to East China in the first place.

"We should have asked you to live with us," she told her father-in-law.

"Not me," Jason Grey said. "I'm never going to California."

It turned out that Jason wasn't paying for hot water any more either, so Lila boiled some water to wash the coffee cups and spoons. By the time she finished and went into the parlor, Jason was already asleep on the couch, and Lila covered him with a wool afghan her mother-in-law had crocheted. Then she turned off the lights. She went upstairs and got into bed, but when she turned off the lamp on the night table there was still a glow from the kerosene heater.

In that bedroom, beneath a heavy quilt, Lila felt perfectly safe. It was quite possible, she knew, to stay here forever. Especially in winter, when it was dark by four and there was wood to be brought in, salt blocks to be dragged out to the yard for the deer, ice on all the windows. She hadn't known quite how much she'd missed winter, and now that she was back she almost felt young in this season, in this house. That night she brushed her hair a hundred times with a wire brush she'd found on the bureau, and she slept deeply as the ice on the windows grew thicker. By midnight you couldn't have seen outside even if you'd wanted to; it was as if nothing existed on the other side of the glass but snow and an old road that led nowhere in particular.

In the morning, Lila woke suddenly. The heater had run out of kerosene and the room was freezing. She reached for her clothes and got dressed under the covers the way she and Richard used to on mornings when it was too cold to get out of bed. Sometime during the night Jason Grey had woken up, put more wood in the parlor stove, then gone back to sleep on his cot. When he came into the kitchen at six-thirty Lila had already made coffee and French toast, which was staying warm on a plate in the oven.

Jason smiled when Lila brought his plate to the table. "I never knew you could cook like this."

Lila turned the oven up higher, then put on a second borrowed sweater, and watched her father-in-law eat. She couldn't quite believe she had been in the house for less than twenty-four hours. In a little while she planned to fix the wallpaper that was coming down in the hallway; all it needed was some masking tape and glue.

After breakfast, Jason insisted on doing the dishes.

"I guess you're going somewhere today," he said when he'd finished. He had used cold water and the cups and plates were streaked.

Lila could feel a tightening in her throat.

"I was thinking about getting some groceries," Lila said.

"That's not what I mean," Jason Grey said.

Lila had the sudden urge for a cigarette. There was a pack of Marlboros on the table; she lit one, but the smoke only made her throat feel worse and she handed the cigarette to her father-in-law. She just wasn't ready to go out. Maybe after some time in this house, after the winter when there was something else in the world besides snow, maybe then she could think about it.

"We both know you didn't come out here just to see me," Jason Grey said. "I'm not asking why you're here, you understand."

Jason sat down across from her and Lila pushed a glass ashtray toward him. He smoked only half the cigarette before he stubbed it out and coughed for what seemed too long a time. If Lila didn't go after her daughter soon, she would never do it. And if that happened she would never be able to leave this house; she might be able to go as far as the driveway, but then a feeling of pure terror would force her to run back inside and lock herself in the upstairs bedroom.

"I figure you'll need my car," Jason Grey said. "Just remember to pump those brakes before you make a stop. They work. They just work better if you pump them."

Lila pulled on her boots and left the house. The thermometer nailed to the porch was at fifteen degrees. It took ten minutes for the car to heat up enough so that it wouldn't stall out every time she put it into gear. Jason had always said that it was an auto mechanic's duty to have a car that always needed repairing—that way if he had no business he could always give himself a job. As she sat in the idling car, the smell of gas made her sick to her stomach. She drove down the driveway carefully, and when she pulled out onto the East China Highway she skidded; if there had been oncoming traffic she wouldn't have been able to pump the brakes in time.

She had forgotten how small the place was—two long streets and a marina, then the circle of residential streets on a hill above the harbor. On one of these streets was a small housing development that had been built the year before Lila first came to East China. It was easy to find the right address, but, once she had, Lila turned the key in the ignition and just sat there, looking at the house. All along she'd imagined a two-story house, and here it was a ranch in a neighborhood that was so deserted that when Lila finally got out of the Ford and the car door slammed behind her, the sudden noise made her jump.

The ground was frozen and there was a cover of ice on the asphalt driveway. Lila tried to tell herself that the worst part was over—she had found the house where her daughter had grown up. But already it felt wrong to her. She walked up to the door and knocked. She could hear something inside—a dishwasher or a washing machine. She realized then that she had expected some signs of children—a bicycle or a set of swings. The idea was ridiculous—it was winter, and her daughter was a grown woman—she probably only came back to this house on holidays, two or three times a year.

Lila could hear someone walking down the hallway, but it wasn't until the door opened that she believed it was finally happening. A woman stood looking at her through the storm door. The sound of water was even louder, and Lila could tell now—it was a dishwasher.

"I'm Lila Grey," Lila said right away, as if that explained anything.

The woman nodded, expecting more, a sales pitch for cosmetics or vacuum cleaners. Lila could tell that she had already decided to say no and was just being polite.

"My father-in-law used to own the first gas station on the highway," Lila said. She was talking too much and too fast, but she couldn't seem to stop herself. "He lives just past the station, in that old green farmhouse you can see from the road, and that's his car out there. I knew I shouldn't have borrowed it, but I did, and now I'm stuck and I have to call him."

When the woman looked out at the parked Ford it was easy to believe that Lila had indeed had car trouble. And then she actually did it; she unlocked the storm door and let Lila inside.

"Everything's a mess," the woman said apologetically as she led Lila to the kitchen. There was a wall phone above the table, and the woman turned the dishwasher off so that Lila could hear. Her name, Lila knew from the file, was Janet Ross, and she had been thirty-three years old when cysts were discovered in both her ovaries. When the cysts were removed the surgeon found that the walls of her ovaries were depleted and thin. Janet Ross had come to see Dr. Marshall for a second opinion, and she had broken down in his office when he told her she'd never be able to have a child. When the doctor phoned her a few months later to tell her he had found a baby for her, it was late at night and the ice storm had made driving impossible. They took a train into Manhattan at five that morning. By seven they were in Dr. Marshall's office at Beekman, and the doctor couldn't help but notice that Janet Ross had dressed so quickly she was still wearing a nightgown underneath her dress and the flowered hem hung down past her knees to the tops of her boots.

Lila held the phone down with her finger and dialed; she kidded Jason for lending her a wreck of a car and suggested he bring his tools and meet her out on the street.

Janet Ross was at the table, polishing a silver creamer when Lila got off the phone.

"He'll have to take a cab over," Lila said. "I guess I'll wait in the car. I just wish the heater worked."

"No heat," Janet Ross said sympathetically.

Lila kept looking for a sign: a Mother's Day card taped to the refrigerator, a photograph hung on the wall.

"How about some coffee?" Janet Ross asked.

"Great," Lila said. "But why don't you make it tea. I read tea leaves," she explained.

Janet Ross put some water up to boil, but she gave Lila a look.

"It's a hobby," Lila explained. She waited just the right amount of time before she spoke again. "Why don't you let me read yours?"

"I couldn't ask you to do that," Janet Ross said, taking two teacups out of the cabinet.

"Oh, you have to let me," Lila said. "I'll feel much better about barging in on you."

She took the teabags Janet Ross had put in each cup and tore them open with her fingernail. As water was poured into the cups Lila realized how uncomfortable she was in this kitchen; she had expected it to be much nicer than it was: the walls were covered with something that was supposed to look like slate, and the appliances were all a too bright yellow.

"Lovely place you've got," Lila actually said.

"Do you really think so?" Janet Ross said, pleased. "We moved out here from the city thirty-two years ago—right after we were married."

Lila held up her hand. "Don't tell me any more about yourself," she warned. When Janet looked puzzled, she added, "Otherwise, what's the point in having your fortune told?"

The women smiled at each other, but all the time Lila was thinking what a fool Janet was. First she pretended to be someone's mother, and now she was about to tell Lila everything she wanted to know.

"Can I add milk to this?" Janet Ross asked. Used to coffee, she was having a hard time with the bitter taste of tea.

"Just drink it," Lila said.

She sounded harsher than she'd planned, but Janet quickly finished her tea, as though, for a moment, she'd been frightened of Lila. Lila held the cup and peered into it.

"I see the letter L," she said. "A man who is very close to you."

"I can't believe it," Janet said. "That's Lewis. My husband."

Lila smiled; she had her now.

"This Lewis," Lila said, "he's an engineer someplace where they make airplanes?"

Janet Ross grew rigid. "How did you know that?" she asked.

Lila pointed to the teacup. Dr. Marshall's files were very complete. "See this," she said. "This little airplane in the corner?"

Janet Ross looked and couldn't see a thing.

"Well, it takes years to understand the symbols," Lila said. "Take this one." She briefly passed the cup in front of Janet. "This is clearly the symbol for your daughter."

"My daughter?" Janet said, confused.

"I see here that she is twenty-six—no, twenty-seven years old this month."

She looked at Janet Ross out of the corner of her eye, and kept her voice as even as possible.

"I can't quite make out where it is she's living now," Lila said. "Is it East China?"

Janet Ross seemed to be having trouble breathing. "I don't know what you're talking about," she said.

"Your daughter," Lila said impatiently. "Where is she?"

They looked at each other across the table, and Lila could feel something passing between them.

"I don't have a daughter," Janet Ross said.

Lila sat straight in her chair; her head snapped back, as though she'd been slapped. She had the file in her suitcase and she knew this was the right house. This was the right woman—you could tell she was a thief just by looking at her.

"Wait a minute," Lila said. "I see the symbol for your daughter in the tea leaves, and the tea leaves never lie."

It was all a show for Janet Ross, and so it was even more terrible when Lila looked into the teacup and really did see something. There were arms and legs surfacing, and then, for a moment, a child's face.

"Oh, my God," Lila said. "She's right there."

In the fluorescent lighting of the kitchen Janet Ross suddenly looked much older than she was.

"What do you want?" she whispered.

Lila knew that she could lose it all now; one more out-burst and she might never find out where her daughter was. "You don't have to be nervous now that we've begun to talk about children," she said. But she could tell that Janet Ross wasn't quite as stupid as she'd thought.

"There's nothing wrong with your car," Janet said.

"Of course there is," Lila said quickly. "Just take a look at it."

"I don't want you here," Janet Ross told her.

"You're the one who invited me in!" Lila said.

She could feel the edge of Janet's hysteria as Janet stood up and reached for the phone.

"I'm calling the police," Janet Ross said.

Lila leapt up and grabbed the phone receiver out of her hand.

"Don't you dare call the police," Lila said, and when she let go of the phone Janet obediently hung up. Lila had no time to waste. She went into the living room and began to search for signs of her daughter. Janet followed her and watched as Lila tore through the house. She went through the bureau drawers and found nothing—not a photograph, not an address. She went through the bedrooms, the closets, the medicine cabinet in the bathroom, and all the while Janet followed her, watching. By the time Lila had finished with the last room—a den in which there was a fold-out couch for guests—she was shivering.

"I don't know what you're looking for," Janet said. "We don't have anything worth stealing. Take the color TV if you want it." She took off her wristwatch and her diamond ring and held them out to Lila. "Here," she offered. "Take these."

"There's nothing here," Lila said weakly.

"I could have told you that," Janet Ross said. "You picked the wrong house."

Lila went to the front door and let herself out. It was freezing cold, and Lila just couldn't wait for the car to warm up, so every time she shifted into gear, the engine stalled. She should have known from the minute she walked through the door that no child had ever lived there. If her daughter had grown up in that house she would have left some sign for Lila: a framed picture of a robin, bronzed baby shoes, fingerprints that Janet Ross could never get off the kitchen door. Lila immediately blamed Dr. Marshall for giving her the wrong address to throw her off the track, but maybe it was an innocent mix-up of his files, and after all these years what could anyone expect? Files got lost, names misplaced, children disappeared on cold, clear days. And as Lila drove away she had only one wish: that she had come here last night at midnight with a pack of matches and some kerosene and burned this house to the ground. Then, at least, there'd have been smoke and ashes, and when Lila had picked through the rubble she could have imagined that everything she touched had once belonged to her daughter.

Lila went back to her father-in-law's house and sat down in the kitchen with her coat still on. Jason Grey was in the back, putting out salt licks for the deer. When he heard the Ford pull up he finished and came inside. As soon as he saw Lila he knew she hadn't gotten whatever it was she'd wanted.

"Do you want me to ask you what's wrong?" he said.

Lila shook her head no.

He made her a pot of coffee and set it down on the table, then he left her alone. Lila sat in the kitchen all afternoon. She could hear the TV turned on in the parlor, she could hear footsteps in the hallway every once in a while when Jason came as close to the kitchen doorway as he dared, just to check on her. When it started to get dark, Lila didn't bother to turn on the light. She could sit there in the dark forever, and the colder it got in the room, the less she felt like moving. She let the cold get into her bones and if

she waited long enough, if she really tried, she might be able
to feel nothing at all.

It was seven in the evening when the phone rang, and by
then Lila was so cold that she could barely move. Jason
came in from the parlor and they both watched the phone,
set out on the kitchen counter, as it rang five more times.

"You know who that is," Jason Grey said. "He always
calls me on a Friday night."

Jason went over and turned the oven on.

"You shouldn't be sitting here," he told Lila. "It's too
cold."

The phone began to ring again.

"I take it you don't want to talk to him," Jason said. He
lit a cigarette and leaned against the sink. Bent over that
way he was actually shorter than Lila.

Everything seemed to have a hard edge; when Lila
looked at her father-in-law she could see only his skeleton.

The phone had stopped ringing, and this time Jason
went over and pulled the plug out of the wall.

"You don't have to talk to him if you don't want to,
Lila," Jason Grey said. "But I'll tell you one thing you do
have to do—eat dinner. And I'll tell you what I have in
mind." He was talking to her as if it were the most natural
thing in the world for them to be there together in the dark
with her not saying a thing. "Helen never liked for me to
have Italian food, she was sure it was bad for your heart. But
I've been thinking about going to a restaurant in town. And
that's what I'm going to do—I'm going to take you out to
dinner."

They left the kitchen oven on, so that the house

would warm up. Jason Grey put on his down jacket, and his high boots, and then they walked arm in arm down the dirt driveway toward the Ford. Lila held on tightly to her father-in-law, so that he wouldn't slip on the ice. The stars were brighter than they'd ever been and the sky was so huge it made you aware of how fragile you were, how easy it would be to slip on the ice and break something. As they walked past the pines it grew even colder, and Lila breathed in deeply, but she didn't dare speak. Already, she could feel that the stone had formed and was waiting to drop from her tongue.

· · ·

On the day of her daughter's birthday it was fifty-eight degrees, one of the warmest days in January anyone in East China could remember. By now Lila couldn't go any farther than the end of the driveway, and she knew it was pointless to try. It was as if there was a sudden drop in the oxygen out there, or a pack of half-starved wolves roaming the East China Highway, out for blood.

Of course there were things she could have done: hired detectives, made phone calls, pored over school records in the basement of the elementary school. But nothing outside the yard of Jason Grey's house seemed very real, and California seemed most unreal of all. Richard kept calling. Twice, Lila had overheard Jason Grey talking to him on the telephone, and each time she had been startled by the idea that you could talk to someone who was three thousand miles away.

"I'm telling you she's all right," she had heard her father-in-law tell Richard on the Saturday after she'd been to see Janet Ross. But Richard refused to believe him; he phoned again and again, and when he called one night after midnight, Lila could tell he was thinking about following her. She stood in the kitchen doorway, near the cabinet where the brooms were stored; she dreaded the possibility that Richard might come after her. Jason sensed her presence in the room and turned to her. Lila couldn't seem to blink, and Jason was reminded of the deer who edged closer and closer to the house each season, as the woods claimed more and more of the yard.

"Don't argue with me," Jason had said to Richard. "Sometimes people need to be alone and you can't take it personally."

Richard stopped calling after that. Lila tried to thank her father-in-law by baking him a cake, but she ran out of flour, and she couldn't go into town any more, not even to the grocery on Main Street. Each day she stayed closer and closer to the house, but on her daughter's birthday the weather was so seductive that even Lila went outside. She pulled on a pair of Jason Grey's old boots and began to rake the mud in the front yard. She had been working for nearly an hour, and had broken two fingernails when she heard the car pull into the driveway, its wheels spinning in the mud. The birds had gone crazy with the sudden warmth; there were so many of them searching for worms that from certain angles the earth looked blue. At the far edge of the yard were the shells of two Chryslers waiting for spring when Jason would rebuild them. If he worked slowly enough, he had told Lila, those Chryslers might keep him busy for the rest of his life.

When the car pulled in, Lila stood up and put one hand on her hip. Every time she licked her lips she tasted salt; she had lost so much weight in the past two weeks that her wedding band slipped up and down her fourth finger easily. But now she held on to the rake so tightly that the ring stayed in place. She knew, right then, as the car pulled over and parked, that she was about to find her daughter. The first thing she did was make a quick list of things she had to do: wash her hair, file down the nails that had broken while she raked, look through her mother-in-law's closet for a leather belt, polish her one good pair of shoes.

Janet Ross didn't see Lila out in the yard, and Lila let her walk to the house without calling to her. She enjoyed watching from a distance as Janet navigated through the mud and knocked on the front door and she stood still as Jason Grey invited Janet inside. Lila wanted this exact moment to go on and on. She wanted the same sound of the birds, and the thud of the front door as her father-in-law closed it, and the air so surprisingly warm and sweet it made you feel like crying. And when she finally walked back to the house, Lila made certain to take her time—because, after all, she had been waiting for this moment for more than half her life.

She took off her boots in the hallway and hung her sweater on a hook by the door. It was still chilly in the house, from months of freezing weather. Lila could hear voices in the parlor and, standing in the hallway, she was reminded of the first time Richard had brought her here.

Then it had been Helen Grey's voice she had heard, and the sound of it had made her frightened to go in. She'd had a strong sense of interrupting something, of stepping inside a place where she didn't belong.

"Don't worry," Richard had whispered to her, and he had taken her arm to give her courage. "They're going to be crazy about you."

Janet Ross was sitting on the couch, still wearing her coat, when Lila walked into the room. Jason had just put out a cigarette and was coughing. His cough, Lila couldn't help noticing, was getting worse.

"I guess you lied to me," Lila said, right away, not willing to give Janet Ross an inch.

"I'll bet you ladies are thirsty," Jason Grey said. He had been sitting in the old chair that faced the couch, and now he stood. "What if I offered you both some bourbon and water?"

Lila and Janet Ross were staring at each other.

"None for me," Lila said to her father-in-law.

"None for me," Janet echoed.

"You'll excuse me if I get some for myself," Jason Grey said, and he left the room. They could hear him in the kitchen, but then the back door slammed, and Lila knew that what he'd wanted wasn't a drink but an excuse to leave them alone.

"I guess your father-in-law lives here by himself," Janet Ross said. "You can always tell just by looking at a room."

Lila sat down in the armchair. She could still hear the birds outside, even through the closed windows.

"You can tell from a room when something's gone wrong," Janet said.

She looked at Lila then.

"As soon as I saw you I knew you were Susan's birth mother," she said.

The name cut right through Lila. That was definitely not her daughter's name, not Susan. All during her pregnancy, and even after the baby was born, Lila had not once thought of a name for her daughter. It was only lately that she felt her daughter had to have a name, and she certainly wasn't about to let someone like Janet Ross choose it.

"Not her birth mother," Lila said. "Her real mother."

Janet Ross looked toward the doorway of the parlor after Jason Grey. "Maybe I will have that bourbon," she said.

"I don't think there is any," Lila told her. "He just wanted to get out of the room."

"Well, I don't blame him," Janet said. She unbuttoned her coat, but she was so nervous that she couldn't get all the buttons undone. "It certainly was a different kind of January back then," she said. "It was so cold that when you stepped out for a second to get the mail your eyelashes froze together and you couldn't see a thing."

"I know what it was like," Lila said.

"When the phone call came I thought I was dreaming," Janet said. "I was half asleep, and my husband had worked late the day before so he was exhausted—he didn't even hear it ring."

"Look," Lila said, "I don't care about you or your husband. I don't care about anything you have to say. I just want to know where she is."

"I know that's what you want," Janet said. "That's why I'm telling you this. Because I remember everything about it. I remember thinking, This is going to be the best day of my life. Even before it happens to me, I know it can never be any better."

They were in Dr. Marshall's office when he brought her in to them. At first Janet was afraid to touch her; she had wanted her so much that now if she reached out a little too quickly the baby might dissolve into smoke. Of course, once she did hold the baby she refused to let go. She held her all the way back to East China and refused to speak. Even when her husband asked her a direct question, she just couldn't answer. It was all too perfect to talk about. From the window of the train they could see that the sound had frozen solid, each wave had turned into green ice.

That first night Janet sat in the rocking chair in the nursery, fed the baby a bottle, and sang her to sleep. Lewis had wanted to call the baby Deborah, after his grandmother, but the name Susan came to Janet the moment Dr. Marshall put the baby in her arms, and she insisted upon it.

After that first quiet night Susan couldn't seem to sleep, and Janet had to rock with her for hours. The baby slept peacefully during the day, but as soon as it grew dark she was restless. All the books assured Janet that this sort of fretting was normal, but sometimes, after Susan had finally fallen asleep and her mouth was still puckered from crying, Janet wondered if it was something more, if Susan simply couldn't bear the dark. After a while, they settled into a routine, but Janet still felt drawn to the nursery at night. She stood in the doorway, and even from a distance she could see that Susan's skin was luminous. She nearly shimmered beneath her woolen blanket, and even on moonless nights the nursery seemed brighter than the rest of the house, as if the baby had managed to chase away the night.

Janet's husband, Lewis, may not have been a model husband—he worked overtime too much, and he sometimes didn't listen to a word she said—but he was a good father to Susan. He brought home dresses and toys, and when the baby came down with a cold in February he took turns rocking her back to sleep. Susan's cold lingered for more than a month. It seemed to wrap her in a cocoon, and Janet had the feeling that the baby was far away, even when she was holding her. Janet had Lewis hook up an intercom to connect their bedroom with the nursery, and whenever she heard a hiccup or a cough in the middle of the night she sat up in bed, eyes riveted to the intercom until it was quiet again. She was overanxious, but what had she expected? She had been afraid of losing this baby even before she had her, and now she couldn't escape the uneasy feeling that Susan was somehow on loan to her, and that sooner or later she'd have to give her up.

In early April the weather turned warmer and Susan's lingering cold disappeared. Janet began to take her everywhere, first to the market, and then for drives in the car. They went to towns where Janet had never been before, to restaurants and diners where Susan sat in her infant seat, propped up on the table quietly drinking her bottle without any fuss at all. For the first time in her life Janet began to talk to strangers, and when she did, she lied. She pretended that she was Susan's natural mother; she described her labor to waitresses, she discussed her nursing problems with women at the next table. And all the while she felt Susan watching her, studying her carefully with her wide eyes.

At three months, Susan had smiled for the first time. A few weeks later she actually turned over and both her parents were so overcome they had tears in their eyes. Susan watched everything now, and she looked so knowing that Janet sometimes felt uncomfortable. She had gotten into the habit of talking to Susan all day long, calling out each ingredient as she added to the batter of a chocolate cake, reading aloud from the morning newspaper. Sometimes Janet marveled at her own nerve. How had she ever dared to think she could take care of this child? How could she have pretended to be someone's mother?

Janet felt proud whenever Susan did anything new, as if she had something to do with the child's brilliance. She could sit for hours, rapt, as Susan studied the mobile above her crib, or carefully examined her toes. They were a closed circle, the two of them, and even Lewis sometimes felt like an intruder. It may have been because of those colds Susan continued to have; though none was bad enough for a trip to the doctor, Janet was so protective that even she began to be amazed at how fierce her love had become. There was something about sitting up late at night with Susan that made Janet totally surrender to the child. Each time her daughter reached up and put her arms around her neck the world outside the nursery evaporated, the nightlight on the wall became far brighter than the moon.

There had been a two-month visit to the pediatrician, and there would be another at six months. But even if someone had suggested that something was wrong, Janet Ross wouldn't have believed it. She didn't even notice how small Susan was until the child was five months old. It was June; the mimosa trees were in flower and the air was silky. Janet took Susan down to the playground near the harbor for the first time in her new stroller. That day Susan was dressed in white cotton tights and a yellow dress, and Janet felt she had never seen a more beautiful child. At the park she sat on a green wooden bench with the other mothers. She took Susan out of her stroller and held her on her lap; together they watched two ten-year-old boys on the swings who were making themselves dizzy with height. Across from them, on another green bench, were two other mothers whose children were in strollers identical to Susan's. They waved to Janet and she waved back gaily, and she didn't even have the urge to lie to anyone about her labor and delivery. That's how right she felt sitting there with the other mothers. That's how perfect the day was.

When it was time to go home, Janet put Susan back into the stroller and walked past the mothers on the bench across from theirs.

"Look," one of the women said to her child, "a brand-new baby!"

The children in the other strollers stared gravely at Susan.

"Not all that new," Janet smiled.

"God, I can barely remember when Jessie was that small," the woman said.

"I don't think Paul was ever that small," her friend said. "He was ten pounds two ounces at birth."

Janet bent down to the stroller and smiled. "Hear that?" she said to Susan. "But just you wait till you're as old as these babies are now. I won't even be able to lift you up."

Susan looked so beautiful in her stroller that Janet could hardly bear it. She had the urge to pick her up again; instead she smoothed down Susan's skirt.

"How old is she?" the first mother asked Janet. "About six weeks?"

"Six weeks!" Janet laughed. "She was just five months. She's already wearing size six months clothes."

The two mothers on the bench looked at each other; both knew that a newborn child could fit into that size.

"She was only five pounds six ounces when she was born," Janet said, flustered.

Susan had untied her hat and the two mothers were studying her.

"How old are yours?" Janet said stiffly.

"I love that hat of hers," one of the mothers said. "I never saw anything so cute."

Janet looked closely at the two other children in their strollers; both were twice Susan's size and Janet guessed they were somewhere between a year and eighteen months old.

"I'd really like to know," Janet said now. "How old are they?"

"Jessie is four months this week, but Paul is already six months," one of the mothers said quietly.

"My daughter is very petite," Janet said quickly. She felt as though she'd been slapped.

"That's right." The other mother was just as quick to agree. "Five foot two, eyes of blue. She'll have all the boys chasing after her."

Janet walked home then. Susan fell asleep on the way, and Janet left her out on the porch in her stroller. She went inside and sat down on the couch, but after a while she went and got her baby. It just didn't seem right to leave her out there, asleep and defenseless, because it now seemed that the air was a little too silky, and the sky was almost threatening, it was too bright and too blue.

That night Janet asked her husband to measure Susan. They held her down on the couch and lined up a tape measure. Janet looked up the growth chart in the back of one of the baby books and she found that Susan's length was that of a six- or eight-week-old baby. She had just stopped growing, and they hadn't even noticed. She had been getting four bottles of formula a day and she'd never cried out or complained that she was hungry, but when they weighed her now, sitting her down on the bathroom scale, she was only ten pounds.

Janet could feel something inside her snapping, but after she put Susan to sleep and Lewis wanted to talk about it, she couldn't.

"There's nothing wrong with her," Janet insisted.

But she lay in bed awake all night, and she could tell Lewis was awake, too.

"I've thought it over," he told her in the morning.

"There probably is nothing wrong with her, but maybe she has a hormone deficiency or something. I just want to take her in and get her examined. I want to be sure."

He was right, and Janet nodded her head, but she just couldn't stand it. Lewis took the day off from work and they drove to see the pediatrician. When the doctor saw Susan something in his eyes changed. It passed in a moment, and he calmly examined Susan, but Janet knew then that something was wrong. He never accused them of anything, although now all Janet could think of was why hadn't they thought to weigh her, why hadn't they brought her in one of those times she was coughing and feverish? By the end of the exam the doctor had made an appointment for a chest X-ray that afternoon at Central Suffolk Hospital.

"That's impossible," Janet found herself saying. "Susan takes a nap in the afternoon."

"Janet!" her husband said.

"I don't think you understand," the doctor said gently. "There may be a problem with her heart, and that's what may have affected her growth."

But Janet understood perfectly. They were about to take Susan away from her. When she was taken into the X-ray department Janet had to look away. The technicians had fitted Susan into a sort of glass tube to keep her from moving, and inside the glass Susan looked tinier than ever and so beautiful it nearly broke Janet's heart. She tried to think of a reason why she would be punished this way, and she knew it could only be that she hadn't been a good enough mother. Not a real mother. She had resented the crying in the night sometimes, she had been overwhelmed by the sheer amount of dirty laundry one baby could generate. And now she was being punished, and what's more, she deserved it.

They discovered a congenital heart lesion. It had stopped Susan's growth and made her delicate enough to catch so many colds. The valves of her heart were beyond repair. Janet and Lewis took her to Mount Sinai for a second opinion, but the second opinion was the same as the first. Susan would not last through her first year. The strange thing was that, if anything, Susan became more beautiful, and when Janet took her for walks in her stroller people turned and stared and some of them couldn't stop themselves from coming right up to tell Janet what a lovely daughter she had. Janet herself looked much older. Lewis told her to take it easy, not to work so hard, to sleep more. But Janet just didn't feel she had the time to waste on things like sleeping and eating. She only wanted to be with Susan. She spent all day playing with her, and didn't bother with supper for Lewis or vacuuming the rugs. She taught Susan to eat cereal off a tiny demitasse spoon, to clap her hands together, to wave goodbye. One afternoon, when they were sitting together on the floor, Susan stopped playing with the soft rattle she held, looked up at Janet and said "ma." Janet felt her heart break in half, and all that night Susan ran her new sound together, "amamamamam," and even after she had closed her eyes, when Janet went into the nursery to check on her, Susan turned in her sleep and called out to her.

In July Susan had a cold, and then a stomach virus; she just didn't have the defenses to fight it off. And then, when it seemed that the virus had subsided, it suddenly got worse, and it happened so fast there was no time to think. One moment Susan was well enough to take solid foods, and the next she'd begun vomiting and her eyes had rolled upward so that all you could see was a milky white line beneath each lid. When they rushed her to the emergency ward she was absolutely limp, like a small doll who occasionally took a deep breath, and Janet thought to herself, This is a test. This is to get me ready for all I have to bear. Only a few hours after she was hooked up to an IV Susan revived, and as they took her home Janet realized that she hadn't once allowed herself to cry. Even Lewis could do that, she had heard him in the bathroom, with the water in the sink running to mask the sound. But somehow, crying was an admission of what was happening to them, and Janet would never be ready for that.

She died on the second Sunday in August, when the sky was cloudless and the temperature eighty-two degrees. Janet woke up at five in the morning and, lying next to her husband in bed, she knew. The light that morning was pearl-colored and soft. It was the sort of morning when summer is everywhere, in all the rooms of the house and in every backyard. Janet slipped out of bed, leaving her husband asleep. When he got up at seven, he found Janet in the nursery, rocking back and forth in the chair, holding the dead child. There were always blackbirds in East China, but this morning they called so loudly in the trees that they set all the neighborhood cats howling. Lewis sat down on the carpeted floor of the nursery and put his head in his wife's lap, and because there was no longer any reason not to, Janet finally let herself cry.

They couldn't find a coffin small enough, so they had one specially made. By the following morning all signs that a child had been in the house were gone: the crib and all the boxes of clothes were taken up to the attic; the photograph albums and toys were stored in the cellar behind an old metal sink. But all that first night Janet swore she heard a baby crying for its mother.

The day that Lila had appeared at the front door Janet was suspicious, and as soon as Lila began to question her about her children, she was a hundred percent sure. It wasn't unexpected—why shouldn't Susan's birth mother come back after all these years? Why shouldn't she accuse her of murder? But Janet wasn't about to admit anything, and when Lila finally left the house Janet double-locked the front door, and she didn't dare take another breath until she heard Lila drive away.

But even though she had tricked Lila into leaving, Janet couldn't stop thinking about her, and that night she went down to the cellar and for the first time in twenty-seven years she opened the cardboard boxes. It was cold in the cellar, but when she opened the first box Janet felt a rush of heat, as if some of the air from that August had been trapped inside when Lewis first sealed the boxes. She put her flashlight down on the floor and took out the photo album. She had to force herself to go on past the first picture, taken the first week after they had brought her home. How could they have thought that anything so beautiful, so perfect, could last? In every photograph Susan seemed to be leaving them behind, calmly departing, and it suddenly seemed silly to Janet that she had ever thought of Susan as hers. It was just that for a little while she had been allowed to take care of her, and even if she told Lila the truth she couldn't lose someone she had never really had.

They could hear the scrape of the rake outside as Jason Grey cleared out the driveway. Lila sat perfectly still and although she thought to herself over and over, She's a liar, she knew it was all true. It was the kind of truth you feel in your bones. The sudden knowledge that there was nothing at all wrong with Rae's child nearly made Lila cry out loud; it was her own child who had surfaced from the bottom of the cup. It was her own bad fortune.

"Maybe I've been waiting for you to come back for her all this time," Janet Ross said quietly. "But you don't have to tell me how I failed. Believe me. I know."

That August had been the best time in Lila's life. The sunlight had been so bright you could see only certain things: a thin gold wedding band, the reedy stalks of orange lilies that grew by the back door, the line of Richard's shoulder when he turned to her in bed.

Janet Ross slid a photograph album across the coffee table between them.

"I brought this for you," she said.

Lila planned to say, I don't want it, my daughter is twenty-seven years old, today is her birthday, she lives somewhere right here in this town, she has children of her own, and she's been waiting for me, every day she opens the back door and looks out across the lawn and expects to see me. But when she tried to speak she couldn't, and though she tried to stop herself she reached for the album on the coffee table. The baby nearly jumped out at her. She was sitting in the backyard, on Janet Ross's lap underneath a mimosa tree, and her eyes were so alive they couldn't be held back by the confines of the paper. Lila could feel a sharp pain all along her left side. The child was stunning, but Lila had already decided—she was not her daughter.

"She doesn't look anything like me," Lila said, and as she spoke she could feel the cold, round shape of the words drop from her mouth.

"I brought this, too," Janet said. She took a small white sweater out of her pocketbook and gently placed it on the coffee table. "She looked beautiful in anything you put on her, pastels, stripes, anything at all."

Jason Grey had never believed in using anything stronger than a sixty-watt bulb, though the pines made the parlor dark all day long. But even in the dim light, even though Janet Ross had turned her face away, Lila could tell that she was crying. Lila closed the photograph album and went to sit next to her on the couch. Janet wiped her tears with the backs of her hands and laughed.

"If my husband goes down to the cellar before I clean up he'll probably wonder if a robber's been there. He'll wonder why anyone in their right mind would pick those old boxes to go through."

Lila couldn't take her eyes off Janet, and she found herself calmly thinking: *So that's how it feels.* Janet's sense of loss was all over her, in the way she buttoned her coat to leave, in the angle of her shoulders. When she compared her absolute lack of feeling to Janet's grief, Lila couldn't even bring herself to feel guilt—only uselessness. Outside it was even warmer than Los Angeles on a winter day; the earth had begun to steam, giving off moisture in little gasps. And Lila knew one thing for certain: She was not about to lose her daughter this way.

When Lila slid the photograph album back onto Janet Ross's lap, Janet looked over at her, confused.

"I brought it for you," Janet said.

Maybe she should have felt grateful: here was the woman who sat up nights mixing formula, rocking back and forth in the rocking chair, not daring to go back to her own bed, even though the baby's breathing was fine and the intercom was switched on. But the truth was that the one time in her life when Lila was about to do something that seemed selfless, she was feeling nothing at all.

"You take this all home with you," Lila insisted. "She was your daughter."

That evening Lila and Jason Grey sat in the kitchen and had a supper of coffee and sandwiches. They could feel the drop in the temperature and they knew it was about to snow.

Jason had been watching her all evening and now he said carefully, "I liked that visitor of yours. Nice lady."

For the first time since she'd come back Lila realized just how cold this old house was.

"I think I might go back to California," she said.

Jason nodded. "They're predicting a hell of a February. Wherever you look you're going to see snow."

"I don't see how you stand it," Lila said, and they both knew she wasn't talking about the snow.

"I'll tell you what the hard part is," Jason Grey said. "It's not feeling Helen's not with me—I feel like she's with me all the time. It's letting her go. After all, it's pretty selfish trying to keep her here with me in this house, so every once in a while I just remind myself to let her go."

That night, before she went to bed, Lila went around the house, turning off all the lights. In the parlor, her father-in-law was already asleep, and when Lila went over to turn out the lamp near his cot she saw that Janet Ross had left behind the small white sweater, neatly folded on the coffee table. Lila hesitated, but then she picked it up and discovered that the sweater was warm, as if it had just been worn.

She went upstairs, brushed her hair, and undressed; and when she got into bed she took the sweater in with her and held it against her chest. Everything in the room was faintly orange from the light of the kerosene heater, and outside the window, above the pine trees, the moon had a hazy ring around it, promising snow. Lila brought her knees up to her chest, and she rocked back and forth; in no time at all she was holding her daughter in her arms. She hadn't changed since the day she was born, she wasn't one minute older. And as Lila rocked her baby to sleep she closed her eyes and couldn't help thinking that Jason Grey could do whatever he wanted. It wasn't her baby that Janet Ross had been talking about, and she wasn't about to let her daughter go.

By morning nearly a foot of snow had fallen; the drifts reached the center of the front door and it took Lila and Jason Grey nearly two hours to dig the car out so that Jason could drive her to the airport. The last thing Lila had packed was the white wool sweater, and once they had gotten the car started, she kept the suitcase on her lap. At the edge of the driveway, just before they turned left onto the East China Highway, Lila felt a brief surge of pity for Janet Ross. But then, it didn't really concern her. She had found her daughter after all, and all the way to the airport she kept her left hand on her suitcase and she swore she could feel a heartbeat, as if she had hidden inside her suitcase a child so perfect and small no one else could see her, a baby who needed to be held all night, and gently rocked to sleep.

PART FIVE

$\mathcal{T}$HEY WERE ON THE FLOOR IN the living room, so intent on their breathing techniques that they hadn't heard her come in. As she watched from the hallway, Lila felt a coldness settle around her. Rae lay on a bed of pillows, her knees drawn up, eyes closed. She exhaled rapidly, as if she were blowing out an endless row of matches. Richard was right beside her, staring at his watch and counting out the seconds. On the coffee table there was a tape recorder, but instead of music there was the echo of wind chimes, brittle and cool and clear. It was the kind of sound that went right through you and made you realize that if you weren't lonely already, you would be soon.

When she had had enough, Lila dropped her suitcase so that it fell to the floor with a thud. They both sat up, startled, and turned toward the hallway. It was late afternoon, and so quiet you could hear air currents move through the room. The light that came in through the drapes was opalescent; everyone got lost in its shadows, you had to blink twice just to see straight. Except Lila, to whom everything was now obvious. For the past six hours, as she traveled between New York and Los Angeles, Lila had been wondering how she could walk in and resume her old life. Now, in an instant, she saw that she simply could not.

"Don't let me interrupt you," she told them.

She turned and went into the kitchen, but once the door had closed behind her, she didn't know what she was doing there. She didn't notice that it was too warm to still be wearing her wool coat and her boots. She had a confused, weightless feeling, as if she had stumbled not only into the wrong house but into the wrong time. When she had imagined coming home she had imagined feeling guilty, not betrayed. And she nearly forgot that even though she had not found Richard alone, she also was not alone. She had brought her daughter home with her.

By the time Richard followed her into the kitchen, Lila had decided to act as if nothing was wrong. She filled the tea kettle and put it up to boil. But every casual movement was difficult. The atmosphere was pushing down on her, the way it does in a jet, just after takeoff when the pressurized air suddenly turns fierce.

"Is this it?" Richard said to her. "After all this time you just walk right past me without a single explanation?"

Lila took a lemon from the window sill and cut it into quarters. She looked down and saw that her hand was shaking, and she quickly dropped the knife into the sink.

"Why didn't you talk to me when I called?" Richard

asked. "Why did my father act like everything was a god-damned secret?"

They could hear Rae straighten up in the living room, picking up pillows from the floor, putting on her shoes, rewinding the relaxation tape on the recorder. In the kitchen, the sound of the rewinding tape was exactly like the sound of someone drowning.

"I should have guessed you'd get involved with her," Lila said.

"What is that supposed to mean?" Richard said. "You left and she was stuck without a labor coach."

"Are you sleeping with her?" Lila asked.

"Are you crazy?" Richard said.

"I don't know," Lila said. "Is it crazy to want your husband to remain faithful?"

"How are you doing this?" Richard said. "How can you manage to make it seem like I'm the one who's done something wrong?"

Miles above the earth, somewhere above Michigan, Lila had been struck with the sudden knowledge that she was about to lose someone. If she had to choose, Lila knew who that someone would be. The cabin of the jet had been flooded with light; to look at the clouds or the earth below, you had to wear sunglasses and squint. It was like the instant after you flip a coin, and your heart rate lets you know what you really wanted all along.

"Are you going to tell me why you left?" Richard said.

The tea kettle had begun to whistle, and Lila got a cup and saucer from the drying rack. If she had brought back a young woman she could have introduced her as her daughter, she could have explained. A long time ago, she would have told Richard, on a night that was so cold you couldn't light a match without having the flame freeze, she had given in to something so powerful it was impossible to fight it. She could hold on to the mattress until her fingers turned white, she could scream until her throat was raw, but all the time she did she knew she was just about to surrender. The surrender was unconditional, it lasted forever. But it didn't really matter that she had no proof, no flesh-and-blood child, no one to introduce to him. She was someone's mother, and there was no way to explain that her daughter was a ghost.

"Just tell me what's going on," Richard said. "Is that asking too much?"

Lila opened the cabinet above the stove. She took one look and could feel their marriage dissolving. When she thought now of their wedding day, she couldn't even remember what kind of flowers had grown outside by the kitchen door. There were no longer any teabags in this cabinet; he had rearranged things without once guessing that putting down new shelf paper and moving a few boxes and bowls would make her believe that it was over between them.

"What did you do?" Lila said.

Richard reached for the cabinet nearest the refrigerator and pulled it open. A box of teabags was now stored next to canned vegetables, soup, salt shakers, silverware.

"It's a lot more convenient this way," Richard began to explain.

"How could you do this to me?" Lila said. "How could you go ahead and do this?"

Richard looked at her carefully. He ran one hand through his hair. "This is crazy," he said. "This is true insanity."

It wasn't just the whistle of the kettle that caused the high pitch in the room. It was the tension between them; they couldn't take their eyes off each other, and both of them knew that if they weren't careful someone was about to go too far.

Out in the living room, Rae knew that she had to get out of there, but she didn't know quite how to do it. She had been waiting for someone to come out of the kitchen and dismiss her, preferably Richard. But now she could tell, from the sound of their voices, they had forgotten her. So she did what she thought was only polite. She went to the kitchen door and gently knocked.

"I think I'm going to go now," she called in to them.

"Oh, God," Lila groaned. She could feel Rae draining her energy, just as she had the first time they met. "Will you get her out of here?" she said to Richard.

"She has nothing to do with this," Richard said.

But through the closed door Lila could feel Rae's weight, and the slow movements of her baby as it turned in its sleep. Worst of all she could feel Rae's happiness, and it was that sense of expectation that burned right through Lila, like a jolt of electricity. Without thinking twice, Lila turned to the open cabinet and threw everything on the floor. Salt and silver trinkets saved in a box with a dog's tooth they had found in the garden, three silver knives, a fistful of black tea torn from two teabags, a wishbone, dust. And as Richard watched, horrified by the mess, Lila bent down and mixed it all together, and as she did she secretly wished Rae a labor exactly like her own. Right there in her own kitchen Lila called up pain, fear, suffering, blood, lone-liness, and deceit.

Richard backed her into a corner and said her name three times. But she still wouldn't listen to him.

"Get her out!" Lila said.

Richard swallowed hard, then he went out to the hall-way and helped Rae find her coat in the closet. Lila could hear their voices. Richard was apologizing, she could tell from his tone. He walked Rae to the door, and then Lila heard his footsteps returning. She was pacing the floor when he came back; her nerve endings were so raw that the air against her skin hurt.

"She's gone," Richard said. "We can talk now."

Lila looked at him from the corner of her eye and laughed.

"Please," Richard said. "Just talk to me."

He was begging her, really. But Lila forced herself not to look at him. She couldn't be distracted, not by him or anyone else. When she concentrated she could force her energy out through her fingertips in a flow of heat. She could bring back the ghost of the child who had died in East China.

It was dangerous business. It was walking on the thinnest sort of ice where one false move can make you stumble. And once your foot broke through the ice it was only seconds before you fell through to that place where lost children call to their mothers but can never be found, and even their voices disappear after a while, each cry swallowed whole by the dark. Lila refused to let anything she felt for Richard get in her way, and so she held her breath and she slowly and purposely stepped right over the line of forgiveness.

"Don't you understand anything?" she said to him. "I don't care enough about you to talk."

Richard instantly drew back. Lila had known that he would, but she hadn't expected it to hurt so much. Hannie had had that same wounded look the first time Lila refused to speak to her. Lila had brought over her order of hot water and raisin buns, but when the old woman invited her to join her at the table, Lila pretended not to hear. She had walked away instead, and she hid in the kitchen, near the crates where they stored lettuce. But every time the swinging doors to the kitchen opened, Lila could see out to the rear table and, as she watched, the look on Hannie's face turned to despair—it was a look that assured you the other person knew it was over between you.

Out in the backyard three jays circled the bird feeder before they perched on its farthest edge. Richard stood absolutely still, just as he had on that day she first met him, when the tar bubbled up on the road and sea gulls dared to eat from the palm of her hand. When he left her, Lila tried to hear only one thing—the thin wail of the kettle. But when the front door slammed the sound echoed. And as she stood there, alone in the kitchen, she could not believe what she had done.

She ran after him, but Richard had already gotten into

his car and put it into gear. Lila pushed open the screen door and said his name, but he couldn't hear her now, and she knew it. It was the time of day when the horizon above the city turns violet, the time of year when the air itself is blue and unpredictable. It was easy to forget how deceiving February could be in California—it pretended to be one season just long enough to fool you, then turned itself inside out and delivered what you least expected—a heat wave or a storm. Tonight it felt exactly like summer. There was that lemon-colored light you usually saw in August, and the scent of dried grass and eucalyptus. But for the first time that Lila could remember there wasn't a single rose on the bushes outside the door, and when she looked carefully she could see a milky substance on the leaves, a sure sign of aphids and neglect.

After a while, Lila went inside. She pulled the screen closed and locked the door. Then she carried her suitcase into the bedroom and began to unpack. She had a headache, a bad one. Bad enough so that when she closed her eyes she swore she could see Richard. His car was idling in the parking lot behind the liquor store on La Brea and the radio was turned on. Everyone who walked past could hear it, and it made them self-conscious about going into a liquor store alone. They all wound up buying more to drink than they'd intended, and they thought it was the Ray Charles song on the radio that made them feel like getting really drunk. But it wasn't. It was seeing somebody who looked desperate parked out there in the lot on such a beautiful night that could really get to you, if you let it. Even if the big decision

Richard was working on at that moment was a choice between bourbon and scotch.

Lila took two aspirins from the medicine cabinet in the bathroom before she came back and took off her coat and boots. A jet passed by overhead, and out in someone's yard a dog began to howl. When Lila had unpacked she went to her bureau and picked up the three silver bracelets she had left there. She put them on and they hit against each other, like pieces of ice in a glass. She thought, then, of her father-in-law. It was late in New York, and he was certainly already asleep in the parlor. Richard had told her that on the afternoon of Helen's funeral, Jason Grey had locked himself in a closet and cried. Afterward, they'd had dinner together, a casserole sent over by the wife of the fellow who'd bought Jason's gas station a few years back. Richard had continually looked over at his father, waiting for him to break down again. But he hadn't—he ate some of what was on his plate, had coffee, and went to lie down on the couch in the parlor at a little after eight. Richard slept in his old bedroom. Near midnight he heard something out in back of the house and woke up. He went to the window and saw that his father was out there, digging a hole in the ground with a shovel. The first thing he'd thought, he'd told Lila later, was that his father was digging his own grave. That night the moon was orange and full and Richard had been certain that the reason his father had not appeared to be grieving during dinner was that he'd been planning to bury himself alive.

Richard had stood at the window, unable to move. Outside, Jason Grey stopped digging; he leaned on his shovel and looked up at the sky. That was when Richard could see that the hole his father had been digging was much too small for a grave, even for something the size of a small dog. Jason took something out of his pocket. Richard pressed his face against the window and he could see that his father held a palm full of jewelry. It was Helen Grey's jewelry—her wedding ring, a small aquamarine brooch, a strand of seed pearls, a silver locket in the shape of a heart. Jason Grey knelt down and carefully buried the jewelry in the ground. But then he didn't go away—he just stood there, and he was standing there long after Richard had turned and gone back to bed.

When he'd come home to Los Angeles a few days later, Richard told Lila that at the moment when his father knelt on the damp ground, he'd had the sense that something was about to begin. It wasn't until the following morning that he realized what he'd felt was the start of his father's grief, the beginning of something that would take years to complete.

Lila sat on the edge of the bed and took off her silver bracelets. She felt terribly moved by the thought of her father-in-law out in his backyard, in the dark, opening his hands and trying to let his wife go. But, the truth was, it wasn't the same. Outside, the dog who had been chained up tugged on his lead and whined. The sky was dark now, you couldn't even see the birds who were nesting in the lemon tree for the night. There was simply no loss that compared to the death of a child. It was the one death that contained a thousand more within itself. An unbreakable ring, the end of everything your child might have been, the girl of ten, the woman of twenty, the one loss you just cannot bring yourself to believe.

If Lila had been there, if she'd felt her daughter grow cold, if she'd been the one forced to search all over East China for a coffin small enough, she might have accepted it by now. She might have been able to take her father-in-law's advice to let the dead go, even though afterward there would have been marks on her palms from the wrenching of letting go, small pinpoints that let in air and never seemed to heal. But instead of mourning what had been lost, Lila reached into her suitcase and took out her daughter's sweater. She held it in her hands and she closed her eyes until she couldn't see anything but white light. And as she sat there on the edge of the bed she could feel the material in her hands begin to grow warmer—so she closed her eyes tighter and willed her daughter to come to her.

Richard came home after eleven. He'd had more to drink than he could ever remember. He parked his car in the driveway and carefully maneuvered his way up the dark path. There wasn't a sound in the street, just his unsteady footsteps on the cement. When he got to the front door he just couldn't bring himself to go inside. He sat down on the porch steps, between the two rose bushes, and tried to figure out what had gone wrong.

Lila knew that he was back. She realized that all she had to do was make one move and all the others would follow. Just get out of bed, then put on her robe, then walk down the hallway and unlatch the front door. But she couldn't do it, she couldn't let her thoughts be swayed for a second. Her thoughts had to be as pure as light. And so she didn't move when she heard him push the latch up on the screen door, then unlock the front door.

He stood outside the closed bedroom door for a while, and then he went to the linen closet in the hallway and got some sheets. He undressed in the living room, in the dark. Just before he was about to lie down on the couch Richard realized that he smelled something burning. He followed the smell into the kitchen, where it turned overpoweringly bitter. The kitchen was dark, except for a circle of blue light that seemed somehow dangerous. For a split second, Richard found that he was afraid. But then he switched on the overhead light and saw that the blue circle was only the gas burner on the stove, turned on and forgotten. The water in the kettle had boiled away and the tin bottom was charred and smoking. Richard turned off the gas and put the kettle in the sink. He turned on the cold water and there was a rush of steam as the hot metal sizzled. When the kettle had cooled down, Richard tossed it in the trash, but even after he had opened the window the burning scent was still there, clinging to the curtains and the walls.

Richard didn't bother to put the sheets on the couch. He lay there, unable to sleep, imagining the way Lila used to look. The first time he saw her he knew there could never be anyone else, and the first time he had made love to her, he had actually cried—that's how much he'd wanted her. Every night he watched as she brushed her hair a hundred strokes with a wire brush. And he simply couldn't stop watching her, not even after she had fallen asleep. As she slept she reached out for him, she did it every night, just as every night Richard pulled her a little closer until it seemed there was only one person asleep in their bed and only one heart beating.

But on this night Lila didn't reach out for her husband, she didn't even think about him. She lay in their bed and concentrated so hard that she could feel the room spin. Her blood moved faster and faster; her fingertips began to burn. After a while Lila could feel herself growing weaker, and she knew she didn't have much more to give. The sheets beneath her were soaked with sweat and she could feel she was just about to break—her bones were rising up to the surface like fish, her skin simply couldn't contain energy like this. And just as she was about to give up, Lila felt something move in her arms. She ground her teeth and refused to give up. She concentrated even harder, imagining every tiny finger and toe, recalling each second after her baby's birth—the shape of her cheek, the dark eyelashes, the odor of blood and milk. At last, Lila felt a weight on the bed next to her. She held her breath and when she opened her eyes she could see, even in the dark, that her daughter was finally beside her.

The baby's eyes were closed, her eyelids as white as stones. Slowly, the lids fluttered, and two perfect slate-gray eyes stared up at Lila. There was an outline of light all around the baby. Even when Lila held her tighter underneath a white sheet, the outline remained. And Lila wept when she realized that her daughter knew her, she cried so many tears that in no time at all both she and her child were coated with salt.

Out in the hallway you could see the light that surrounded the baby escape from under the bedroom door. It spread out all along the floor, into the other rooms of the house. Richard might have seen it if he hadn't been on his back, staring at the ceiling. He wished that he were holding his wife, but by now it was after midnight and Richard wouldn't have dreamed of disturbing Lila, any more than Lila would have thought to call out his name. Richard fell right asleep, maybe because he knew that he'd be sleeping out in the living room for a long time. And every night after that, before he went to sleep, Richard stood outside the bedroom door for a moment, and every night Lila heard him. But neither of them could go to the other; a thin sheet of glass had sprung up between them, and it separated them until they were as distant from each other as they were from the stars.

• • •

At the beginning of her eighth month, Rae woke up one morning and decided that she wouldn't go through with it after all. It wasn't being pregnant, she had gotten used to that—the insomnia, the heartburn, the pressure on her bladder, the way she had to get down on her knees every time she wanted to pick her shoes up off the floor. It was the idea of labor that terrified her. Throughout her life there had been a conspiracy, and there was still a secret she'd never been told. Lately, women with small children had begun to smile at her for no reason at all. Rae had thought it was sympathy—she was so lumbering and huge—or a particularly sweet memory of the time when their own child was about to be born. Now she realized it was something more—a moment of compassion for the uninitiated, a spinning backward through time to their own innocence. No one had ever told Rae the truth about childbirth. Not her Lamaze instructor, not her doctor, not her own mother. No one had bothered to suggest to her just how much it might hurt.

She'd done the practical things—read child-care books, renewed her insurance coverage, interviewed day-care mothers, even gone to a parenting course at U.C.L.A., where she'd given a doll a bath in a plastic washtub and pretended to insert a thermometer to check for fever. Still, the idea of holding an infant in her arms scared her. She had never even changed a diaper. The one time when she had baby-sat, she'd been lost. She'd sat for a nine-month-old boy who lived down the block from her parents' house, and he'd been asleep when she arrived. Rae was sixteen, and madly in love with Jessup, and she'd arranged for him to come over an hour after the child's parents had gone to the movies. They were on the couch, kissing, when the baby woke up. There'd been no warning, no slow escalation of louder and louder cries—suddenly the baby was screaming his head off, as if he had been stuck with pins.

"Oh, shit," Jessup had said. He sat up and threw his head back against the couch. "Why did I bother to come over here?"

Rae ran upstairs and peeked into the nursery. A night-light gave off a purplish glow. From the doorway, Rae could see the baby standing up, holding on to the bars of his crib, screaming in a way that turned her blood cold. Rae stood there for a moment, then ran back downstairs. She found

Jessup in the kitchen, looking through the refrigerator for a beer. When he saw Rae he was surprised.

"Why didn't you shut him up?" Jessup asked.

"I don't know how to," Rae said.

Jessup found a six-pack. He took out a can and pulled off the tab. "Did you change his diaper?" he said.

Rae could feel the baby's screams inside her skin. "I can't," she admitted. "I never did it before."

"You can't?" Jessup said. "You took this job and you don't even know how to change a diaper?"

Rae looked away from him and shrugged.

"What about feeding him?"

"I don't know how to," Rae had said in a small voice.

"Jesus Christ, Rae," Jessup said to her. "Don't invite me to any more of your jobs, all right?"

He slammed his beer down on the counter, got a bottle of formula out of the refrigerator, warmed it, then left her there in tears. She felt absolutely desperate—the pitch of the baby's cry had grown worse, and Rae imagined covering his mouth with her hand and shaking him until he stopped. But after a few minutes, the crying stopped, and Rae took off her shoes so she could creep back upstairs. By the time she got to the nursery, Jessup had changed the baby's diaper and he was sitting in the rocking chair feeding the baby his bottle. Rae stood in the doorway and listened to the squeak of the rocking chair and the greedy sound of the baby's swallowing. After a while she felt like an intruder, so she went back downstairs and sat on the couch.

Jessup came down after the baby was asleep. He got his

beer, sat down next to Rae, and put his boots up on the coffee table.

"How did you do that?" Rae said to him.

"Do what?" Jessup said, as though he had never left her side.

They'd heard the key in the lock then, and Jessup had immediately leapt to his feet. He ran into the kitchen and was out the back door before the baby's parents had set foot in the house. But they saw the open beer can on the coffee table and, to Rae's great relief, they told her they'd see to it that she never baby-sat for anyone in the neighborhood ever again.

Afterward she tried to get Jessup to explain how he'd known what to do.

"I've got a couple of cousins," Jessup had said with a shrug. "Every kid is the same—when they pee you change their diaper. Then you give them something to eat so they can pee again and you can change their diaper again. It's no big deal."

Still, there was one thing Rae couldn't figure out—how Jessup had known to put the baby over his shoulder after he'd had his bottle, and gently rub his back until he fell asleep. Rae had been right there, standing in the doorway, but the room had been dark and there had been that purple, misleading glow of light, and after a while she guessed that she'd been seeing things. Maybe Jessup hadn't been as gentle as she'd imagined. Maybe he hadn't actually been humming, and she had also imagined the sound of a lullaby that was so sweet you knew you weren't meant to overhear.

She was missing him more these days, she was even dreaming about him. She dreamed that she was out in the desert, late at night, when there wasn't a soul around. The Oldsmobile was parked in a dusty field, and Rae sat on its hood, looking at the sky. She heard hoofbeats then, and she knew even before she saw it that it was one of Jessup's horses, smaller than a pony, with a coat that was the same blue-black color as the night. The horse came up right alongside her, and Rae could tell that Jessup had sent him to her. She waited, and after a while the horse spoke to her and told her that Jessup was being held captive. They stood there in the dark and both of them began to cry. Their tears formed a pool, and when Rae bent to look she saw that there were silvery fish swimming in circles, shimmering in the dark water. And when Rae looked even closer she noticed that where each fish's gills should be there was a tiny arm, and a hundred babies' hands paddled in the water.

Another time she dreamed that she and Jessup were making love, and when she woke she missed him more than ever, and all that morning she was weak in the knees, as though she had just come from her lover's bed. Missing Jessup was bad enough, what made it worse was that everyone around Rae was so distant and preoccupied. Freddy Contina didn't even go home any more. He worked till midnight and slept in his office, and he still couldn't figure out why no theater would release the films he'd brought back from Europe. Rae couldn't talk to him, and she couldn't talk to Richard any more either. Something was so wrong with Richard you could feel it just by touching his hand. When he knelt down beside Rae in Lamaze class his unhappiness interrupted Rae's concentration, and she often lost count of how many breaths she had taken. After class, as they walked out to the parking lot together, Rae always felt as if she were alone. She tried to talk to Richard about Lila, but he refused. "Don't even think about her," he told Rae. "Don't be concerned." But Rae couldn't help it, she was concerned. And sometimes, late at night, Rae wondered if she might have to pay for the sorrow on Lila's face when she walked in and saw them in the living room, a look that made Rae think of the way she used to look at Jessup when she knew he was about to go somewhere and leave her all alone.

She still couldn't quite believe Jessup wasn't coming back. She began to actively try to erase him from her mind. She took all his old clothes to a mission downtown and filled out a change-of-address card for him at the post office. She no longer ran to the window when she heard something that sounded like his footsteps; on the anniversary of the day he'd first kissed her she went to the Chinese take-out place around the corner and ordered everything he hated: shrimp with black bean sauce, spicy eggplant, mysterious flavored chicken.

On a Sunday early in March, when she had nearly managed to forget him, Rae got out of the shower and heard a knock at the door. She just stood there with a towel wrapped around her head. For a moment, right before she threw on her bathrobe and answered the door, she felt a surge of heat near her heart. She knew exactly who she wanted it to be out there in the courtyard, and after she opened the door and saw that it was only Jessup's partner, Hal, she was so disappointed it showed.

Hal had been out there for a while, trying to summon up the nerve to knock. He had brought her carnations which had been dipped in red dye, and the flowers made it impossible for Rae to turn him away. She made him some coffee, then went into the bathroom and got dressed. When she came back to the kitchen he was still stirring his coffee, and he seemed much more interested in the way Rae arranged the carnations than he did in having something to drink. She sat down across from him at the table and watched him carefully.

"Jessup didn't send you here, did he?" Rae asked. "Maybe he wanted you to see if I was all right or if I needed anything."

"Jessup?" Hal said, confused.

Rae put her elbows on the table and tried to smile. "I didn't think so," she said.

"I guess I just feel guilty," Hal said. "If he had told me about you I would have never asked him to come in on the ranch with me. To tell you the truth, I'm sorry I did ask him." Hal took a sip of his coffee and shook his head. "That goddamned Jessup. Whenever he runs out of something— like dishes or clean clothes—he acts so damned surprised, like there's an unlimited supply of everything. I'm telling you—no one can live with him."

"I did," Rae said.

"Well, you were in love with him," Hal said. He spooned more sugar into his coffee. Then, as if something had suddenly dawned on him, he said, "Don't tell me you still are?"

"If you're here because you think you broke us up, forget it," Rae said.

"I'd just like to help you out," Hal said.

He wasn't looking at her, so Rae could study him all she wanted. "Why?" she finally asked.

He seemed genuinely surprised by her question, and it took a while before he answered.

"Why shouldn't I?" he said.

"I don't know," Rae said.

"I could come visit you once in a while and take care of things," Hal said. "Maybe I just feel like doing something for you."

Rae promised him she'd think about it, and when there was a knock on her door the following Sunday, she didn't have any expectations. She knew exactly who it was. She let him carry the laundry downstairs and change the oil in the Oldsmobile, but it just made things worse. And when she walked him out to the pickup he and Jessup had bought, Rae felt a rush of desire. The truck was red, and Rae was certain that Jessup had been the one who'd chosen the color. She sounded sincere when she thanked Hal for all his help, but all she could think about was Jessup, sitting at the counter of the Dunkin' Donuts in Barstow, watching that waitress, Paulette, from the corner of his eye.

Later, when she got into bed, Rae could tell she would have nightmares. She thought she would dream about the men in her life: Jessup would turn his back on her; Hal would knock at her window, waking her from a sound sleep; Richard would drive to the wrong hospital, leaving her waiting at the admitting desk, in labor and all alone. But that night Rae dreamed of Lila, and when she woke she was frightened the way she had been as a little girl, when she cried in her sleep and wanted her mother and no one else would do. Night after night Rae dreamed of Lila: she had a fever that could not be broken until Lila appeared; she was lost in a garden, and even though she could see Lila's house in the distance, every path led right back to the same locust grove. When she had been plagued by bad dreams as a child, Carolyn had taught her some tricks to chase them away. On the nights she felt she might have nightmares she was to wash her hair with lemon juice, and take some sewing or embroidery to bed, to work on just before she fell asleep. But now when she rinsed her hair the lemon juice always smelled bitter, and every time she picked up the embroidery needle she bought at the drugstore, she stuck her finger and drew blood.

After a few nights, the drops of blood that had fallen as Rae tried to work her embroidery formed the shape of a heart on her sheets, and she knew that if things kept on this way there would be only bad luck. But even when she willed herself not to have any dreams during the few hours each night that she slept, it wasn't enough. She did not expect Lila to agree to be at the baby's birth, but she might at least get her blessing. And so one evening, when she had cooked dinner but could not eat, Rae got into her car, and she drove without stopping to Three Sisters Street.

Richard's Volkswagen wasn't in the driveway, and that made Rae hesitate. But he was rarely there any more. Whenever he couldn't find a good excuse to work overtime he went and parked in the lot behind the liquor store. He didn't bother to go in and buy something to drink. He just parked and listened to the radio and avoided going home. When he did finally come home, Lila always knew. She froze the instant his car turned the corner, she could feel his weight as he came up the brick path to the door. It was not as difficult as she had thought it would be to live in the same house with someone and have nothing to do with him. If she and Richard met accidentally, in the hallway or the kitchen, Lila lowered her eyes and silently counted to a hundred, and by that time Richard had usually left the room. Every time Richard came into the house, and before he fell asleep on the couch, Lila made certain to keep the dresser drawer where her daughter slept closed. But as soon as she could she opened the drawer and picked up her baby, and sometimes, when she felt particularly brave, she took her outside and they sat together underneath the lemon tree.

The evening that Rae came to see her, Lila was sitting in the chair in her bedroom, rocking her daughter to sleep. She could feel someone walk up the brick path, and she knew it wasn't Richard. She got up and carefully put her daughter back in the drawer and covered her with a silk scarf that was so soft it slipped through your fingers. Then she put on her robe and went into the living room. She stood close to the wall, beside the drapes, and she lifted a fold of material so that she could look outside.

Rae's weight made her walk off-balance, and when she came up the porch steps she held on to the banister. Lately, she had developed a fear of falling, and she took each step gingerly, her left arm circling her belly protectively. Lila could almost see inside Rae to the baby she was carrying. Its eyes were closed, but it was moving its fingers, making a fist, then letting go. Already it had eyelashes, fingernails, a cap of soft down on its head. Beside this baby Lila's own child grew more ghostly, and Lila could tell, just thinking about Rae's baby sapped her child's strength: in the dresser drawer her daughter was right now struggling for breath.

When Rae rang the bell, Lila stood behind the drapes and hid. Rae waited on the porch for longer than Lila had expected—nearly fifteen minutes. When she'd been there long enough to feel foolish, Rae turned and walked back to her parked car. Lila stood with her back against the wall; she wiped her eyes with the hem of the drapes. And later, when Lila summoned up the courage to pull back the drapes and look outside, there wasn't one single sign that anyone had come to see her, and no one who wasn't looking carefully would have noticed that there were at least a dozen new buds on the rosebushes at the front door, and that each and every one of them was blood red.

· · ·

Hal and Rae had spent an entire morning shopping for a crib, going from one baby store to another. As the morning wore on, Rae began to feel more and more defeated. Everything was so expensive, so foreign. There were things she had never seen before—crib bumpers, walkers, infant seats with buckles and bells. All morning the baby had been pushing against her ribs, and when Hal asked her if she liked a particular crib, Rae turned on him.

"Why can't you just leave me alone?" she said before she stomped away. The pressure inside her grew worse then, and she wound up sitting on the floor, knees pulled up, hands shaking. She didn't know if she liked the crib or not because she didn't know what there was to like about it. In the end, she just pointed a finger at a wooden crib that didn't look any different from the rest and said she would take it.

As Hal loaded the crib into the rear of the pickup, Rae practiced her deep breathing in the parking lot. On the way home she was certain that if Hal said one word to her she would jump out of the moving truck. He wouldn't let her help him carry the crib across the courtyard, and once he had managed to get it inside they were both amazed by how much room it took up. They stood there watching it, hypnotized. Finally, Hal cleared his throat.

"That's some crib," he said appraisingly.

"I guess so," Rae said.

She sat down on the edge of the bed and ran one hand through her hair.

"I must be crazy," she said.

"I'll tell you what's crazy," Hal said. "We're making money. It's especially hard to believe because it was all Jessup's idea—we started advertising in *Variety* and in the *Times*. Go on and guess what *the* birthday present for kids in Beverly Hills is these days."

Rae looked up at him.

"Our horses," Hal said. "We deliver them wearing birthday hats."

Hal reached for his wallet and carefully peeled off ten hundred-dollar bills. He placed them at the foot of the bed.

ALICE HOFFMAN

"Don't do this," Rae warned him. "Don't you feel sorry for me."

"I'm not," Hal swore. "Listen, this is Jessup's money—only he doesn't know it."

"Really?" Rae said, interested.

"I'm in charge of the finances," Hal told her.

They smiled at each other then.

"I guess he owes me something," Rae agreed.

"I told you to get those bumpers for the crib," Hal said. "I told you they weren't too expensive."

"You know, you shouldn't be here," Rae said. "You should be out finding somebody of your own."

"That's okay," Hal said.

"I really mean it, Hal," Rae told him.

"I know you do," he nodded. "And I'm not expecting anything."

So Rae picked up the money he had given her, and she counted it twice. But she knew that you could easily say you weren't expecting anything, and still not quite believe you weren't really going to get it if you waited long enough.

That night they went out for an early dinner to celebrate the crib. The restaurant had once been a guest house on the edge of the Sisters' estate; they sat in the garden at a white wrought-iron table, and Rae insisted they order the most expensive items on the menu, since it was Jessup who was really paying. At first it was a joke, but by the time they had ordered dessert, Rae couldn't get Jessup off her mind. She actually ordered apple pie, which she hated, just because it was Jessup's favorite.

"Not that I'd take him back," she told Hal. "Imagine me

250

having a baby with Jessup in the room watching. I'd have to worry about how awful I looked, and he'd be so horrible he'd probably ask me to jump off the bed and run out to get him a glass of ice water."

"You won't look awful," Hal said innocently. "You'll be beautiful."

"Oh, yeah?" Rae said coldly. "You're just the type of man who thinks a woman could be beautiful while she was up there on some hospital bed being tortured. I'll bet you want the woman you're with to be beautiful all the time— I'll bet that's why that girlfriend of yours left you."

Hal put down his fork. "Who said she left me?"

Hal wasn't the one she wanted to hurt, so there really was no point in this. "You know what?" Rae said tiredly. "I think I want to go home."

Hal looked so distraught as they walked through the parking lot, that Rae took his arm.

"I'll tell you how I knew," she said. "I was left, too, and it takes one to know one."

"I thought I was giving you a compliment," Hal said.

"I know you did," Rae said. "Don't pay any attention to me. It's living with Jessup for so long—it's made me mean."

As they drove back on Sunset, Rae felt nervous. Everything was reminding her of Jessup—the sand on the floor of the truck, the shadows on the street. After a while she noticed that Hal was studying something in the rearview mirror. She leaned over and looked.

"Oh, shit," Rae said. "Is it him?"

Hal nodded and kept on driving. "I can't believe this fucking guy—he's got my car," he said.

For some reason, they both had the feeling they had done something wrong, and they spoke to each other in whispers.

"What are we going to do?" Rae said.

"What can we do?" Hal said, because by then they were stopped at a red light.

Jessup got out of Hal's Ford and slammed the door behind him. He left the Ford idling hard and came up and knocked on Rae's window. Rae looked at Hal and he leaned over and rolled her window down.

"What the hell is this supposed to be?" Jessup said.

"We went out to dinner," Hal said.

"Oh, really?" Jessup said. "How long has this been going on?"

"There's nothing going on," Hal said. He looked at Rae for a second, measuring what he was about to say. "But you know, while we're at it," he said to Jessup. "How about Paulette?"

"Paulette!" Jessup said. "Paulette is nothing."

"Come on, Jessup," Hal said. "Who do you think you're talking to—idiots?"

"I'll tell you what I'd really like to know," Jessup said. Rae wasn't looking at him, but she could tell by his tone that he was talking to her. "I'd like to know why you're too afraid to look at me."

Rae turned to him then, and as coolly as she could she said, "I'm looking at you now."

"Yeah?" Jessup said. "Well, take a good look."

As they stared at each other the light turned green; behind them someone sounded a horn. Without turning,

Jessup raised his arm and signaled for the driver to go around them.

"Do you know what today is?" Jessup said to Rae.

The driver behind them leaned on his horn. Jessup jumped away from the pickup.

"Drive around us, you asshole," he called.

Hal leaned over toward Rae. "We don't have to sit here and take this from him," he said.

Jessup stuck his head in Rae's window again. The muscles in his jaw were tightening, the way they always did when he was upset.

"Today's my birthday, Rae," he said.

"Do you believe this?" Hal said. "Who does this guy think he is?"

"Do you really want me to spend my birthday alone?" Jessup asked Rae.

"What about Paulette?" Rae said before she could stop herself, and anyone could tell how interested she was no matter how cool she sounded. Next to her she could feel Hal sink down a little behind the steering wheel.

Jessup knew he had just had a small victory, and he grinned. "Come on," he said. "Let's go celebrate."

Rae swallowed hard, then turned to Hal. "I'm sorry," she said. "It's his birthday."

Jessup was walking around to the driver's door. He opened it and waited for Hal to get out.

"I appreciate everything you've done for me," Rae said to Hal.

"I don't need your appreciation," Hal said.

He got out, and Jessup stood aside so that Hal could

walk back to the Ford. Then Jessup got into the truck. He pulled the door closed and took off. Rae leaned over to look in the rearview mirror and she could see Hal getting into his Ford, waving his hands at the line of cars waiting behind him.

"Well, I did it," Jessup said. He lit a cigarette and rolled down his window. "Just under the wire, before I turned thirty. I made it." He reached into his pocket, and for a moment the truck veered into the oncoming lane. "Take a look," Jessup said. He held up a billfold and smiled. "Thirty years old and I'm a success."

"Congratulations," Rae said.

"I told you I would be," Jessup said.

"I don't know," Rae said. "I just feel terrible about Hal."

"Let me tell you something about Hal," Jessup said. "He wants what anybody else has."

Rae gave Jessup a look.

"Or used to have," Jessup amended. "You know what I mean—whatever happens, we'll always be involved. It is my baby you're having, if I'm not mistaken."

"You're not mistaken," Rae said.

"There you go," Jessup nodded.

He pulled the car over when they passed a liquor store.

"Wait right here," he said, and he was gone before she could tell him not to.

Waiting there for him felt wrong. She had the feeling that this had all happened a hundred times before, only she'd been a different person.

Jessup jumped back into the pickup and put two bottles of Spanish champagne under his seat.

"What is that?" Rae said.

"That is champagne," Jessup said. "We're going back to the apartment to get drunk."

"I can't drink," Rae said. "I'm pregnant."

Jessup turned to her, annoyed. "It's my birthday," he said.

"I know," Rae said. "You keep reminding me."

"Yeah, well you sure didn't remember on your own."

Then Rae felt contrite—she had never forgotten his birthday before, but lately the only date she could remember was her baby's due date.

"All right," Rae said finally. "Let's go home."

They didn't talk for the rest of the ride. Once, Jessup caught Rae staring at him, and they both laughed, and it almost seemed like it was going to be all right. But as soon as Jessup had parked the car, Rae could tell it just wasn't the same as it used to be. She simply didn't trust him.

Jessup followed her across the courtyard, a champagne bottle in each hand. He was studying her as she unlocked the door and finally he said, "You sure do look pregnant."

Rae looked at him briefly, then pushed open the door.

When Jessup saw the crib, he put the champagne bottles down on the bureau, then walked over and ran his hand over the wooden bars. Rae had the strongest sense that he was about to say something important. But when he spoke it was only to tell her he was dying of thirst.

She went into the kitchen for glasses. Later she managed to act as if she was drinking by occasionally raising her glass to her lips. She was right to assume that Jessup wouldn't even notice that the only glass he kept refilling was his own.

"Why are you staying so far away from me?" Jessup asked her.

He was sitting on the edge of the bed. Rae was in the easy chair, watching him drink.

"I'm comfortable here," Rae shrugged.

"Like hell," Jessup said. "You're afraid of what might happen if you come a little closer."

Rae got up and went to sit next to him; balancing on the edge of the bed with nothing to support her strained her back. As he leaned toward her Rae thought about the first time he had ever kissed her. It was so cold that icicles had formed on all the streetlights. She really hadn't expected it; Jessup had been waiting for her outside the high school, and Rae left the girls she usually walked home with on the steps and ran to meet him. They walked along in silence, Jessup didn't even look at her, and Rae had to struggle to keep up with him on the slippery sidewalk. Then he'd turned on her, for no reason at all.

"Did you see the way they looked at me?" he said.

"Who?" Rae asked. They hadn't passed anyone on the street.

"Your friends," Jessup said. "That's who. You'd have to be blind not to notice."

"They didn't look at you," Rae said, although she expected they had, and that, by now, they had already dissected him right there on the steps of the school.

"Don't give me that crap," Jessup said.

"All right," Rae said. "They looked because they're jealous."

Jessup looked over at her.

"They are," Rae insisted.

"Bullshit," Jessup said, but she could tell he was buying it.

"I swear," Rae said, "they are."

"There's nothing to be jealous of," Jessup said then. "We're nothing to each other."

Rae looked down at the sidewalk.

"I'm warning you right now," Jessup said, "so you don't get hurt."

When he kissed her Rae knew that she was supposed to close her eyes, but she couldn't. She had to look at him to make certain it was really happening to her because she knew that when this first kiss was over, Jessup would back away and act as if nothing between them had changed.

This time, Rae was the one who backed away. Jessup looked at her, then reached down and pulled off his boots.

"What are you doing?" Rae said.

Jessup stood up and unbuttoned his shirt.

"What does it look like I'm doing?" he said.

"You really do think I'm stupid," Rae said.

"Go ahead," Jessup said. "Try and tell yourself you don't want me here."

"You should have gone out with Paulette," Rae said. "You would have had a much better birthday with her."

"Will you just forget about Paulette?" Jessup said. "In the first place she just got engaged to some cowboy."

Rae bent down and got Jessup's boots, then she walked across the room, opened the front door, and threw them out into the courtyard.

"Wait a minute!" Jessup said.

Rae stood at the open door and fanned herself to cool off.

"I told you this was going to happen to you," Jessup said. "I told you if you went ahead and got pregnant everything would change. You're not even thinking straight."

"You selfish bastard," Rae said. "If you think selling a few crummy horses means you're not a failure, you're wrong."

Jessup looked at her for a moment, then he buttoned his shirt and tucked it in. "Nobody talks to me like that," he said, and he walked right past her.

"Get out!" Rae said, even though she knew it sounded ridiculous—he already was standing in the courtyard. As she was about to slam the door behind him, Jessup grabbed it so it wouldn't budge.

"You had to go and do this on my birthday," he said. "You had to get back at me."

He spoke softly, almost in a whisper, but all the same Rae could tell that his voice was breaking. That was when she knew that he had come back because he needed her. On any other night it would have felt like a victory, but tonight she just felt sorry for him, and feeling that way about Jessup was the worst sort of betrayal there was. When she watched him walk across the courtyard he seemed hunched over, and Rae had the urge to run after him. But instead she closed the door and listened for his truck to start and drive away. She wondered if on that night in Boston when he told her he was leaving he had been holding his breath, desperate for her to beg to go with him. He had hidden it so well, all Rae had seen was endless courage, hot nights, a look that could make her do anything. But tonight Jessup was a thirty-year-old man who couldn't stay still long enough to last in one place. Someone who, when there was no one beside him in the passenger seat on the long ride out into the desert, wound up talking to himself for comfort. Someone who was totally exhausted when he got into the lower bunk bed in his trailer and found he still couldn't sleep.

Rae had been sure that she wouldn't be able to sleep either, but she was in bed and fast asleep long before Jessup reached the freeway. It wasn't that she didn't care any more—she did. But everything was different, in spite of what she felt. As she was falling asleep, Rae tried to picture Jessup's face and couldn't. Instead, she kept seeing the crib that was pushed up against the wall. With her eyes half closed the slats of the crib cast blue shadows across the room, and every time the headlights of a car out on the street flickered the shadows moved like water.

Sometime near dawn, Rae dreamed that she was with her mother at the house in Wellfleet. It was low tide, and you could hear the birds in the salt marsh beyond the house. They were out on the porch, and Carolyn was wearing a white summer dress, one she had owned years earlier, before Rae was born. They were facing the channel beside the marsh. It was an inlet, which whales sometimes mistook for deeper water; often, they got lost among the reeds and beached themselves, one after another. Now the channel was empty, and as smooth as glass. After a while, Rae realized that her mother was no longer beside her. When she found she was alone, Rae felt unusually calm. She leaned over the porch railing and listened to the birds, and when she looked again toward the reeds she saw that her mother's white dress was in the water, floating at the edge of the marsh, luminous as the moon.

In the morning, Rae woke up slowly. There was already the echo of traffic out on the boulevards, and a buzzing sound from one of the kitchen windows as a bee bounced against the screen. It wasn't until she got out of bed that Rae began to feel that something had changed: swinging her legs over the mattress was more difficult, walking across the room to get her robe was treacherous. Even when she looked at herself in the full-length mirror in the bathroom, it took a while before Rae realized that it was her own body that had changed. Before, all her weight had been high up, her belly pushed up toward her breasts. But sometime in the night everything had moved down—the baby had dropped, its head was down so far Rae could feel it resting against her pelvic bones. Rae let her bathrobe fall onto the tiled floor just so that she could look at herself. She stayed there so long that anyone would have thought she was terribly vain, but it was just that for the first time that she could remember she didn't wish for anything other than what she already had, and what she had was less than four weeks to go before her baby was born.

. . .

Lila and Richard had learned to be polite to each other, but their civility was so chilling it made their skins crawl. When they really tried they could actually manage to have a meal together in the same room. All they had to do was remember not to look at each other, not to ask each other for the simplest favors, not even to pass the salt, and under no circumstances could they even begin to think about what they had once had.

Nothing on earth could have made Lila turn to her husband, nothing could force her to go to him now and admit that something frightening had begun to happen—she had begun to have visions. These were no orderly prophecies that appeared when beckoned, they came suddenly, at odd hours of the day and night, and they turned time into a wicked thing. There was no way to tell if something was about to happen, or if it had already come to pass. Lila never knew if she was really in her own kitchen, pouring juice into a glass, or if she was on the banks of a frozen bay, watching her first lover, Stephen, walk past the ice fishermen on his way home. In the afternoons, when she went out to water the geraniums, Lila saw her mother out on the patio with two other girls, all of them so young you could practically hear them counting the days until summer. When she dusted in the living room there was Rae, leaning over a bassinet to croon her restless baby to sleep. Each time she went into the bathroom and turned on the light she saw herself putting the stopper in the sink and running the cold water, before she reached for the straight-edged razor and studied her own submerged arm.

These visions brought blinding headaches and a peculiar chill that wouldn't go away. Now Lila knew why Hannie had always worn too many layers of clothing: black skirts, leather boots, sweaters, shawls. Time, Hannie had told her, grew more delicate as you got older, it was so tissue thin you could hold your hand up to the light and see how tapered the fingers had been at twenty-five, how the palms had been scratched by a fall into the brambles on the morning of your eighth birthday.

Sitting at the rear table, Lila had felt more and more uncomfortable as Hannie talked about getting old.

"There must be some way to stop it," she said.

It was a foolish remark, but Hannie didn't laugh. She nodded and bit a sugar cube in half, keeping one half between her thumb and forefinger, the other in her cheek to dissolve.

"There is a way," she told Lila. The fortune-teller's eyes were small, and a little too bright, so that people sometimes had to look away from her for no reason at all. "But I wouldn't wish it on you."

Lila got it into her head that Hannie knew some secret way to stay young, and already, at eighteen, she knew that certain men, like Stephen, couldn't tolerate a woman's growing old. Lila imagined that the secret was a lotion, a cream made of roses and diluted water and fruit, or a powder you dusted over each eyelid before you went to sleep. For days she pestered Hannie; she swore she wouldn't tell another soul. Hannie avoided answering; instead she told Lila the ingredients of the beauty treatments women in her village had sworn by: egg whites left on your face for one hour, cinnamon under your pillow, tea leaves mixed into your shampoo. But none of this was what Lila wanted, and she brought it up again and again, until Hannie finally gave in.

"When I was a child," Hannie told her, "there was a

woman who was so beautiful that ravens used to come to her window just to see her. At night when she went inside the moon grew duller, the frogs who sat on her front porch never made bellowing noises like the ones by the river— they sat there silently, as though they were waiting for a glimpse of her feet underneath the crack of the door. Her husband adored her, her children refused to let go of her skirts because she smelled like lavender and sweet butter. She was so beautiful that no one was jealous of her, and others enjoyed her good fortune as if it were their own.

"But then something went wrong. She cried all day and all night, there were dark circles around her eyes and her skin looked like ashes in the chimney. This is what happened: She had found some gray hairs, and that had caused her to look even closer. When she borrowed a mirror from her mother-in-law she saw wrinkles that she had never noticed before, she saw that she had begun to grow old. She wrapped herself in a quilt and slept on the wooden floor, weeping in her sleep. Her children grew thin, her husband began to lose his hair. And then, one day, she suddenly seemed herself again, only now she smiled shyly, as though she had a secret. Everyone in the village watched carefully, everyone knew that something was about to happen, and sure enough, on their way to the schoolhouse one morning, the children found her body hanging from a pine tree. She had hung herself with a white silk scarf, the same scarf she had worn at her wedding. They buried her the very same day, and from then on she was talked about so much that everyone could still see her: all they had to do was close their eyes. In time her husband came out of mourning, her children recalled her tenderly, the men in the village talked about her each time they sat down by the river and got drunk. All the women in the village knew that she had managed to stay beautiful—she had simply paid a price she would have had to pay anyway, a little later on when her skin was all wrinkled and her hair so white you couldn't see her when she bent over in the snow. And all the young women envied her courage, but the old women looked at each other and knew her for the fool that she was."

Lila knew it was true—her daughter was the only one who didn't get lost in her confusion of time. The baby was always the same, quietly sitting on Lila's lap out in the garden, or waiting to be picked up from her bed in the dresser drawer. But the visions drained Lila's energy, and she went to her daughter less and less often. Sometimes she simply pulled a chair up beside the dresser and watched her daughter sleep. All day long she sat on a hardbacked chair, guarding her daughter, and when she went to sleep her dreams were murky so that in the morning she could never remember them.

Each day she was more on edge, and one evening in March, when the air was light and clean and the acacia tree in their neighbor's yard had begun to flower, Lila suddenly couldn't stand to have another dinner alone. She knew Richard wouldn't be back from the shop until sometime after eight, and so she took a tray out to the table on the patio. She was wearing corduroy slacks and one of Richard's wool sweaters; the evening wasn't very cool but she began to feel a chill. At first she thought it was the kind of coldness that accompanied a vision, but it was different, it was more like a steel knife that cut down her left side, from her fingertips to her chest. For some reason she couldn't smell the lemon tree, she couldn't hear jets when they passed overhead.

She was at the table, the tray of cottage cheese and fruit and iced tea right in front of her, when she began to feel paralyzed. She told herself that all she had to do was move and she'd be all right. But once she was back inside the house, it was worse. Her blood was ice. She went to the phone in the kitchen to call Richard at the shop, but she couldn't remember the number she had called a thousand times before. As she stood there Lila could swear that it was August, the air was so warm and still. She could hear someone down the hallway stir in bed. It was Janet Ross—she couldn't sleep so she got out of bed and went to the closet for her robe as the birds out on the lawn began to sing.

Lila reached up and dialed for the operator.

"I need to reach my husband," she said as soon as the operator answered.

"Can't you dial him directly?" the operator said.

"I can't," Lila said.

"Tell me his number," the operator said.

But that was just it—she couldn't remember.

Outside, the birds were making a terrible racket. Lila knew that any second Janet Ross would come to the nursery, so she crouched down, next to the crib. At first she thought her daughter was sleeping, but then she saw that the baby's eyes were open. Lila leaned her face against the wooden slats of the crib, and when her daughter exhaled, Lila swallowed it in. The taste was so sweet that she knew it was a last breath. As she crouched by the crib Lila heard her baby's heart stop. Just like that, on a morning when people all over East China were sleeping beside their husbands or wives, her daughter's heart stopped beating.

The curtains in the nursery were drawn, but anyone could tell it would be an ideal day, it had been that kind of summer. Eighty-two, and cooler in the shade. Eighty-two, and Lila was freezing. Her daughter's arms trembled slightly and rustled the crib sheet, and then, much too quickly, her body grew heavy as a stone, and pale as the sky in early morning. Lila cried out only once, but that one cry could break glass, it could break through time itself.

"Oh, please," Lila said. She was holding on to the phone receiver so tightly that her fingers were numb.

The operator recited Lila's number and asked for her address. But Lila couldn't answer, and by the time the operator had looked up the address herself, Lila had dropped the receiver on the floor. Everything was failing her now—her lungs, her eyes, her ears. She ran back out to the garden, desperate for air. Snails had begun to wind their way across the patio, but Lila couldn't see them; she stumbled and stepped on several and their shells broke beneath her feet. Her headache had taken over; it shattered into pieces that cut into her temples. She could feel herself falling, and although she had always expected herself to give in gracefully, she tried to hold on.

• • •

That evening was the last Lamaze class. They'd finished learning breathing techniques and tonight they were seeing a film. As soon as the lights were turned out and the credits came on the screen, Rae closed her eyes. Richard reached over and held her hand, but neither of them could stand to watch as the husband and wife on screen welcomed their infant son.

Later, as they walked out to their cars in the parking lot, Rae looked through her bag and couldn't find her keys. "Oh, shit," she said, and she sat down on the curb, disgusted.

Richard sat down next to her. "You don't really want me to be your labor coach, do you?" he said.

"Sure I do," Rae said, but she didn't look at him. She found her keys at the bottom of her bag and nervously swung them in a circle until the jangling made Richard put his hand on hers to stop it.

"Headache," he explained. "I can tell you'd rather have Lila."

"Well, she obviously wouldn't rather do it, so I appreciate the fact that you will."

"You could go talk to her," Richard said.

Rae looked over at him.

"She needs somebody and it sure isn't me," Richard said.

"I've already been to talk to her," Rae admitted. "She wouldn't open the door."

Richard got up and pulled Rae to her feet. It was just getting dark and the rest of the people in their Lamaze class were already on their way home to supper.

"I just want you to know I'm not insulted," Richard said.

"You've got nothing to be insulted about," Rae told

him. But when he looked at her she had to laugh. "All right," Rae said, "maybe I would rather have another woman there with me."

But that wasn't the only reason, and she knew it. She still had the feeling that without Lila there she'd have nothing but bad luck. On her way home she drove past Three Sisters Street; she circled around and drove past again, and when she finally pulled over and parked she was surprised to find that her heart was beating fast.

When no one answered the door right away, Rae considered leaving. She leaned over to the window; with her face pressed against the glass she could see through the house to the kitchen—the back door was ajar. There was already the sound of a siren somewhere close by when Rae walked around to the garden, although the ambulance didn't arrive until Rae had covered Lila with her sweater and knelt down beside her. She screamed to the attendants when she heard them bang on the front door; they rushed the stretcher to the back of the house and found Rae kneeling over Lila, who was sprawled on the cold patio, unconscious. As the attendants lifted Lila they couldn't help but notice the gashes in the slate next to her, left by her fingernails when she tried so hard to hold on. And although it grew less noticeable with time, from that day onward the slate was scarred by fine lines, like the marks you find on wrists that never quite heal.

It wasn't until three days later that Lila was aware of anything, and then it was only a dream. She was in a place where the sunlight was blinding and tropical. The sky itself seemed white, and it took a while before she realized that it wasn't the sky at all but a thousand snowy egrets. The landscape was flat, and there were enormous trees that dripped moss into a bayou. In the water there were huge flowers, each one larger than the largest sunflower. And even while she was dreaming Lila knew that there was no place on earth where egrets fly straight toward the sun, nowhere where the water in a bayou is turquoise, where tropical flowers are as cold and as white as milk.

It occurred to Lila that she might be dying. She had always thought death would come for her in the form of a man dressed in black silk. He would be waiting in an alley on an icy night, lanterns would burn, and wolves would howl so horribly that the sound would send shivers down the spines of children as they tossed in their sleep. It seemed impossible for the end to happen here, in this tropical place. The only escape was to wake up, and she seemed to be stuck here, in this dream. When she did finally manage to wake up it was agonizingly slow. The bayou dried up and receded by inches, leaving behind a gray tiled floor that seemed to have ripples in it, perhaps because she looked at it through the curtain of an oxygen tent.

Richard had sat at her bedside for three days, waiting for her to die and blaming himself. At the end of the third day he seemed to have shrunk a little—he was wearing the same clothes, but they were all too loose for him now. Rae came to the hospital after work and relieved him so that he could go home and shower and sleep for a few hours on something other than a hardbacked chair. She had been there for nearly two hours when she heard the sound of something moving against the bedsheets—it was Lila, struggling to lift her arm under the weight of the IV. Rae leaned closer to the bed, and as soon as Lila opened her eyes Rae rang the buzzer on the wall.

"Don't call for the damned doctor," Lila said, but her voice wouldn't rise above a whisper and Rae couldn't hear her through the oxygen tent.

"She's awake," Rae called shrilly when the nurse responded through the intercom.

Lila tapped on the oxygen tent with one finger and Rae leaned toward her.

"Didn't you hear me?" Lila said. "Don't call the damned doctor."

"You don't know how worried we were," Rae said.

"Nobody has to worry about me," Lila said, but her voice betrayed her, and when Rae pressed her hand against the plastic tent, Lila didn't move her hand away.

While Lila was being examined, Rae went out to the hallway of the Intensive Care Unit and telephoned Richard. He was there in less than twenty minutes, and he told Rae it was all right for her to leave. Lila's doctors cornered him in the hallway. They advised him that even though Lila's heart attack had been mild, there was always the chance of a second, more brutal attack. Richard nodded when they told him her recovery might be slow; he really tried to listen, but all he wanted was to see her. Although when he finally went into her room he was suddenly shy, a twenty-year-old all over again. He stood near the door, ready to back out into the hallway.

"If you don't want me here, I'll understand," he told Lila. His voice sounded hoarse, even after he'd cleared his throat. "Maybe you don't want me to be your husband any more."

For the first time Lila realized that she was in pain. She pushed the oxygen tent away and signaled for him to come closer. Richard stood by the side of the bed.

"I've been going crazy," he said.

While Lila was unconscious Rae had brought her a potted blue hyacinth. In the overheated hospital room its scent was hypnotic—you could almost imagine yourself on the East China Highway during that one week in April when everything suddenly began to bloom.

"They're going to release you at the end of the week," Richard said. He still could not look anywhere but the floor. Yesterday he had forgotten to call his father, and when it was midnight in New York Jason Grey had phoned him. As soon as he'd heard his father's voice he'd started to weep, and ever since then he couldn't seem to control himself.

"I'm glad my doctor is talking to someone," Lila said. "He hasn't told me a thing."

"I don't want to lose you," Richard said.

When neither of them spoke they could hear the click of the IV as glucose dripped into Lila's vein. Lila tried to think about her daughter, left alone for days in the dresser drawer, but all she could see was that flat, white landscape of her dreams. It was so lonely there you could die of it, it made you want to turn and throw your arms around whoever it was you loved best.

Richard pulled up a chair and sat close to the bed.

"We can start over," he said.

Lila shook her head.

"Sure we can," Richard told her. "Even people who get divorced get back together sometimes, and we never even got divorced."

"Maybe we should," Lila said. "Maybe that's the answer."

Richard leaned toward her. "Is that what you want?" he asked. "A divorce?"

On the day he picked up that bucket of water he did it so easily, as if it was nothing more than a china cup. She knew she shouldn't have stood there for as long as she did, she shouldn't have looked at him twice.

"Why do you keep asking me such stupid questions?" Lila said.

Richard knew that it was now all right for him to lean over and take her hand. "I'll come and get you Friday," Richard said. "I'll close the shop and take you home."

The pillow under Lila's head was so soft it made her sleepy. As soon as Richard left she planned to close her eyes, she might even be able to sleep for an hour before they brought her dinner in on a tray. As she fell asleep she'd tell herself that she'd given in because he'd just badger her anyway until she agreed. But she had already begun to count the days until Friday, and really, after all these years together, she just couldn't imagine going home without him.

• • •

In the twenties, when the block was owned by the Three Sisters, pelicans nested on the roof and foxes came to sleep on the veranda at midday. The chaparral in the foothills was thick with manzanitas and wild morning glories. The aqueducts from Owens Valley had been completed, but you could still feel the desert every time you walked out your front door. Everyone was thirsty all the time—you could finish a pitcher of water and still have the urge for more, you just couldn't get enough to drink.

The Sisters regretted coming to California the instant they stepped off the train. The smell of citrus groves and the hollow clanking of oil riggings just made them more homesick. At night they dreamed of New Jersey and cried in their sleep. One sister had been persuaded to leave her fiancé behind, the other two had both passed thirty and they'd assumed they had nothing more to lose. But the odd afternoon light coming in through the windows was enough to frighten them so badly that they lost their voices from two until suppertime. Every day the real-estate boom grew closer to their estate; they could hear cottonwoods and eucalyptus being chopped down, and all night long, workmen hammered out the wood frames of new bungalows. In time the Sisters became fiercely protective of their property and they built an iron fence whose gate had only three keys. But they could never tolerate the luxury of their house, and the fact that the brother who had brought them out to California had designed it only made them more bitter. They fired the gardeners, drained the turquoise-colored cement fountain, sold the pair of screaming peacocks at auction. Most of the furniture was taken away in huge wagons, and the screening room was torn down before they had viewed even one of their brother's pictures. After a while their brother stopped inviting them to parties at his own house up in the hills. Instead he sent them handwritten notes once a month, and although he received polite replies he soon gave up altogether. In the end the Sisters rarely left the confines of their property.

Except for one. The youngest of the Sisters ran away and was married for a brief time. Years later she returned quite suddenly, and she lived on the estate long after the two older ones had died. Because no one in the family had left a will, the city claimed the estate and sold it off, parcel by parcel. But no developer seemed to want to touch the house itself—it stayed empty and intact until the Long Beach earthquake split the foundation and tumbled the turrets onto a grove of Hawaiian palms. In the neighborhood, people liked to say that the youngest sister had given birth to a child during her time away from the estate, a true heir who would one day return to claim the property. Then they would all have to move out of their houses and the block would once again be planted with eucalyptus and juniper trees and thick old rose bushes imported from New York and France. People actually seemed to look forward to this time when they'd be removed from their houses, either because it seemed so unlikely or because they were so tired of working in their fruitless backyards that they were willing to give it all up just to see somebody succeed.

For the most part people who owned houses on Three Sisters Street had the sense that their homes didn't really belong to them. Yet since Lila had come back from the hospital she felt more at home than she ever had before. The bungalow seemed simple and clean, and when the afternoon light came in through the windows it was so sharp it took your breath away. It was the nights that were difficult, because at night Lila could tell that she was losing her daughter. It was a case of neglect: she just didn't have the strength to will her daughter to life. Every night the baby was more transparent and her skin grew colder by the hour, even after she'd been covered with a towel to keep her warm. When it was very late, and everyone in the neighborhood had been asleep for hours, Lila could hear her baby struggling for breath. But there was nothing she could do. Richard wasn't sleeping on the couch any more, he was right there beside her, and because she was afraid of waking him all Lila could do was bite her lip and listen to her baby's chest rattling.

She knew that the kindest thing to do would be to let her daughter go. It seemed so simple and rational when she thought about it during the day. But at night she couldn't bring herself to give the baby up, and sometimes she took a terrible risk—she dragged herself out of bed and went to open the dresser drawer. But each time Lila held the baby the weight in her arms was lighter, and after a while she realized that her daughter could no longer open her eyes.

Richard insisted on treating Lila like an invalid and she didn't try to stop him. He'd changed his schedule and hired another mechanic so he had to go into the shop only in the afternoons. In the mornings he made certain Lila stayed in bed; he brought her tea and muffins and magazines. Her visions and headaches had never returned and her doctors insisted she was getting stronger, but after lunch, when she was alone in the house, Lila found herself listening to her own heart, waiting for an irregular beat. It was awful to want so much to be alive; it left you with no pride at all. When Rae phoned and said she could arrange to leave work early Lila found herself agreeing and let her come visit, although when Rae got there Lila wouldn't talk to her—the most she would tolerate was being read to from the L.A. *Times*. Rae would let herself in the front door with a key Richard had hidden under a terra-cotta flowerpot, then go to the kitchen and get one glass of milk and one glass of lemonade before going into Lila's room. Richard left a chair for her near the bed, and she kept her feet raised on the edge of the mattress. She usually began by reading the headlines, then the editorial page, the horoscopes, the TV listings for that night. Reading aloud reminded Rae of those nights when her mother would read her recipes listed in French cookery books as they dined on baked beans and hamburgers. Maybe that was why she felt homesick whenever she left Lila's house, and she looked for excuses to stay. If Lila fell asleep while she was reading, Rae went into the kitchen and finished reading the newspaper, and then, if there were no dishes in the sink to wash, she simply stood by the window and watched the light.

Even when Lila didn't fall asleep there were times when she didn't seem to notice Rae was there. But once, as Rae was reading the TV listings, Lila sat up straight and turned to her.

"I may be trapped in bed, but I don't have to listen to this garbage," Lila said. "Who in their right mind would read the plot summary of *Charlie's Angels*?"

"I think it's kind of interesting," Rae said. "The way they can reduce everything to one sentence. It's in my line of work—if I ever do anything more than file and answer the phone."

"Anything but TV listings," Lila said, and Rae felt as though they'd had some sort of breakthrough that afternoon. It was almost as if they'd had a real conversation.

The next day Rae brought a book of baby names instead of the *Times*.

"I can't seem to find a name I like," Rae explained.

"I'm sorry," Lila said, "this is not an appropriate thing to read to a sick woman."

But once Rae began, the litany of names was mesmerizing, and when she left off—at girls' names beginning with M—Lila felt disappointed. All through the weekend Lila looked forward to hearing the rest of the names, but on Tuesday Rae was late. At three thirty Lila actually got out of bed and went to the window to wait for her. For no reason at all she felt slighted, and as soon as she saw Rae's car pull up she got back into bed. When Rae came in with the tray of lemonade and milk, Lila pretended to be sleeping. Rae waited till four thirty, but Lila still refused to open her eyes, she closed them so tightly they hurt.

That night Rae began to have strange little spasms and her womb tightened until it was hard as a rock. Suddenly the birth of her baby seemed much too near, and by the time she called her doctor's service she was so hysterical that she lost her voice and had to croak out what her symptoms were. Her doctor insisted it was nothing for her to get alarmed about, only Braxton Hicks contractions—false labor. Still, the contractions changed something—it was no longer possible to imagine that this pregnancy would go on forever. She was really going to have this baby.

After that Rae couldn't concentrate on anything. At work she filed contracts into the wrong folders and disconnected everyone who tried to reach Freddy. One afternoon Freddy invited her along to a screening of a Canadian film—in it a woman named Eugenie was widowed after following her husband to a place that was so far north the snow was twelve feet deep; she fought off wolves with a shotgun, and loneliness with strong Indian tea. As she watched Rae was reminded of her own mother, Carolyn, and by the time the picture was over she was in tears.

"Give me a break," Freddy said when the lights came back on.

"Seriously?" Rae said as she wiped her eyes with the cuffs of her blouse. "You're not going to distribute it?"

"This is a picture for Canadians," Freddy told her. "In Toronto they think sitting around and waiting for spring is exciting."

Maybe it was because business was so bad, or because Rae felt the sort of daring that comes when you think you're about to lose your job anyway—Freddy had certainly never promised her a job to come back to after the baby was born—but when Rae went back up to the office she forged Freddy's signature and bought rights to *Eugenie*. When she drove to Three Sisters Street after work Rae was still flushed with the excitement of having done something rash. Not even Lila's flat-out refusal to let her read aloud from the book of names could dampen her spirits. But it didn't last long—on the way home Rae stopped at the Chinese take-out place, and while she waited for her order she had an overwhelming sense of disappointment. The only man she had ever loved would never be true, the labor coach she wanted wouldn't even discuss names for the baby, and the coach she had was so distracted he hadn't even talked to her in a week, he just left her notes taped to the refrigerator: *She's in a good mood today* or *Watch out—she woke up on the wrong side of bed for sure*. When she got back into the car the smell of eggrolls on the seat beside her made her feel queasy and even more distraught. Parking the Oldsmobile, all she could think about was the fact that her own mother was three thousand miles away, and she backed into a Mustang and had to leave a note wedged in behind one of the windshield wipers with the name of her insurance company.

She was still making a list of everything that had gone wrong since last summer as she crossed the courtyard, but halfway to her apartment she stopped cold. Just ahead of her, standing in the shadows, was the wild black Labrador she had seen in the courtyard before, just after the heat wave. Rae knew that the one thing she should not do was run. She stood there and held the brown paper bag of Chinese food to her chest. The air seemed cold, not like April at all, and even from this distance she could hear the dog growl. Anyone could see it was underfed; when it began to walk toward her, Rae could count its ribs.

"Good dog," Rae said.

Jessup had told her once that dogs always brought down deer by attacking their delicate legs. They had been driving along the Skyline Drive, to see the changing leaves, when they sighted a pack of dogs, running through the woods, after prey. Rae had been surprised that Jessup knew anything about deer, she'd doubted him until they heard the dogs yapping wildly, and then she'd begged him to step on the gas and get them out of there, fast.

This dog's tail was up, and she knew that wasn't a good sign. She could feel something sour in her mouth, and she wondered how a pregnant person could possibly be given rabies shots. Inside her the baby moved; when it turned on its side like that it was almost as if there was a wave trapped within her.

"I'm going to keep walking," Rae said to the dog. It was close enough so that she could feel the heat of its body. "I want you to stay," she told it.

Her legs were shaking, and maybe that was why it seemed to take such a long time to get to the front door. As soon as she heard the lock click she pushed the door open and ran inside. She stood there with her back to the door, shivering. Then she put the bag of Chinese food down on the bed and went to the kitchen window. The dog was still out there, in the exact place where she'd told it to stay. It looked around, confused; if it had come down from the canyons during the heat wave last summer it had spent the last months hiding, coming out at night to turn over garbage cans and search for water in birdbaths and gutters. But someone had once trained this dog well and it was compelled to obey Rae's command. It might have stood out in the courtyard all night if Rae hadn't filled a plate with fried rice and eggrolls and opened the door to call to it.

It was a female, and not quite as vicious as it had first seemed. It watched Rae, puzzled, but when she closed the front door, it ran to the food and devoured it. Rae sat in the easy chair and ate the rest of the food out of the containers; later, when she went into the kitchen to boil water for tea, she looked out the window and saw that the dog was still out there, curled up on her doorstep. That night, Rae took her embroidery into bed with her and she used a cross-stitch and red thread to make a border of hearts along the hem of a baby blanket. Through the locked front door she could hear the dog breathe in its sleep, long easy intakes of air that sounded like sighs. It was amazing how the sound of another creature's breathing could get into your dreams and bind you together. In the morning Rae set a bowl of milk outside her front door, and after a little while she found the courage to reach down and pat the stray dog as it drank.

The next morning she took the dog in for a rabies vaccination and bought it a collar and leash. She walked the dog three times a day. Her doctor agreed that it was good exercise, but she also suggested that it was time to start taking it easy, maybe time to stop working.

When Rae went to visit Lila, the dog climbed into the car and insisted on going with her. She left it tied to the garage door. Lila was crankier than usual, and after a while Rae gave up trying to read to her. At a quarter to five Rae went into the kitchen; she washed out some cups and cleaned the counter with a paper towel. When Lila heard the front door open she thought Rae had left, and she sat up in bed, frightened at being alone. But Rae had only gone out with a bowl of cold water for the dog. She came back and rinsed out the bowl, then stood in the doorway to Lila's room.

"Didn't you leave yet?" Lila said.

"Not yet," Rae said. "But I guess I won't be coming back any more."

Lila reached for the remote control and snapped on the TV.

"My doctor wants me to take it easy," Rae said. "It makes me wonder if there's something wrong with my baby," she blurted.

"Of course there isn't," Lila said. "They tell everybody to relax in the last weeks."

"Yeah," Rae said, unconvinced.

Outside the dog looked mournfully at the front door and then began to bark.

"Sounds like a big dog you've got," Lila said. She just couldn't bring herself to look at Rae.

"I'm scared," Rae said.

Even if Lila had tried there was no way for her to tell Rae just how much agony giving birth would be or how, in an instant, the pain would be so forgotten that it wouldn't even be like a dream, but more like a dream someone else had had. It was easier, of course, when you had someone there beside you to remind you how quickly it would all be over, how much you stood to gain: one child who reached out for you even before it opened its eyes.

Rae stood where she was in the doorway, and Lila knew that if she took one more step it would be impossible to turn her away. She wouldn't even want to. Rae held her car keys in her hand; the metal bit into her fingers until she couldn't stand it. Then she let go. She walked over to the bed, and together she and Lila listened to the dog outside, tied to the garage door, barking.

"I'm really, really scared," Rae whispered.

Lila leaned over and touched her hand. "Don't be scared," she said.

· · ·

Each day Lila was able to get out of bed for a little while longer. Richard went back to work full time, and the doctors told Lila that her recovery was complete. But she still felt unsteady, as though bedrest had softened her bones. And she still couldn't bring herself to open the dresser drawer—it had been shut tight for nine days in a row—although sometimes she heard a rustling sound among her nightgowns.

Early one afternoon, when Lila went into the kitchen to make herself some tea, she looked out the window and noticed that all the birds in the yard had suddenly taken flight. For a moment the sky was filled with birds, and feathers fell to the ground in backyards and vacant lots all over Hollywood. When the birds disappeared the sky was still and gray. Everything was much too silent; Lila could hear a lemon as it fell from the tree and rolled across the patio.

Richard hadn't bothered to replace the teapot Lila had burnt when she first got back from New York, so she filled a saucepan and set it on the stove. As soon as Lila lit the flame the water in the pan appeared to be boiling. The water bubbled and swirled in a circle, first to the left, then to the right. Without thinking, Lila stuck her finger into the water to test it, and she would have been much less shocked to have burnt herself than she was when she discovered that the water was ice cold. It was then Lila knew that this was an earthquake. Tremors had begun to move up through the earth, through the foundation and the linoleum floor right through her bones. Lila held on to the countertop as the kitchen floor shifted. Dishes rolled out of cabinets, spices fell from their rack, glasses in the sink broke without being touched. A hot wind blew in through the open window, scorching the curtains, burning Lila's face. The lemon tree in the yard fell over, but it wasn't until it hit the ground that Lila realized the wrenching sound she had heard a moment earlier hadn't been thunder but roots being torn from the ground.

Richard was in a panic to get home; he left his mechanics to sweep up the broken glass, got into his car, and took off, leaving a hot trail of rubber behind him. It should have taken fifteen minutes to get home, but it was over an hour—the roads were jammed with traffic, and all over the freeways and side streets there were hundreds of frogs no one had even known existed until now when they fled from sewers and aqueducts. Richard pulled into the driveway so fast that he missed the asphalt and the tires tore up the lawn. He looked for her first in the bedroom. The mattress was tilted off the bed and the lamps had overturned and fallen to the floor. The house was so silent that Richard could hear his own pulse. He found that he could still feel some of the same fears he'd had as a boy, when the woods just behind the house seemed too dangerous and dark. As he looked into the empty bedroom, Richard had a sudden longing for his father. It seemed that everything he had ever done he'd done with his father in mind—not the old man back in East China, whose health and unpaid bills he worried about, but the man who'd seemed taller than everyone else. It was possible, Richard knew, to be away from home too long, to forget all the things you once knew by heart. He didn't want just his father, he wanted the boy he used to be, someone who could be comforted by the sound of his parents talking in the next room, someone who refused to come into the house for supper until after dusk because that was the hour when deer mysteriously appeared in the driveway.

He found Lila in the kitchen, and he felt as if he had never needed her quite as much. She was staring at her wind-burned hands, puzzled, and as soon as she saw him she lifted up her hands so that she seemed to be asking for help. Richard led her back to bed, then got some vinegar to cool off her burns.

"It's a good thing you weren't in bed," Richard said. "You would have wound up on the floor."

He got a handkerchief and Lila watched him fold it into quarters and pour out some vinegar. When he dabbed her skin the vinegar was so cool that she shuddered.

"I think I'd better start by cleaning up the kitchen," Richard said. He recapped the vinegar bottle and started to go, but Lila put her hand on his arm and stopped him. When he got into bed beside her Lila knew that it was possible to love two people best, and when he put his arms around her both of them could imagine that they were in the bedroom of his parents' house in East China, and that it was the time when orange lilies bloomed right outside the kitchen door, and without even trying to, they both fell in love all over again.

Later they learned that Los Angeles had felt only the outside circle of the earthquake. Its center was miles away, in the desert, and there the tremors were so strong they could lift a trailer right into the air and leave it lying on its side.

Rae was at work when the earthquake struck and immediately she thought: Jessup. It was her last day at the office, and Freddy had called her in after lunch. Rae assumed she was about to be fired. At least, she'd thought, he'd had the decency to wait long enough so that her hospital bills would be covered by the health insurance.

"Guess what?" Freddy said after she sat down on the couch and put up her feet on the coffee table. "Six theaters want to show something called *Eugenie*—which they tell me I own."

"Really?" Rae said innocently.

"I trusted you," Freddy said.

"I swear to God I don't know what made me do it," Rae told him.

She'd been so preoccupied, taking the dog for walks three times a day, getting the apartment ready, talking to Lila every morning on the phone for an hour, that she'd nearly forgotten she'd forged his name.

"It won best picture in Germany," Freddy told her.

"*Eugenie?*" Rae said.

"Lucky for you," Freddy said. "If luck's what it was."

Rae had to ask him to repeat himself when he told her he wanted her to come back after the baby, not as his secretary but as his assistant.

"Are you trying to squeeze more money out of me?" Freddy said.

"I'm not sure I heard you right," Rae said. "What did you say?"

"All right!" Freddy said. "You'll get a raise, but it won't be much at first."

He reached for a bottle of wine to celebrate with and was opening it when the tremors began. The steel girders in the building began to vibrate, the file cabinets all tilted to the right. Rae sat up straight: she imagined Jessup trapped in the trailer, pinned underneath furniture that couldn't be moved. Freddy held the wine bottle in the air and tried to dodge the spray of rosé. Afterward, they stared at each other.

"Did that just happen?" Freddy said.

They left the building together, by the rear stairway, and then, along with nearly everyone else in the city, they went home to see how much damage had been done. Rae could hear the dog howling inside her apartment as soon as she got out of her car, but when she unlocked her front door the dog was nowhere in sight. A framed print had fallen off the wall, and the glass had shattered and left shards in the bed; the blue-and-white dishes they had bought in Maryland had fallen out of the cupboards and cracked. Rae looked under the bed and in the front closet; she could still hear the howling, as if the sound had been trapped in the walls. The dog was in the bathroom, huddled in the tub. A long time ago, when they had lived in Florida, Rae had bought glass canisters of bath salts that had been so expensive she'd never been able to bring herself to use them. Now the bath salts were spilled in the tub, and the dog had left pawprints in the orange and blue crystals. Rae grabbed hold of the dog's new collar and helped it out of the tub. It sat obediently on the tiled floor, still shivering, as she toweled off the bath salts that clung to its fur. She had always begged Carolyn for a dog, but after lengthy discussions with Rae's father, the decision had always been no. It wasn't that Carolyn didn't like dogs, she did; on Saturday afternoons she and Rae often drove out to kennels in Concord to look at litters of golden retrievers and spaniels. But Rae and Carolyn both knew that in their house a dog was out of the question. One argument over fleas or chewed-up shoes would be enough to disrupt a peace as fragile as theirs.

Two weeks after they ran away to Maryland, Rae went out and got a puppy, but it turned out that Jessup hated dogs. They were all right if they served a purpose—a guard dog or a sheepdog was fine—but spending his paycheck to keep a poodle in dog chow was out of the question. It wasn't a poodle, just a mixed breed, but Rae didn't bother to correct Jessup. She stood out on the curb as he lifted the puppy into the back seat of the Oldsmobile, and while Jessup drove back out to the animal shelter, Rae threw out the plastic water dish and the five-pound bag of dog food she had bought that morning.

Now she was the one who wasn't so sure she wanted the responsibility of a dog, even one that was used to no attention at all. When the phone rang, Rae told the dog to stay in the bathroom, and she ran to answer, hoping that it was Jessup calling to tell her he was all right. But it was only Richard, checking up on her—Lila had told him that a change in the atmosphere could bring on an early labor. Rae assured him that she was fine. But all over the city things had started to go wrong. Everyone said it was the earthquake; it disrupted atoms in the air, bringing out the worst you had hidden inside. The newspapers were already reporting several knife fights—each time a suspect was picked up and questioned about how the fight had begun he always looked sheepish and didn't seem to know. The supermarket where Rae shopped was held up at gunpoint, and in a parking lot behind the drugstore a young girl was beaten and left unconscious just beyond the spot where the asphalt had buckled. There was still a trace of that hot wind, and everyone had the jitters—when you drank a glass of cold water you were likely to spill it.

Rae didn't bother to clean up the apartment, she sat on the bed, hoping that Jessup would phone. The phone did ring late in the evening, but it wasn't Jessup, it was Hal, phoning from the interstate on his way back to Montana. They had lost everything. Hal had been out in the barn, Jessup inside the trailer, taking a nap. Earthquake weather had just sort of sneaked up on everyone, even the buzzards and the hawks were taken by surprise and some of them were tossed nearly half a mile from their nests. The bunkbed had overturned on top of Jessup, and after he'd gotten out from under it, he'd kicked down the door to the trailer and climbed outside. Hal watched from the doorway of the barn as Jessup ran toward the corral, but it was too late. Anyone could have told him that. They'd never rebuilt it, and the wooden fence had split in two. Horses ran through the opening, the herd so close together it seemed like one animal. As the earth shifted, the sand moved like water, the wind was getting hotter all the time, and you could hear wind chimes in the distance, rattling like mad. Jessup had run over to the corral so fast that he had to bend over, low to the ground, just to catch his breath. By the time he stood back up, the horses were running toward the mountains, a trail of sand rising up behind them like a white wall.

Hal and Jessup had just stood there for a while, then Hal had gone into the trailer to see what he could salvage. As he picked through the mess Hal heard the engine of the pickup start, and when he came out, holding an armful of laundry, he saw Jessup driving away from the ranch at top speed. Hal filled the trunk of his car with everything he owned that hadn't been broken or ruined; then he drove into town. He'd managed to talk the sheriff into letting him go up in one of the helicopters searching for missing livestock.

From the air they could see cracks in the earth, and to Hal it seemed that those cracks were already filling with sand. In no time it would seem as if the earthquake had never even happened. There were a few cows and sheep up in the mountains, stumbling along the unfamiliar territory, and Hal found himself wondering if their horses had ever existed, that's how absolute their disappearance was, not one hoofprint, not one hair from a tail or a mane. There was no chance that the state emergency fund would reimburse them for the lost horses. Jessup had had his own ideas about tax evasion, so they'd listed their stock with the authorities as six horses rather than thirty. Hal was heading back home, and if he ever found anyone stupid enough to buy the land, he'd send Rae a check for half.

"And the thing that really gets me about Jessup," Hal told her, "is that he didn't see me standing behind him. He didn't even stop to find out whether or not I'd broken my neck. He just took off."

After she hung up the phone, Rae cleaned up the worst of the mess in the apartment. She had forgotten about dinner, so now she opened up two cans of tuna—one for herself, the other for the dog. She called to the dog sharply, but when it came into the kitchen she patted its head, and they ate dinner together and then went for a walk around the block. Outside you could hear buzz saws all over the city as road crews began to remove the fallen trees and telephone poles. In the distance there was the sound of sirens, and once the dog startled Rae by throwing back its head and howling along with an ambulance. They walked around the block slowly; the air turned foggy and thick now that the hot wind from the earthquake had settled down; the ground was steaming.

When they got back to the courtyard the dog turned toward the street and barked, and Rae looked behind her. For a moment she thought she saw a pickup truck, parked near the entrance to the apartment complex. The fog had grown so thick that Rae couldn't see any farther than the forgotten strand of Christmas lights stretched across the dark courtyard; tonight they were as disconcerting as fallen stars. The dog headed to the apartment, and Rae followed. Once they were inside, she double-locked the door.

The earth had already begun to settle, but that night everyone moved with caution getting into bed, as if anything might happen while you slept. The dog lay down beside the bed; it was so quiet that twice Rae reached down and touched its head, just to make certain she wasn't alone. She felt more a captive of her own body than ever—she longed to sleep on her stomach, her ribs and back ached. In the dark she could hear her own pulse, and it seemed too loud and too fast. Her pregnancy felt like a bottomless pool, and now that she had jumped and the water was almost over her head, she could not imagine why she had ever made this leap. Even though she now knew that Lila would be there with her in the labor room if she wanted her, something was missing. It wasn't just that Jessup had disappeared, it was the feeling that she was having this baby without having had any past of her own. Who would send presents, who would look for photographs of her as an infant so that she could compare and see if the baby took after her?

As she fell asleep Rae found herself trying to imagine Carolyn on the day of her own birth. She knew only this: It had taken two days for her to be born. For two days her father had sat in the waiting room, he had shaved in the visitor's washroom and ordered sandwiches delivered from a deli down the street. Down the hall, Carolyn had to be strapped into her bed. At the very end, when she couldn't stand it any more, they gave her Demerol, but it didn't last long enough, and when it wore off she begged them for more. For an hour they left her there, strapped to the bed, and when it came time for the baby to be delivered they told her about something called twilight sleep and then hooked an IV to her arm. After that the pain grew worse, too enormous to respond to, but she wasn't really there. She could hear herself screaming, yet she was detached, and although the nurse swore they had shown her the baby the moment she was born, Carolyn couldn't remember a thing about it, and when she was given her daughter to hold she held on tight, for fear it might be discovered that she hadn't really had a baby at all.

That night Rae had no dreams, as if she'd been given twilight sleep herself, and when she woke in the morning she realized that she'd been crying in her sleep. She had a cup of tea, then gave the dog two of the Pet Tabs she'd gotten at the vet. When they went out for a walk the air seemed back to normal, the flawless blue air of April. The dog carefully kept pace alongside Rae, but the one habit Rae hadn't been able to break it of was chasing birds, and it took off, behind some bushes, after a pair of jays. Rae clapped her hands and whistled, and as she waited for the dog to grow tired and trot back down the sidewalk she decided that she wasn't quite as prepared for the baby as she'd thought. The nightgowns and crib sheets were laundered twice and carefully folded, the hats threaded with ribbons were stacked in a neat pile, the medicine chest was stocked with Vaseline and cotton and rubbing alcohol. But there was still one more thing she needed, and she clipped the dog's leash on so that it wouldn't run off again, and went right back to her apartment. She got her car keys and her pocketbook, and then she went out and spent the rest of the day shopping for a pair of red shoes.

. . .

By the time Rae was ten days overdue, Richard and Lila had played a hundred games of gin rummy. They played at the kitchen table and they kept score. There was anticipation in everything they did, and each morning when Rae phoned to tell them still nothing had happened, they looked at each other and sighed. At night they both heard Rae's relaxation tape in their dreams—the sound of wind chimes, two flutes playing scales. Richard had taught Lila all of the breathing techniques, and he didn't hide his great relief that both of them would be there in the labor room with Rae. But secretly Lila wasn't certain that she'd go through with it.

Richard had decided to take care of the earthquake damage himself; instead of calling the tree service Lila had found in the phone book, he borrowed a saw from their next-door neighbor and began to cut the lemon tree into logs. He had already collected all the lemons from the ground, and each day Lila made a fresh pitcher of lemonade. When there were only three lemons left, Lila made one last pitcherful, and as she stirred in a cup of sugar she suddenly realized that if they had had a child together it would have been long gone, to a separate life, to a family of its own, and it would have been just the two of them in this house anyway. When she took Richard a glass of lemonade he switched off the buzz saw and drank the whole glass without pausing. All around them the air smelled sweet; if they saved the logs and rationed them carefully in the small fireplace in the living room they might be able to capture the scent of lemons all that next winter. They could hold hands in the dark and watch the wood burn from November to March, and each time it rained it would seem like April in their house.

Richard bent down and put his empty glass alongside the tree stump. When he stood up his back cracked. He couldn't use the saw for more than an hour without feeling it that night, and the job was taking him days longer than he'd planned.

"Maybe I should have hired a kid to do this," he said now. "Maybe it was a mistake not to call a service that would come and dynamite the stump." He surveyed his work and looked puzzled; the more logs he cut, the more wood there seemed to be still left to cut. "I should have been able to cut this all in one day," Richard said.

He seemed so fragile that Lila put her arms around him, and she stayed out there with him, sitting in the sun while he cut more wood. She thought of Hannie, who had been married less than a year when her husband had gone off with the other men in the village to buy grain, and had then disappeared. A sudden autumn storm had trapped the men in the woods; at night the people in the village could hear wolves howling, but there was nothing they could do. Later, four of the men were found in the woods, buried under new drifts of snow. All of the sixteen women who had become widows mourned their husbands together, but as she sat on a wooden crate in the ashes with the line of other women,

Hannie had felt nothing at all—she was already pregnant but she barely knew her husband, she couldn't even remember what his favorite meal had been.

When Lila looked at Richard, she remembered everything about him. The way the bed creaked when he sat down and pulled off his shoes, the smell of blueberry pancakes, his favorite breakfast, on Sunday mornings. When she looked at him carefully she could see the boy he used to be, right there beneath his skin, and she had the urge to kiss him. Soon Richard finished cutting logs, and he came to sit next to her in a wrought-iron chair. Lila felt herself grow excited. When he looked at her that way she knew he was seeing her for who she really was.

That night they went to bed early, and they took off their clothes under the covers and laughed the way they used to when it was freezing cold in their bedroom in East China. When they made love they felt each other's bodies, but they also could feel the way they used to be, and the delight of knowing somebody so well was so staggering it made them weep and hold each other tight all night long.

On the morning when Rae was eleven days past her due date, Lila woke up with a lump in her throat. All that night she had dreamed of Hannie, and now she remembered the reason Hannie had come to New York in the first place: she had lost her son in the war. It had been the worst winter anyone could remember; the ice was thick enough to swallow you alive. Thousands had been left homeless and they wandered from village to village, stealing from root cellars and begging for food. When the mayor came to tell Hannie that her son had been killed, she couldn't contain her grief, her screams could be heard all over the village, and mothers held their hands over their children's ears. Hannie's son had been a soldier, but to her he was still a boy. Her neighbors built up the fire in her stove, but once they had gone out to bring her some soup, Hannie locked her door and wouldn't let them back in. She sat there by the stove, with a blanket around her, and as the night grew later, her grief grew as well. When her neighbors pounded on her door, Hannie ignored them. What good were they to her—they couldn't tell her what she wanted to know. She was obsessed with finding out the way her son died—if he had been in pain, if the end had been quick, if he had called out for her as he lay dying. After a while she convinced herself that he had—he had wanted his mother, and no one had come to him.

There was a storm that night, and the wind was fierce. Every now and then, Hannie heard a pounding on her door, but she didn't move to answer it. Her despair was blinding, it did away with time. When she called out to her son, she swore she could hear his childish voice answer and call her Mama. Finally, she fell asleep, and as she slept the drifts outside grew higher and the fire in the stove went out and a trail of smoke floated between the ceiling and the floor. When she woke up, Hannie opened the window and waved the smoke outside. Then she went to the door. It was jammed, and she had to push harder and harder. At last it fell away. The sunlight was so harsh that Hannie held one arm over her eyes to shield them, but of course she could see what had been against her door, and her blood drained away. It was a boy of ten, one of the many homeless, and he'd been frozen to the ground, his hands still reaching for the door. It had been his voice she'd heard all night, he'd been the one crying for his mother, and no one had come to him, no one had lifted him out of the ice to carry him home.

Hannie left her village the very next day, and during the two years it took her to reach New York, she decided to concentrate on the future. That's when she began to read tea leaves, at first for no money, and later for only a token.

When Lila had heard Hannie's story, she had not known how to react. It was too awful, condolences could never be enough. But Hannie had seemed so detached it was almost as if she had been telling a story about someone else. Hannie called for the waitress and ordered toast and jam, although when her order came she only spread butter on her bread very thinly, with the brittle motions of some-one who knows she can't explain her grief any more than she can describe the moment when she knows she has held on to her grief for too long.

Lila knew that it was sometimes quite impossible to account for some very simple things: how your life can go on after you've lost your child, how the clear blue sky of an early morning can move you to tears, how a woman can stand by her own kitchen window and watch her husband go out to gather wood and not want anything more than that one moment—that instant when the man she loves sees her watching through the curtains, and turns to wave.

• • •

On the twelfth day after her due date Rae began to have chaotic cramps that came and went and a feeling that wire was being pulled taut all the way around, from her belly to her backbone. She drank herbal tea and read magazines. There was no point in alerting Richard and Lila because Rae thought it might be nothing more than back strain, something gone wrong with her spine. But the cramps grew stronger, and when they began to come at five-minute intervals Rae knew they were contractions. She phoned her doctor. She was ready to leave for the hospital then and there, but her doctor told her to call back when the contractions were two minutes apart.

Late in the day, when nothing had changed, Rae grew calmer. She got out the mop and washed the kitchen floor, then took the dog out and watched it chase birds in the courtyard. She did all this between contractions, which had begun to feel familiar, separate from childbirth, some flaw in her body she'd have to learn to live with. Then they changed. They were still coming five minutes apart, but they were hot, as if someone pressed a burning bar of iron into her flesh at regular intervals. She took a cold shower and let the water beat against her spine. But she was still so hot that she opened every window in the apartment, and as she leaned out the kitchen window, to gulp down some cool evening air, she saw that a pickup truck was parked at the curb.

Rae threw on a dress, then held the dog back by its collar until she could run out the door. All week she'd felt Jessup had been there, late at night, at hours when Rae didn't go out. Now she'd caught him. He was sitting behind the wheel, eating his dinner out of a McDonald's bag when Rae pounded on the passenger window. Jessup looked at her through the glass; he held his hamburger in the air and for a moment he seemed to be considering turning the key in the ignition and stepping on the gas as hard as he could. Rae knocked on the window again, and after he'd looked at her a little longer, Jessup leaned over and rolled it down. Rae held on to the base of the window and lifted herself up to get a better look.

"I knew you were sneaking around here," she said triumphantly.

"I'm not sneaking anywhere," Jessup said. "I just don't happen to have an address right now. That's all."

"So you've just been parking here," Rae said.

"That's right," Jessup told her.

"You just happened to pick my street out of all the streets in Southern California? How dare you park here and eat a goddamned hamburger? How dare you think you can do this to me?"

"All right!" Jessup said. "I happen to think I have a right to see my kid."

"Oh, really," Rae said.

"Are you going to let me see him or not?" Jessup said.

Rae was holding on to the edge of the window; she pulled herself up and held on tighter as she felt a contraction begin. For seven nights Jessup had been watching the apartment, but because he didn't want to be found out, he never saw more than what might happen in any apartment after midnight: a light switched on, a window opened, a shade lowered. Now, all he saw was Rae's face, her fingers, her narrow shoulders.

"It was a boy, wasn't it?" Jessup said.

She stepped away from the truck and let him see how huge she was. "It hasn't been born yet, but when it is I'll send you a telegram." She began to walk away. "If you have an address by then," she called over her shoulder.

When she heard the door of the truck open and slam shut, Rae began to walk faster. She could feel that this contraction was different; the wire around her was so hot and tight it was impossible to move.

"I want to talk to you," Jessup called.

Rae tried to keep walking but couldn't. She inhaled slowly and counted to five, then exhaled and counted again. By the time Jessup had run across the courtyard, she was doubled over.

"Are you okay?" Jessup said.

Rae took his hand and placed it on her belly so that he could feel the contraction.

"Jesus Christ," Jessup said, withdrawing his hand. "Rae."

Jessup leaned toward her so she could support herself on his arm until the contraction was over. Afterward, he tried to follow Rae into the apartment, but the dog stood in the doorway, barking.

"Get this dog away from me," Jessup said.

Rae looked through the drawer in the night table for an old watch with a second hand. Jessup tried to push the dog back with his foot, but each time he did its barks were worse than before.

"I'm going to have to kick the shit out of you," Jessup told the dog.

"Stop it!" Rae said.

Jessup and the dog looked over at her.

"I thought you were supposed to have already had this baby," Jessup said.

Rae went to the doorway and held the dog by its collar. She could feel the vibration of a growl low in its throat.

"That just shows how little you know," Rae said.

It wasn't just the dog's growl she was feeling, she could feel vibrations in the air.

"I need something to drink," Rae said. "Herbal tea."

Jessup looked at her confused. "You want me to make you tea?"

"I think you could manage it," Rae said. "They've trained chimpanzees to make tea—all you have to do is fill the kettle and turn on the burner."

Jessup went into the kitchen, and Rae could hear him rummaging through everything, making a mess.

"Mint," she called. "In the first cabinet."

After she sat down in the easy chair Rae realized she was still holding on to the dog's collar. The metal felt cool, like the chain-link fence that marked off Rae's parents' house from the next-door neighbors'. When Jessup came in with the tea, Rae waved him away. It had been a little more than two minutes between contractions, and this last one had gone on for nearly a minute. The blood had drained from Jessup's face, and all you had to do was look at him to see how scared he was.

"Let's go," Jessup said. "I'm taking you to the hospital."

"I have to time the next one," Rae said. She still couldn't let go of the dog. "I don't want to get to the hospital and have to turn around and come back home."

Jessup took the wristwatch and sat on the edge of the bed, facing Rae.

"You really have nerve," Rae said. "What makes you think I want you here?"

She could feel the next one beginning, low in her back, spreading out in a circle.

"Is it starting?" Jessup said. "Should I time it?"

Rae nodded and began to breathe deeply. She kept her eyes focused on the center of Jessup's forehead. As the contraction subsided she thought of how Jessup couldn't wait to be born, how they'd had to stop the elevator and deliver him right there. After twelve days of hesitation, Rae's baby suddenly seemed to take after its father. She could feel its urgency inside her, and she knew that the time had come. She let go of the dog's collar, and when the dog whined and rested its head on her knee, she gently pushed it away. And then Rae felt a pop, like the sensation you feel in your ears when a jet suddenly drops and the pressure changes.

"Something's happening," Rae whispered.

Jessup ran over to her, but before he could reach Rae her water broke. Her dress was drenched, and beneath the easy chair there was a pool of liquid.

"Oh, Jesus," Jessup said.

He knelt down beside her, stricken. It took Rae a moment to realize that he hadn't the faintest idea of what had just happened. As far as Jessup could tell she was dying, first water, then blood, then her bones might begin to dissolve.

In spite of herself, Rae smiled. "Don't be an idiot," she said. "This is supposed to happen. Get me a towel and the blue dress in the closet."

When she stood up to phone her doctor she was still dripping, amazed by how much fluid had actually been inside her. She left a message for her doctor that she would meet her at the hospital, then changed her dress.

"I want you to listen to me," Jessup said, but Rae couldn't. She held her hand up in the air to silence him and Jessup began to time her contraction. This time Rae imagined the moment when the horses escaped from the corral. The sound of their hoofbeats on the flat sand was deafening, the sand rose up like a twister, burning the horses' eyes, making them wilder and a hundred times more desperate to escape.

"That one lasted for a minute and a half," Jessup said.

Rae went into the kitchen and put out fresh water and dog food.

"Are you crazy?" Jessup said. He pulled his keys out of his pocket. "Let's go," he said.

"If you really want to help me you can take care of the dog."

"Shit," Jessup said under his breath.

"She needs to be walked three times a day."

The dog was lying near the bed, nose buried in its paws. It watched Rae carefully, following every move she made with its eyes. Jessup glared over at it.

"All right," he said. "All right, all right."

But just to make sure the dog wouldn't be locked up indefinitely if Jessup didn't live up to his word, Rae left the kitchen window open. That way the dog could escape if it wanted to: all it had to do was climb up on a kitchen chair and leap over the window ledge. The drop was only a few feet, and under the bamboo there were soft weeds and grass.

When the next contraction came, Rae leaned up against the refrigerator and rocked back and forth. All of a sudden she wanted Lila, she nearly got lost in between the waves of the contraction.

"We're leaving right now," Jessup said as soon as it was over.

Rae went to the telephone, but before she could dial, Jessup took the receiver out of her hands.

"Don't start up with me now," Rae warned him. "I swear to God I'm dangerous."

She grabbed at the phone, but Jessup wouldn't let go.

"I have to call my labor coaches," Rae yelled.

"Let me go with you," Jessup said.

They both held on to the receiver and stared at each other.

"Please," Jessup said.

She thought then of the one time she had gone to the apartment where Jessup had grown up. It was before she moved out to Newton; she'd been hanging around the front door of his building, hoping to see him, when his mother came home from work, carrying some groceries.

"I know you," she said to Rae, and she'd insisted Rae come up to the apartment. Inside, the hallways were dark, and they had to walk up four flights of stairs. The apartment itself was tiny, Jessup slept on a fold-out couch in the living room. Jessup's mother had sat Rae down at the kitchen table and made her a glass of chocolate milk. She was apologetic about everything—the lack of heat, the fact that she came home from work after six and didn't know where her son was—as if Rae were another adult, someone she had to impress.

"I'm so glad that Jessup has friends," his mother confided, and for a moment Rae didn't understand. Jessup never had any friends. Then it dawned on Rae that his mother meant her.

Jessup's mother put the groceries away, then slipped off her shoes and got herself a cup of coffee.

"He's told me all about you," she told Rae. "The girl with the red hair."

Rae was too shocked to speak; she gulped her chocolate milk as she listened to the details of his birth. When, at seven, Jessup still hadn't arrived, Rae told his mother that she had to go home. Jessup's mother walked her to the door, and as though by agreement they stopped to look at the couch that folded out to become Jessup's bed.

"He started walking when he was nine months old," Jessup's mother said proudly.

Rae's throat had begun to hurt. She knew that if Jessup found out she'd been there, he'd never be able to face her again.

"I meant to surprise him," she told his mother. "So maybe we'd better not tell him I was here."

Jessup's mother looked at Rae for a moment before she understood. "It will be our secret," she said, and Rae knew that she was talking about more than just this one visit.

"I know I've made some mistakes," Jessup was saying to her now.

"Several," Rae agreed.

"I know it," Jessup said. "I wanted things. I'm not going to lie to you—I still want them."

Rae held her hand in the air so that he would stop talking. This time her contraction lasted for nearly as long as the space between it and the last one.

"Are you all right?" Jessup asked when it was over.

Rae nodded and blew out air. She had expected it to hurt, but she'd never expected this.

"I want to tell you something, so you'll understand," Jessup said. "I always thought you'd leave me."

"This isn't fair," Rae said.

"I know," Jessup said.

He put his arms around her when the next contraction came, and counted the seconds.

"You can drive me to the hospital, but that's all," Rae told him. Jessup looked so grateful that she would have laughed out loud if she could have. She pointed to her overnight bag. He picked it up and stood in the doorway, waiting, until she waved him out.

"Go on," she told him. "I'll meet you in the truck."

When he left Rae could see him out the window as he crossed the courtyard; he was the exact same distance away as he'd been on those nights when Rae had looked out her bedroom window to see him out on the sidewalk. But she'd never noticed how frightened he looked from this distance, or that he had a nervous habit of rubbing his fingers together, as if he was worried that she might not appear.

Jessup threw the overnight case in the cab of the truck, started the engine, then got out and waited for her. It was dark by now, and the exhaust from the pickup was inky, the color of winter nights in Boston just before the snow begins. Rae went to her closet, steadied herself by holding on to the wall, then slipped on her red shoes. This child really was a lot like Jessup—it could hardly wait to be born. So she hurried—she bent down to stroke the dog's head, and before she went out to cross the courtyard, she phoned Richard and Lila to tell them she was ready at last.

They both heard the phone at the same time. Richard jumped up from the couch to answer it and, out in the garden, Lila knew it was time. That afternoon she had baked a cake—she had thought she was making it for dessert that night, but when Richard went to cut a piece, she stopped him. She'd been particularly careful with the ingredients: sweet butter, a cup of sugar, milk, a spoonful of lemon rind saved from their own tree. Lila wrapped the cake in waxed paper, knowing it was a gift for Rae. As she stored it in a metal tin she wondered if she would feel jealous when the call finally came, but now that it had she was actually relieved. It was a comfort to know what you did and did not have.

While Richard made arrangements to meet Rae at the hospital, Lila heard a rustling in the grass. She knew exactly what it was. A little girl with slate-gray eyes crawled across the patio, then lifted herself onto Lila's lap. Holding her was like trying to hold on to light, or water, or air. But when she reached up and put her arms around Lila's neck, Lila could feel the heat of her body, and no mother, in any nursery, could have loved her child more.

Inside the house, Richard hung up the phone and rushed to the bedroom to pack the few things they might need: a change of clothes, white washcloths, a good clock with a second hand. They had already begun to plan a trip to East China, and once they went back it would be nearly summer, the lilies would have already begun to send up green shoots. Richard planned to spend most of their visit helping his father work on the house. He'd be so busy with wallpaper and leaking pipes that he'd never notice when Lila took their rented car and disappeared for an afternoon. And even if he did notice, he'd know enough to let it pass. He and Jason would replace the gutters on the north side of the house and fix the rotten floor boards in the porch, while Lila drove out to a place where last winter's salt and ice had been so powerful they had cut through stone. A place where if you were standing in the right spot you could see the shadow of the moon in late afternoon, you could run your hand along a small headstone and imagine it was made out of memory and pearls and bones.

And so when the baby began to inch away, Lila didn't try to stop her. She bit her lip until she drew two drops of blood and watched as the baby lowered herself back onto the patio. Above them the sky grew darker. The baby moved along the flat stones, past the hedges, into the neighbor's yard. At this hour the potted gardenias next door smelled sweeter; the air was cool enough to make you shiver. Lila reached down and touched the warm slate, but when she went to look beyond the hedges there wasn't a sign of her child. Just another garden that had to be coaxed to grow, a row of thin tomato seedlings and a bent magnolia tree.

Richard was at the screen door watching her. She could feel his presence, and when she turned he called out that it was time. Lila motioned that she would meet him in the driveway,

ALICE HOFFMAN

and when Richard went to start the car Lila went inside to get the cake tin from the kitchen counter. Into this cake Lila had baked three gifts: a cool hand to test for fevers, a kiss with the power to chase away nightmares, a heart that can tell when it's time to let go.

Outside, the car was idling and Richard had left the passenger door open. Everyone else on the block was already in bed. It was a still, blue night with no wind, a good night for sleeping, and the neighborhood was so quiet that if you listened very carefully you could hear the roses outside the front door unfolding. You could take one look at the sky and know it was the perfect time of night for a miracle.